# ADA'S REALM

Sharon Dodua Otoo

# ADA'S REALM

*Translated from the German by*
*Jon Cho-Polizzi*

MACLEHOSE PRESS
QUERCUS · LONDON

First published as *Adas Raum* by
S. Fischer Verlag GmbH in Frankfurt, Germany, in 2021

First published in Great Britain in 2023 by MacLehose Press

This paperback edition published in 2024 by

MacLehose Press
An imprint of Quercus Editions Limited
Carmelite House
50 Victoria Embankment
London EC4Y 0DZ

An Hachette UK company

The translation of this work was supported
by a grant from the Goethe-Institut

A CIP catalogue record for this book is available from the British Library.

ISBN (MMP) 978 1 52941 904 7
ISBN (Ebook) 978 1 52941 903 0

2  4  6  8  10  9  7  5  3  1

Designed and typeset in Palatino by Patty Rennie
Printed and bound in Great Britain by Clays Ltd, Elcograf S.p.A.

Papers used by Quercus Books are from well-managed
forests and other responsible sources.

*For Tyrell*
         *. . . finally!*

Se wo were fi na wosan kofa a yennkyi

*Sankofa, Adinkra symbol of the Asante*

Return and retrieve! It is not taboo
To return for what has been forgotten.
Learn from your past.

## THE FIRST ORBITS

## BETWEEN THE ORBITS

## THE NEXT ORBITS

## EPILOGUE

# THE FIRST ORBITS

# Ada

*Totope, March 1459*

During the longest night of the year, blood clung to my forehead and my baby died. Finally. He had whimpered in his final moments, and Naa Lamiley had caressed his cheek. How lovely, I had thought, that this would be his final memory. She lay just beside him, the child between us, and her head resting next to mine. Naa Lamiley's eyes shimmered as she assured me it would not be much longer now, "God willing". She whispered because all of our mothers were sleeping on the other side of the room, but Naa Lamiley's voice would have given out at any moment anyway. Together, we had cried and prayed at my baby's side the last three nights. I could barely hear her, and I understood her even less. While she caressed him, she had stared at me, as if surprised by my confusion – though the words *How would you know?* never left my lips. In an already unbearable situation, this moment was particularly absurd. Naa Lamiley *always* knew. But in that moment – it was quite literally a matter of my own flesh and blood – I did not want to seem clueless to her. To distract myself,

I scratched my forehead. I scratched and forgot I had blood under my nails.

The few candles Naa Lamiley had gathered and placed before the doorway flickered.

"It was this way with Kofi, too," she breathed softly, as if she did not wish to disturb my son while he was dying. Shame on me. This was not so long ago. The ensuing silence resulting from my shame and her sympathy accompanied us through the final, tortured breaths. The candles wept.

Outside, Naa Lamiley had prepared a tiny pad of palm leaves to lay him out in the moonlit courtyard. She spread a white cloth over it. There would be no grave. The boy did not even have a name; he was only five days old. And yet he had still tarried longer than my first child. Also, a boy. *He* had opened his eyes immediately after birth, looked around, and evidently, not liked what he had seen. That little one had left us before I could even take him in my arms.

Naa Lamiley squeezed my hand once, briefly, then shifted to her knees and stood. I wanted to, as well, but with great effort I only managed to make it halfway – a squat. It was about time to carry out his body – I remained on the floor. She bent over one of the flames – I remained on the floor. She blew one candle out, then the next, and then another. Finally, she lifted the baby's body and carried him from our room. I remained on the floor. The darkness comforted me.

Through the open doorway, I watched how Naa Lamiley weighed my baby in her arms, how she lay his body gently down onto the palm leaves, how she adjusted his head lovingly, pressing his lips together. How she blinked her tears

4

away. I leaned back against the wall, closed my own eyes, and dozed off.

By sunrise – his body was still warm – the older women, toothless and spitting, had assured one another that I had best forget about it all as quickly as possible. They sat together on the bench directly in front of our hut, watching the morning unfold. The one whose eyesight was poorest nodded emphatically in Naa Lamiley's direction as she pronounced that I was still young and could, God willing, bear at least three more healthy children one after another.

"Or," Mami Ashitey cackled, shaking her broom, "perhaps all three at once!" And as if this were the best joke of all time, they began to laugh in unison. Their ribcages shook, and their eyes wept tears of laughter. I bit my lip. Did they not know the prophesy had foretold that I – the woman they all called Ada – would accompany only *one* child into adulthood?

Naa Odarkor, who was frying up the masses of shrimp which would later be brought to market, threw her fan to the ground and leaped over the coal stove. She had to prop up the toothless one whose hearing was poorest, as she began to laugh so mightily, she almost fell from her bench.

*Forget it all as soon as possible?* I fought to hold on to every memory I had of him! I clung with all my strength to the sour scent of my son. His murmuring still resounded in my ears, as though he had only just stopped nursing. And I longed for this again, o! My swollen breast all but robbed me of my breath. As chapped and tender as my nipples were, I wished for nothing more than to exchange the agony in my engorged breasts for the torture of nursing. Naa Lamiley shook her head and chewed at her cracked

5

thumbnail, while the toothless ones began to laugh at me once more. But it was really true that I could still feel how he had gazed at me as I had held him in my arms. Like a promise he would stay with me for ever. Or perhaps, a promise that I had never really lived without him.

"Eh-eh!"

"He's not your HUSBAND, o!"

I turned away. So, then I should only mourn someone with whom I once had lain? Pfft!

I did not want a grave. There should not be another forgotten, overgrown place for which no-one would care after we had departed – and that would be soon, after all: We were only waiting for a sign. No grave. But there should be a ritual, Naa Lamiley knew which one.

Not until early evening, after the hearth fire had been fanned, the soup cooked, and the yams mashed – not until all of us had eaten, only then would one of my mothers "take care of the baby". Unless I could steal away with him while the toothless ones – surrounded by plucked feathers and slaughtered hens – continued to chatter on excitedly. I would walk to the great water, approach its edge, and permit the tiny, peaceful body to glide out upon the waves. This was my wish.

Because I did not yet want to show myself at market – it was still too soon – I sent Naa Lamiley instead to collect the two or three yams we needed for the ritual. She nodded, first in exhaustion, then in determination – disappearing with a basket of smoked fish. I also threatened to disappear. Before my eyes an all-encompassing blackness spread. A hole. Were I to fall into it, there would be no escape.

The toothless ones calmed themselves, and the hens,

too, ceased their clucking and flapping. Mami Ashitey cackled on, hobbling about and fluttering her arms in the air.

"Naa?" she cried, her right eye tearing.

Naa Odarkor shook her head. Seconds before, she had watched as Mami Ashitey rubbed her face with her dusty hand. I should have removed whatever it was that ended up in her eye – it would have been better, for Naa Odarkor's fingers shook – but it was still too soon. I could not tolerate Naa Odarkor's loving gaze upon her wife, the tenderness of her touch, the pettiness of Mami Ashitey's pain. By the time I had turned away, it was already over.

Gradually, they all resumed their activities – the sweeping of the yard, the fanning of the flames, or the chewing of kotsa. That the toothless ones still used kotsa at all! Even I only used the chewing sponge after meals or occasionally to remove a particularly foul taste from my mouth. But these elders? If they had had one single tooth to share amongst them, it would have been a lot! And yet they chewed day in and day out, as if they were trying in vain to grind down a piece of gristle.

My baby was covered with a white cloth and was safe from both the swirling dust and their flying spit. I just should have waited for Naa Lamiley. Even centuries later, I still will not know what I was thinking. In any case, the bracelet was already untied. I held it in my right hand and counted the golden beads with my thumb.

Thirty, thirty-one, thirty-two . . . thirty-three moon phases ago, when I had noticed that the line below my belly button was beginning to darken again, I had left no stone unturned. At first, I had prayed to Jehovah, the God

of the whites, for I had been told that he was a jealous God, and thought He might appreciate that I had turned to Him first in my hour of need. And so, I had closed my eyes, folded my hands together, and moved my lips zealously. Still kneeling, the thought came to me that it would be prudent to next venerate the coastal deity, Ataa Naa Nyɔŋmɔ, because the combination of the masculine "Ataa" and the feminine "Naa" were surely more powerful than Jehovah's one-sided masculinity. In the end, I could merely offer Ataa Naa Nyɔŋmɔ *one* song in Ga. My voice could not quite reach the high notes, but at least I had known the words. Then I had put on the bracelet, hoping this time that the golden beads might convince the dead to protect my unborn child. That, at least, was the subject of another hasty prayer in Arabic, which my first mother had taught me a long, long time ago. In the quiet after the duʿāʾ, I poked my distended belly button, and I was confident that my efforts could also please Allah. But all these efforts were in vain. My baby died anyway.

What was so wrong with me that my children did not come to stay? I saw nothing, for my lashes were too heavy with tears and pain, but at least I could still pray softly with my fingers and lips. And then, as I began to count the beads of the bracelet once more, it dawned on me: My son did not have to return naked to Asamando, like his brother before him. The golden beads, which by no means belonged to me alone, should adorn his waist. And the thought that in this way, the bracelet would finally return to my foremothers, comforted me a little. I sat beside him. The bracelet was not quite long enough, and so I carefully removed three threads from the seam of my cloth. With

the tips of my fingernails, I bound them to the wire. The white cloth rustled in the light breeze. It had only a slight bulge beneath it, looking almost innocent. I touched this tiny mound. How hard it was. Like a stone, it was.

"Oh!" I moaned, as I retracted my hand. My left hand again. The toothless ones were furious. In two strides, Mami Ashitey was at my side. She struck at me mightily, instantly disappointed that the fibres of her broom were too weak for this application. Then she cursed, turning the broom in the palm of her right hand and striking at me again with the wooden handle. Her movements were quick and precise, as though she had been practising for this all her life.

"O Mami!" My hands encircled my head. "Please stop, o! Please STOP!"

Of course, she heard me, but she acted as though the cries of the other toothless ones drowned out my own. Naa Odarkor nodded at each blow and made no effort to restrain her wife from punishing me.

Then Mami Ashitey struck me on the knee on a particularly tender spot, so that my leg gave out. It simply happened: Strike. Kick. Suddenly the white cloth under which – until that moment – my son had rested peacefully, lay beside a stiff, baby corpse. Astaghfirullah.

A few excited hens.

Four toothless elders, one with broom.

A young woman with a bleeding forehead.

A recently deceased child.

This is how he likely first came upon us, the white man from the sea—

9

## Stratford-le-Bow, March 1848

I glanced back at him.

While he dressed. First the stockings, then the trousers. Never the other way around. Then his undershirt, shaken out two times. He worried, otherwise, that his overshirt would not sit properly. The tips of his elegant fingers encircled the buttons, one after the other. And he quivered with rage. *Cher Charles*.

I could have avoided this argument if I had merely conceded to agree with him unconditionally. And often I did, especially in those days, because it had become exceedingly exhausting to quarrel with men like Charles. Men who actually considered themselves to be "the good ones", and yet – between the Africans on one side and the women on the other – never knew where to expect the next challenge to their God-given authority, and therefore fought pre-emptively on every front at once. The confidence with which *he* had presumed to tell *me* something of probability theory was actually quite comical. It would seem the constricting impact of a corset affected both men and women alike. I kept my internal commentary – "Darling, what actually goes on in that little head of yours?" – to myself, and counted silently to ten.

He held one of my calculations for the Analytical Engine in his hand, reading glasses balanced on the tip of his nose.

"Hmm."

He tapped on one of the lines with his index finger. Perhaps it had been rather unconscionable of me not to acknowledge him at once.

"You've made an error here," he said. "There's a comma missing."

I examined the spot without turning my head, then returned my gaze to him. I decided on the response:

"Thank you, my dear."

I sat at my writing desk, quill pen in hand, and dipped the nib into my inkwell. I appended the missing comma to the sentence: *"As soon as an Analytical Engine exists it will necessarily guide the future course of the science."*

He had nodded, removing his reading glasses and cleaning them with his cotton handkerchief.

"And what, precisely, does *analytical* signify in this context?"

I remember looking up at him, misinterpreting his earnest stare. Admittedly, my subsequent lecture was a bit longwinded.

His eyes had glazed over by the time I arrived at my conclusion: "One day, we will even be able to compose music with it!" I had raved. "The applications are limitless!"

What had prevented him from simply delighting in this with me? What a pitiful little man, I had thought. How he toyed sulkily with his goatee as he countered:

"If what you are describing were possible, a real *scientist* would have developed it!"

If I had merely kept my peace, we could have continued lying together side by side in the warmth of my bed. But after a certain point, even the last spark of artificial humility fizzles out.

"Yes," I had nodded. "You're quite right. I am that scientist."

His cheeks had flushed. In answer to his question, as

to what I meant by this, I could only look away, lowering my gaze. And of course that had not sufficed as an apology for Charles. I rose from my writing desk as he turned away and began to pull on his trousers with great, theatrical gesticulations.

I know I should have said something. I struggled to find the proper words. But I did not want to show how much his outburst had amused me. My forehead began to itch, precisely at that moment when his faith in me began to erode away once more. It was, for the umpteenth time, the beginning of the end.

In silence, I watched the conflicting voices struggle for dominance inside his head. Some roared, emitting withering tones. They harshly condemned his "special friendship" with me. Others – admittedly the quieter ones – spoke conciliatorily, attempting to excuse away the incident, bemoaning the overpowering allure of unrequited love. But the most powerful voices belonged unambiguously to his lower lip. They concentrated on my cantankerous insistence on being right: "Insolent!" and "Impudent!" and "Ignoble!" were only the first denouncements beginning with "I".

"*Ach, Charles . . .*"

He loved the way I pronounced his name: *Charles*. Between my lips, with the French accent I reserved solely for his name, it sounded like a poem. A song of praise. There was a time when Charles had referred to me as "*Notre Dame*". His eyes were closed, he had caressed my forearm, leaning his head upon my shoulder. I cleared my throat – just once – immediately and definitively assuring that he would refrain from ever calling me by that name again.

". . . Let us not concern ourselves with such trivial matters as mathematics."

I stood behind him, my breath tickling the place on his neck between his collar and hairline where his pale skin was exposed. "Tell me rather of David." My lips brushed against the nape of his neck. "What is he doing? And his new father, Mr Murd . . . ?"

Of course, I already knew his name. Charles read to me from his most recent manuscripts at each of our rendezvous. And thus, he forced the reality of the London streets time and again into the privacy of my bed chamber. In those moments, I was wont to close my eyes. I allowed his stories to swirl about me – carried by his visions, through his voice, beyond my comprehension, deep into my heart. In this way, I came to appreciate all of his literary figures – more, even, than I appreciated my own family. I would have adopted the darling David in a heartbeat, who certainly did not deserve Murdstone as a stepfather. The fact that England possessed innumerable *real-life* orphans was something I could block from my mind with ease. We rarely spoke of my birth family. Or his seven children. Or my own three. We spoke only of those peculiar figures to whom we ourselves were married when it was positively unavoidable.

"Edward Murdstone."

"Murdstone." I nodded, kissing him again on the same spot. "Why must he be so awful, so *dreadful*?"

I felt how his heart threatened to burst. I perceived the sweat gathering above his upper lip. Charles, I thought, come back and lie with me. We could have pondered over literature and poetry and other immaterial things. We

could have laughed while caressing each other. We could have fallen silent while missing each other. So long as we discussed nothing of the fundamentals of our "special friendship", these rare, early-morning hours were healing for him. Beside me. Where he belonged. Of course, he underestimated how much energy this dance around uncomfortable subjects cost him, *cher Charles*. He circled them in ever-smaller orbits, drawing ever closer in recent days, until he got burned. The comforting security he felt with me was, unfortunately for him, the most dangerous part of the whole affair.

And yet, before this conciliatory side of my mind could take hold, the defiant thought arose: Why should I grant Charles my attention anyway? Simply because he always felt the need to share *his* feelings with *me*? *He* was a storyteller, after all! It was his calling to seduce and to confound. What did I stand to gain from such a person who spent his days manipulating people to acquire his wealth? To bring untruths and exaggerations into the world and, of all things, to be rewarded for these efforts? Not to mention his obsession with the poor.

My arms brushed gently against his hips. There was no need to hurry. Who would miss me? My lady friends? Perhaps. But only if they knew how I was spending my time. My mother? Hardly. She no doubt was enjoying her time in Ockham with her grandchildren, precisely *because* I was not there. William? Well. Since he had decamped to France two months before, I had only infrequently received word from my husband, and never with a mention of an impending return. I had no idea what he was doing there. Perhaps Lizzie would miss me. The dear thing. She had already made

herself scarce yesterday morning, without my so much as asking her. Astonishingly, she often seemed to recognise what I needed, even before I did so myself. My mother was right: I would never find a better chambermaid.

"I'm off to see my brother," she had winked with a little too much familiarity for my taste. "I'll be back promptly for luncheon tomorrow." There were a good nine hours in between, and I had some indecent notions of how Charles and I might spend them together. Patient and expectant, I played with his shirt buttons. My fingers tugged at them, I had almost opened the first and then – poof!

He freed himself quickly from my embrace, his necktie still open. The way I knew him, he would declare this to be the last meeting between us and I would finally experience – for God's sake, just this once – his resolve. As he opened the door, his eyes fell upon my desktop. His eyes narrowed, his nostrils flared, he cursed me in colourful terms. I did not listen, and I understood him even less. His voice faded away behind my mental calculation:

$$h = \tfrac{1}{2}gt^2 \rightarrow t = \sqrt{\frac{2h}{g}} = \sqrt{\frac{2 \cdot 5.75}{9.8\frac{m}{s^2}}} = \sqrt{1.17\,s^2} \approx 1.08\,s$$

(Or, how long it would take before a book landed on the street, if Charles were to throw one from the window, ignoring the current wind resistance, his left hand at shoulder height: 5.75 metres above the level of the footpath below.)

He stomped down the stairs, and I rushed to the window. A few moments later, I watched as he crossed the street, disappearing in the silence of the breaking dawn.

I did not mourn his departure. I already knew my way around Charles's attempts at determination, and I remained, as yet, unconvinced. He was an artist, after all.

The flame from the candle on the windowsill danced on, utterly indifferent to the recent goings-on. My reflection appeared like a spectre in the windowpane. Naked branches drifted through my hair; the faint glow of streetlights shone through my dressing gown. I had to laugh. I, who neither believed in ghosts nor religion, priests nor clairvoyants. I believe only in numbers, for those never lie. The spectre smiled back—

### Kohnstein bei Nordhausen, March 1945

and then it vanished.

I don't even know what pain is anymore. A bruised elbow. A broken heart. A burning sensation in the anus. All that would suggest this body still belonged to me. What a strange notion! I don't even know where to begin. All the signs that I could bring life into this world are gone. It's like a scolding from my uterus: "Yee ne'er pay the slightest heed, yee've loost yer past, they thieved yer present – Ah cannae bide it, Ah'm fer away an' takin' yer future wae me!" Even my mother's bracelet is gone. "Property of the German Reich." Like me. Nothing belongs to me anymore.

In this collection of moments that are not my own, I mostly flee into a floating, crimson room behind my

eyelids. From there, I can observe the situation from something like an objective distance. I can. But I don't want to. I never will.

If it happens at night and I can turn – head to the window – I often make it to the moon. I linger there, hopping about nimbly and licking the ground in curiosity. It would taste like powdered sugar. Lovely. If it happens in the early morning and I can wear the hair down, I shake – the head – imagining infinitely long and ashy blond hair. It would smell like cherry blossoms and lavender. Dreamy. In the afternoons, I'd be a track and field star, running faster than the speed of light! "*Übermensch!*" they would cry joyfully if I were Aryan. "Just like a man!" They would scream furiously if I were African. During the evenings, when the sessions are organised into fifteen-minute segments and should take no longer than two hours in total, I think up recipes. Culinary creations with asparagus in summer, or with chanterelles when the weather starts to shift towards fall. I'll tell this one to Cuddle Bear, I think: Linde and I love to exchange recipes. Even though we hardly gain any weight, she calls me Fatty and I call her Cuddle Bear. I allow myself to develop feelings for her, because without her, I wouldn't survive another day in Thirty-Seven. Besides that, I don't have emotions.

And that's why it's possible for another stripe to be standing in my room without me even wondering for how long. Or even wondering how. It's miraculous. They come – every fifteen minutes – and I don't even notice. This one doesn't look older than sixteen. He's even scrawnier than I am – and it makes me think:

See him flying through the room, a footprint on
    his ass—
a fist would shatter his already crooked nose—
fingernails would be painted red by it
the cracked lips would slowly
spread over the face while
the hands would wind around his neck. Tighter.
    He'd look
at the lips while he gasped for air. Finally, he'd
hear endless, shrill laughter—
I'd watch everything from close by—
I'd wish longingly that
I could regain the sense of touch
for this beautiful execution . . .

I sit on the edge of the bed. I observe that he can still feel pain. And that's the only reason I talk to him.

"We have names for you," I whisper, as he undoes his pants. Hastily. He only has fifteen minutes, after all – at this point, probably less than thirteen. "We have names for all of you. That might surprise you. But we can count, too."

Now his penis hangs between his legs, awkward and full of sadness. I wonder what it's doing there. It's supposed to be between *these* legs. I make the appropriate preparations and spread the respective body parts. His penis remains limp, and the fifteen minutes are almost up. The stripe descends into a cycle of *victim or perpetrator? Perpetrator? But I'm way more of a victim than she is. Right?* I know the look. Well, well, I think. You can't be that much of a victim if your dick still belongs to you. And since I don't have any possessions, I can't really have an opinion. I just look on:

18

a neither-victim-nor-perpetrator, a neither-good-nor-evil, a neither-man-nor-child, a nothing.

A pupil appears – encircled in grey-blue – in the hole in the door which provides the illusion of privacy to my visitors and me. I see the black pupil shortly before someone hammers on the door. I hear it, and I understand. I already know that they have their fun watching from out there, but the boy stares back wide-eyed at the jet-black pupil. Cute. He pulls his trousers up around his hips and ties them so tightly around the waist it seems like he'll never take them off again. He disappears before I can even fully memorise his number. The first digits: nine, zero, eight.

The next one enters. What a red face! He's dripping with sweat and smells like a dead fish. I barely take note of him, I just keep sitting on the edge of the bed. Because of Nine-Zero-Eight's lack of action, I have no reason to wash or disinfect anything, freshen up, or set anything straight.

"Dzień dobry," the next one says, closing the door behind him. It's strange. Even though I have no past, a surprising number of people recognise a faded connection to Poland hanging over me. I'm not sure where it comes from. But it happens so often, it can't be a coincidence. I don't answer. There's nothing "good" in this collection of moments, and I don't think in units as big as a "day".

The Pole sits next to me on the bed. He's bigger and older than the scrawny one. I notice that he lays his hand on the leg and strokes the thigh. His palm is sticky. He clears his throat, kisses me on the cheek, and asks what he should call me. I hear moaning and creaking from next door. I understand everything.

"Jak masz na imię?" he asks again. That damn jet-black

pupil appears at the hole again. This next one is lucky. I'm not going to try to hurt him. I just lie back and fixate on that goddamn jet-black pupil. I don't blink.

"Będę cię nazywał Ada," he whispers, as he lies down beside me. He licks the earlobe with the tip of his tongue. Call me whatever you want, I think. Yes, do with the body what you will.

This candle burns on.

# Among the Toothless

*Totope, March 1459*

No matter how tightly Mami Ashitey held me in her hand, no matter how quickly she swung her arm or how often she spun me about, she did not succeed in hurting Ada with her blows. Which, of course, gave me a certain pleasure.

In 1459, I was – as yet – unable to choose which object I would become, but as a brushwood broom, I still possessed a bit of leeway. At that time, at that place, my role was utterly uncomplicated. Most of the time, I lay about outside in a shady corner beside four or five clay pots and several piles of charcoal. I was put to use at least several times per day, but the space between the three small houses on the property was quite manageable. Even those who made the utmost effort to shirk from further household chores could sweep the dust, the chicken shit, and the fish scales together and haul them to the waste heap in no more than the span of two work songs. Naa Lamiley usually managed it in only a few breaths. And since it was typically her task to keep things clean around the yard, I had a lot of time on my twigs.

It was in just such a quiet hour, as I lay sun-drunk and dreaming, that Mami Ashitey put me to use. She swept and laughed and swept-laughed more, and I suspected no ill will. I remember that my twigs were all quite stiff and orderly – this was something in which I took particular pride. The toothless ones liked to tell one another that I looked so good because I was made of palm fronds while all the other brooms had been made of coconut leaves. And until that morning, I had had no cause to convince the women of anything to the contrary.

Mami Ashitey paused. I noticed that she was growing angry, as her grip around me tightened. A low rumble issued from her lips. And in the next moment, I flew through the air towards Ada's shoulder.

"What is wrong with you?!" I heard Mami Ashitey cry. Her eyes squinting as her mouth twisted in rage.

"For! The! Last! Time! Use! The! Right!" Each word was emphasised with another whack.

Naa Odarkor nodded to her wife, her otherwise placid forehead distorted by her narrowed brow. Although she was typically considered the more lenient of the two, it had grown customary for even Naa Odarkor to smack Ada on the upper arm with her stick rather than remind her at every opportunity – whether eating, cooking, or in greeting – to use only her right hand.

"Be quiet!" she would threaten. "Otherwise, I'll give you a *real* reason to cry, o!"

The women of Totope treated Ada as though she had emerged from Mami Ashitey's own loins. In their eyes, her daily floggings were glowing proof of familiarity and love.

I was not pleased to be misused for such purposes, and

so I always slowed my flight just before I was to strike Ada. And while Mami Ashitey continued demonstrating her love for Ada with ever-growing eloquence, a stranger was approaching the compound.

. • . • . • . • .

Guilherme Fernandes Zarco, an ill-tempered (and now for more than two years, insolvent) Portuguese merchant, had clambered down that very morning from the deck of the *São Cristóvão* and swum with great effort to the mainland. (How I knew of this, I will explain to you all in good time. I beg for your patience here: But let's stay with Guilherme for the moment.) As he stood upon the edge of the sea and glanced back at his ship, it seemed as though the freshly mended topsail rose directly from the depths of the blue water. Except for the fluttering sails, there was nothing but a great emptiness, a rustling and swirling, a spiral of blue and dazzling green, and sunlight gleaming like scattered diamonds on the surface of the waves. An endless shhhhh . . . it could all have seemed so peaceful – but for his suffering.

A few short days earlier, Guilherme had gambled away his every possession – lost everything but the clothes upon his back and the black sword at his side. He had tinkered his last shirt into a poor excuse for a sunhat to shield his bald head, his ears and even the tip of his disproportionally long nose. Everything else – especially his shoulders, chest, underarms and legs – had been surrendered to the merciless heat. As the *São Cristóvão* had approached the Costa do Ouro, his skin had smouldered as if in warning

to the other so-called explorers: "Do not tarry here on pain of death!"

Guilherme's every unnecessary movement resulted in a harsh punishment for whomsoever caused it, or if the culprit were not at hand, for whomever came within his reach. He had become a wandering pillar of pain, and why oh why oh why had he not remained lying aboard the ship? Why had he agreed in the first place to embark upon this journey? Africa? A second voyage? He gnashed his teeth as he thought about his creditors. Guilherme suppressed all too gladly any reminder that he had been *forced* back upon the high seas to escape his many debts.

The village in which Ada lived lay less than half an hour by foot through the rainforest from the coast. Of course, Guilherme could not have known this. But he supposed that the people who had laid their fishing nets upon the beach could not live far away. He kneeled down and rubbed one corner of a net between his fingers. It was stiff and warm, and obviously well maintained. Here and there, a few patches glittered a vigorous green from freshly woven strips of tree fibre. But where were their boats? He shielded his eyes and frowned. There was nothing to be seen to his left; to his right, only a single, sun-bleached canoe. From a distance it looked like nothing more than an odd piece of firewood.

Guilherme would have preferred to leave for the settlement at once. He was not sure how long it would take for his remaining colleagues – at least those who still had the strength to swim ashore – to reach the beach. Their heads bobbed up and down on the surface of the water, their arms straining against the distance. And where was Afonso?

Had he leaped from the *São Cristóvão* at all? As soon as he had identified the tiny figure among the struggling swimmers, Guilherme turned away from the commotion, stabbing with his sword into the sand. If they were all so useless as to drown immediately, he at least did not wish to observe the spectacle.

But there was no reason for Guilherme to maintain such thoughts. The sailors were all especially motivated – believing, as they did, that their mission was all but complete. They had set out in search of a certain Mansa Uli II and were of the opinion they were mere hours from their goal. Early that morning they had all already congratulated one another on their success. Everyone but Guilherme. He had folded his arms across his chest and scowled tight-lipped at his comrades – the paupers could not be dissuaded from this abstruse idea.

Their obsession was the direct result of the persuasive power of Diogo Gomes de Sintra, "Navigator, Explorer and Writer". This recently disgraced customs official had convinced them all to come along on the journey to Africa in the first place, promising that they would return with unimaginable quantities of gold. His claim – that this Mansa ruled over the entire continent – was an inauspicious embellishment of an otherwise carefully constructed lie which danced along in parallel to the truth of things. According to Gomes, Mansa Uli II was nearly as fabulously wealthy as the esteemed Mansa Musa, well known to be the richest person of all time.

And so, the men who were now labouring to drag themselves one by one onto the beach could not be convinced otherwise that – even if Africa were, in fact, simply

one kingdom – its king would not necessarily condescend to trade with a simple captain like Gomes. And even if this could, against all odds, be achieved – for after all, nothing is quite so consistent as constant change – it remained unthinkable that this Mansa would be found on a measly island or an impoverished coastal strip on the far margins of his empire.

Months later, Gomes would grind his teeth in recognition that Guilherme had been right. *Years* later, in the closing hours of his life, Gomes would cast the entirety of his career as an explorer in a favourable light in his memoirs. And decades after that, it would be forgotten entirely that Diogo Gomes de Sintra, "Navigator, Explorer and Writer", would never have given up his search along the coast and set out on his march into the interior of the continent, had it not been for Guilherme and his distinctive obstinacy.

Nevertheless, the incorrigible captain had cried "Lançar âncora!" on that fateful morning. And so they had dropped anchor a third time, at random, in the Gulf of Guinea.

The first sailor reached land as Guilherme's sword gleamed dry as a bone. But it still took several more minutes before all the men had assembled before him – Afonso hung back at the rear of the group. Only then was it conveyed to Guilherme that Gomes, due to "health complications", had remained onboard the ship. Guilherme suppressed a disparaging snort, for it was no secret that Gomes – in frustration – had emptied the final keg of wine during the night.

Guilherme did an about turn and began his march. He carried himself as though he were the rightful owner of

the entire land. The remaining sailors, all on the continent for the first time, struggled to keep up with his unyielding pace. They would first need to acquire something of his conduct: He soon left them behind, and that was fine with him. Guilherme slogged his way alone through the humming underbrush. Battered shrubs and mangled trees crashed to the earth behind him. Distraught parrots lamented in shrill tones as they took shelter in the crowns of neighbouring trees.

When he reached the dusty path which led from the jungle to the village, Guilherme's laboured breathing calmed. Pearls of sweat cooled his brow and glittered on his chest. He had left the others far in his wake, and he could no longer hear their voices. He continued along in the direction of the settlement and remained standing when he reached the edge of the first plot. He watched as Mami Ashitey punished Ada with the help of the broom. He shaded his eyes with his right hand, grateful for the distraction – the screeching and chattering. His gaze swept over the oddly familiar terrain.

Three tiny houses arranged about a round plot of land. Rounded cob walls, garments spread out to dry on the thatched roofs, and a freshly swept courtyard. The light – peaceful and clear – was unperturbed by the wisps of smoke rising from the coal stove. Strains of sound, rhythmic and shrill; a quiet breeze which caressed and embraced Guilherme where he stood. And untold quantities of fish. Smoked herring, dried sardines and fried shrimp: gleaming and aromatic, ready for the market stands.

He had only wanted to whisper "articulately", but as he turned, seeking, at the very least, for Afonso, he found

himself unable to keep his voice under control. He felt the hunger in his belly all too persistently, was too tormented by the waves of heat upon his face; it had been much too long since he had issued a command in anything resembling a normal tone of voice: "AFOONSOOO!" he cried.

About time! I thought. It was important that Ada and Guilherme met before the storm broke.

And so, the toothless ones became aware of his presence. They stared at Guilherme with huge eyes and open mouths. Mami Ashitey held me in mid-swing, high above her head, her gaze fixed upon the white man. Ada fell silent.

Guilherme removed his provisional headdress and glanced down at the dirt. In doing so, he caught a glimpse of the beads on the bracelet Ada still held in her hand. Perfect, I thought. Now it shall begin at last! The golden hue of the beads did not shine with their usual splendour and pretence: They glowed, rather, with the humility of moonlight. Guilherme had never seen such quality, not even in the mines of Obuasi. He took a step forward.

"Eh-eh!"

He understood nothing else.

Mami Ashitey raised her eyebrows.

This he understood at once.

Guilherme glanced about himself once more to be certain that his boys had not yet caught up with him – of course not, where were they anyhow? – then he began. Somewhat half-heartedly, he pointed with his right index finger at his chest:

"Guilherme Fernandes Zarco."

Nothing happened. He coughed. Still nothing. He pointed to himself once more:

28

"Eu – Guilherme Fernandes Zarco – *GIL-YER-ME*."

The jaw muscles of the toothless ones moved up and down; Naa Odarkor, squatting beside the fish, clutched her knife more tightly in her fist. Guilherme exhaled through pursed lips. Although this was certainly not the first time that men like himself had come ashore on the Costa do Ouro, these women still had not learned to speak properly.

As Guilherme drew his breath to begin anew, a flood of sounds streamed forth from Mami Ashitey. She gesticulated, rhythmic and frantic, as if to ask him why he had not brought someone with him who had mastered both his own vernacular, as well as hers. He had decided, at least, to interpret her many hand and finger movements so.

Guilherme sought after Afonso one final time in vain. (But actually, it was not ordained for him to appear on this page of the book.) Guilherme's movements pleased Mami Ashitey even less than before. Her tone became more forceful, the individual syllables shot forth staccato from her mouth. The other toothless ones agreed. Guilherme's gaze swept from one elder to the next. He watched as their thin eyebrows danced up and down across their foreheads, how their grey heads turned to and fro, their fine lips barely keeping time with the unrelenting pace of their words. Most of all, he observed that they were not truly angry, but seemed, rather, motivated by some exaggerated anxiety. *Some kind of threat*.

The baby, now uncovered, was attracting all manner of flies which danced around his nose. Mami Ashitey struck Ada one final blow to bring the matter to a decisive end, and placed me back in my corner. Ada rubbed her head

discreetly as Mami Ashitey bent over the body, swatting at flies and reaching for the white cloth once again.

It was shaken vigorously, this cloth. And he was inspected thoroughly, this Guilherme. A wad of spit flew conspicuously from her mouth and landed a few inches from his feet. It frothed boldly on the red dirt floor before disappearing, bubble by bubble, in the dust. Guilherme acted as though he had not noticed. However, the baby's corpse received a bit of the spit as well. Mami Ashitey bent down once more, this time to envelop Ada's child in the cloth. As she rose, Guilherme saw tears in her eyes. At first, they were only a few drops which vanished swiftly against the heat of the ground. Or perhaps he was mistaken? The heavy sky seemed poised to release an impressive display, of this he could be certain. Behind the delicate blue, coal-black strands of gossamer were gathering.

And then the rain broke loose with such fury that Guilherme could hardly make out his own outstretched hand. Water ran frantic red around the coal stove, between the stones, over the ants, pooling in puddles. He had not caught the swift transition from a reluctant "What was that?" to a rash "Let's go, o!" The hens, the goats, the lizards had all vanished in an instant. The toothless ones had made their way at once into the shelter of one of the small houses, salvaging nearly all the food along the way – a single fish head failed to make the exodus from the courtyard to the cover of the buildings and sulked alone, forgotten in the mud.

Ada had not stirred from her seat. The storm rain pelted against her eyes, her chin, her cheeks, but she remained seated next to her son. Soon he will be completely free, she

thought. The beads of her bracelet would protect him on his final journey. Yet she laboured to tie it around him, the cloth clinging to his body like a second skin. And as Guilherme – hope in his heart – signalled to her with a few hand gestures that he could lift the child in order to ease her task, she nodded. And as Guilherme – corpse in his arms – signalled to her with a few movements of his head and shoulders that he knew a good final resting place, she nodded again, grateful that Ataa Naa Nyɔŋmɔ – or whosoever – had sent Guilherme to her. Perhaps it was relief I felt as Ada struggled to her feet: relief because my work for this part of the story had been done. Ada stumbled along behind Guilherme, and he carried her treasured belongings away from the hut.

And the toothless ones were not alone among the living to observe this strange scenario from a rain-sheltered hiding place.

## Stratford-le-Bow, March 1848

Incarnating the head of a lion was no easy feat for me, for I had never been a living being. It neither helped that I was cast in brass nor that I bore a heavy ring in my proud jaws. I had never wanted to be an animal, much less approximate the appearance of one.

In 1848, the shape of a lion's head had been selected to adorn the doorknocker at 37 Elm Road. It was meant to exude certain attributes like fortitude, protection and strength. Things I knew nothing about. Once again, the

object I became had been determined without my consent. I had not yet begun to question this customary procedure.

My opportunities for influencing events were limited to daily contact with refined houseguests. Those with riding gloves often had no chance at all and thought I was defective. Those with fingerless, embroidered gloves of silk had to knock many times before attracting the attention of the exhausted chambermaid. This was amusing, but also trying over time, and I longed to be an ineloquent brushwood broom once more.

From my perch at the entryway, I commanded an admirable view of Charles's angry departure. And not I alone. It may have appeared so to outsiders, but it was no coincidence that Ada's husband had arrived mere seconds before on Elm Road. He tarried a few moments by the corner of Number 37, long after his rival had vanished in the fog – and presently he no longer felt weary. His hunger had evaporated, too, along with his heretofore urgent need to locate the next gutter or tree. The recent chain of events had gone too far: He had seen Dickens!

Naturally, scuttling after the scoundrel would have been below the bearing of Lord William King. He would not confront him; no, the time for friendly exchange had passed. He would not imprecate him. It was even too late to slap him across the face with a glove – a lovely fantasy which, for a moment, brought a smile to William's lips. He fingered the pistol in his coat pocket.

Communications concerning his wife's behaviour had reached him in Paris, including word that she was entertaining an "unconscionable friendship" with a novelist. Had this remained at just one or two whispered

commentaries, he could have dismissed it as simply more Ada hearsay. He could – at his next convenience – have taken the knave aside and advised him to take care that no further rumours of the kind proliferated. But it was clearly too late for a civilised solution. Now he had *seen* the rascal with his own eyes.

Ten times it was that William chafed for not being able to bring his reason better under control; ten times more he felt the same sharp twinge in the pit of his stomach. At the eleventh, he slammed his right fist against the wall and managed not to cry out. The skin over his knuckles split, and he welcomed the external pain. How ironic that he had returned unscathed from the catastrophe known as France only to be wounded in slumbering England. The whitewashed façade had seen a rude, red awakening. He examined his bleeding fist and snorted. He would tend to Mr Charles Dickens in good time. *First things first.* Where was Ada?

William assumed she would already be sitting at her writing desk at this intolerably early hour, obsessed as she was with her mathematics. Secretly, he suspected that she was not so much a countess, but rather some kind of counting machine in human form. He almost wanted to see this woman – his wife, the mother of his children – run weeping, perhaps even pleading, from the house after Dickens. To see that the unscrupulous rogue meant something to her at least. That she maintained the ability to feel deep-seated emotions like desire, ardour, or even hatred for another human being. That she possessed a heart of flesh and blood at all.

The moon was already fading, but the mist had not yet

fully risen. William faltered, recognising moments later that it was merely shadows he saw lingering defiantly in the alleyways. A few birds twittered – could they already be house martins? What cause did they have to be so merry? The time was ripe for a dramatic scene to unfold! To hammer on the ring in my mouth at Number 37 until the heads of households appeared in their starched night-shirts at the neighbouring doorways!

William shook his head. No, he was consideration per-sonified: He would never do such a thing to his comrades in misery. In but a few hours they would be leaving their homes – neatly dressed, prepared and in high spirits. To be sure, only after first offering some words of consolation to their anxious wives. The latest developments in Paris were enough to raise concern even in female heads. They also read the headlines. They, too, could put one and one together. No. *William* would by no means rouse these fine men from their precious sleep. It was the "good ones" like Dickens who had no sensibility for their fellow man. This hero of the toothless masses was, in principle, worse than a simple egoist. With his so-called art he deluded everyone into believing he intervened on behalf of the rights of the poor. He could certainly arouse passions. But what more? Who truly cared about Oliver Twist? Surely even the most obstinate Chartist must acknowledge that the average worker in Great Britain was far better off than in any other European land. Why, in France he would not even have freedom of assembly! Paris was burning for good cause!

William grasped my ring a little too tightly and pounded it three times against the door. I knew he was expecting Lizzie. Where else should she be? He anticipated her

sleepy footsteps on the spiral stairway and was planning to instruct her – after a portentous moment's pause – to summon her mistress. But a few moments later we heard, instead, how Ada herself sprung down the few steps from the first floor to the foyer. William's restive heart skipped a beat.

"You may only come in if you promise me not to run away again . . ." Ada grinned as she opened the door. She had prepared to continue her teasing, but the words caught in her throat at the sight of William. She stood gaping at him. It was written all over his face: This man – her husband, the father of her children – had seen Charles.

She grew pale. After a good half minute, he cleared his throat.

"I will not run away," he said. "It is about to rain."

I could sense how every single hair on Ada's body rose. There had been no indication in his last message that he would be returning so soon. At times, she had even thought he might have perished in the Parisian flames – and she had been startled because she had felt neither grief nor shame at the thought. His appearance robbed her of her speech.

"But where . . . ? How . . . ? Since when have you . . . ?"

I was impressed that William could retain such composure. He said only:

"Where is your bracelet, Ada?"

In this way, we arrived at the matter without delay, and I was grateful because the storm had already announced itself with the first drops of rain. Of course, in 1848, Ada possessed any number of bracelets. Luckily it was not in her nature to stall for time with unnecessary questions. She

knew he meant his wedding gift to her: an exquisite trinket made of beads which exuded a splendid, rare white-golden hue. A bracelet he had inherited from his mother. According to tradition, she had received it from her husband, William's father, on their wedding day.

And William knew that Ada knew that he knew: She had not the foggiest idea where the precious bracelet could be.

## Kohnstein bei Nordhausen, March 1945

At first there were no designated rooms in the *Sonderbaracke*, the so-called special barrack. Everything in or around the Dora labour camp was quantified, measured and recorded seamlessly. From the outside, it was all but indistinguishable from the other wooden huts in the bleak compound: ten-point-five metres wide, twenty-three-point-seven-five metres long, one-storey; the Tommies would have deemed it "unaccommodating". The building would have been entirely inconspicuous had it not been for the flowers in the windows. Its residents were hesitant to describe their lodgings as the "special barrack". And although Ada would have had a far more fitting designation for the place (she called it the "Gates of Hell"), they all eventually agreed – inspired by the administrative number – on calling it "Thirty-Seven".

When they had arrived – they had still been women then – each had been allocated a six-digit number. This was even sewn into their underwear, and it was not to be altered for

the length of their internment. Clothing, haircuts, meals, breaks, positions – everything had been determined and mandated by the camp commander. Everything but the designation of rooms. Ada often wound up in the last room to the left at the end of the hall, where – if she opened her eyes at the right time – the evening twilight took on a particularly lovely sheen. She found herself there so often that it came to be known as "Ada's Room". And, of all things, I was this room.

Friederike Lindauer or Linde, Cuddle Bear to Ada and 972621 for camp records, was one of eight – they had still been women then – selected in March 1945 "for pleasurable use" by the innumerable prisoners. "Still, it's better here than at Ravensbrück" had been the unanimous assessment. At any rate, the food was better at Thirty-Seven, they had warmer clothes, and there was at least the possibility of washing oneself.

Upon her arrival in Dora, Linde had become involved with a thin-lipped, bald-headed prisoner for no other reason than because he, too – in a manner of speaking – came from Göttingen. His name was Waldemar, he had been toiling in the crematorium since the beginning of the year, and he smelled as atrocious as he looked. He used every resource at his disposal in order to win her for himself alone. Because he could. His delicate position within the camp hierarchy allowed him – shall we say – certain privileges. Between making lewd comments and shoving his tongue down her throat, Walde assured Linde that he would personally ensure that she was taken good care of in the special barrack. He sneered after she had repeated the word "good" doubtfully, the gaps in his teeth underscoring the

dereliction of his haggard face. Thirty-Seven was, without a doubt, less horrid than the three days in the Ravensbrück standing cell, but the best that Linde could say of the place where she now found herself was far from "good". Very, very far. Nevertheless, she tolerated this questionable deal with him in order to maintain even a chance of surviving the hell that was Dora. She rejoiced over his countless small gifts, she satisfied him with her hand or mouth as required, and otherwise did her utmost to ignore his brutal transgressions upon the other prisoners.

One day, Walde bestowed her with an exceptional bracelet. They were in the room directly next to me when she received it.

"What kind of beads are these?"

"Hoho!" Walde laughed. "This again. You always want to know everything, don't you?"

"Oh, leave me in peace," she stammered. Even after all these years, she still had not managed to match her language to the circumstances. Besides Linde, no-one in the camp ever spoke of "peace" or "quiet".

As Walde's laughter transitioned into a painful bout of coughing, Linde weighed the jewellery in her hand. It felt heavy between her fingers. Somehow burdened.

"How should I know," Walde wheezed, at last. "I guess it must have slipped out of the warehouse."

Of course, her suspicions about the bracelet's origins were justified.

"Well, do you like it?"

He vanished after she had nodded. He obviously had not noticed her hesitation. As usual, Walde had no time for nuances.

Linde put the bracelet on. The silvery glimmer of the beads seemed out of place on her child-sized wrist. She thought about the place under her bed, the loose board where she hid her treasures. It would be prudent, and certainly more secure to stow this re-stolen bracelet away at once and only admire it by candle- or moonlight. But she was enjoying this moment far too much: Someone had done something on her behalf. Risked his life to give her this small pleasure. She grew lax, intoxicated by feelings of happiness and revery. She forgot that she was no longer a woman.

But God had other intentions for her. By happenstance, Linde was wearing a long-sleeved dress, a bit too big for her. Its cuffs danced about the ends of her fingernails as her room suddenly filled with a row of SS officers. They were as identical as the brass buttons on the front of their uniforms: rigid jaws, faces like iron, steely-pupiled eyes.

The six-digits were to assemble on the parade grounds at once. Wordlessly, with only a cock of an eyebrow, Linde was permitted to put on her shoes. But in such haste, she only managed to shove her feet into the openings. She kept her eyes to the floor, stumbling along past the officers who please, please, please should not observe how her heart pounded in her throat. As she reached the threshold of the room, an officer cleared his throat. Linde did not want an interaction, and she did her best to act like she had Nothing. To. Hide. As she glanced to her side, she locked eyes with him: a watery, almost translucent blue. She was in grave danger of making eye contact for too long ... But the officer beside him – a timid, anxious man who could no longer bear the horrors of Dora and would later shoot

himself – struck her in the ribs with the butt of his rifle. Just hard enough to save her life. Linde vanished through the door.

Just why exactly, in 1945, I had to incarnate a room in a concentration-camp brothel was not obvious to me at the time. My walls were so thin that every cry, every moan resonated through me corporally. I was condemned to witness everything and yet remain unable to hinder anything. To conceal everything, and yet erase nothing. My short tenure as a doorknocker struck me, then, as infinitely preferable. And yet I needed to get on with things: If at all possible, the transfer of the bracelet was to be achieved before the storm! And so, Linde was sent to the parade grounds.

The wind outside! It bit into the ears of the assembled six-digits and lashed against their cheeks. It brought no promise of healing, but a mere assurance of the sleet to come. Ada's face was already glowing snow-white with cold when Linde picked her out from among the crowd. They were commanded to march along past the prisoners with outstretched arms.

"Cuddle Bear," Ada whispered. "What are we doing here?"

Linde looked up at the sky without moving her head. Allegedly, "the girls" were supposed to be spared the attendance of public executions, but how should she reply to Ada with such a comically banal response? And since when had they been elevated to the level of "girls"?

"I suppose they must protect our femininity," Linde said at last, and was grateful that Ada did not ask further questions.

Of course, the more observant readers among you

might be wondering how a room within a concentration-camp barrack could possibly bear witness to events happening in front of the camp's gates. And you would be right to do so. But here, again, I'll have to ask for your patience. In any case, the six-digits stood that morning before the gates of Dora and did their utmost not to listen to what was happening inside. And yet they still saw, in their minds' eye, how the corpses fluttered like Reich flags in the wind. Everyone but Ada and Linde. As usual, they were exchanging recipes:

"Kaiserschmarrn: the ultimate sugared pancake!"

"With or without vanilla custard, Cuddle Bear?"

"Who cares? The most important thing is the rum!"

At that very moment, a Mercedes Benz W 138 – production year 1937 – stopped at the security check point in front of the gates of the camp. The freshly polished automobile glowed as if someone had recently attempted to wipe clean the collective filth which had gathered upon it since the beginning of the War. A fine-boned, serious-faced man in uniform sat in the back of the vehicle, gazing indifferently out of the window. Two SS officers spoke to the driver in staccato tones. He seemed unimpressed by their choleric manner, answering their many questions calmly and objectively:

– They were on their way to the Tunnel Facilities.

– They had all the appropriate documents at hand.

– Of course, they could search the trunk of the vehicle.

And while the two officers paraded self-importantly around the vehicle, the driver stared into the distance through the windshield. His gaze was both peaceful and indomitable, and he fit perfectly into the treacherous

landscape: stately fields as far as the eye could see, proud rows of European beech looming over the horizon – a stubborn mockery of serenity. His only movement was to – occasionally and discreetly – rub his nose.

"I knew it," Linde hissed.

"Hmm?"

"Take a look! He's new here."

Ada squinted at the stiff figure behind the steering wheel. She did not notice anything of interest. He was a man who followed orders – just like every man here.

"He's breathing our air for the first time . . ." Linde whispered, falling silent as the SS officers finished their inspection of the vehicle.

– They could confirm that the automobile was in proper order.

– It could be on its way in a moment.

– But it would first require the appropriate stamp.

The driver pressed his lips together until they became two thin lines. His cheeks paled.

By March 1945, the stench of Dora had achieved a particular quality. A rot hung in the air, clung to the skin, poured into the lungs and airways. It did not stink of immediate death. It did not stink of torture or murder either – for these could only rarely – and certainly not with human senses – be perceived. No. The thing which had begun on the parade grounds with fear and desperation – an aroma which, in 1943, had hung most notably about the entry gates – now wafted far and wide beyond the fences of Dora. A constant, lurid cloud hung over each and every person who lived in or around Kohnstein – yes, even over those who would later claim that they knew nothing.

A few weeks before her imprisonment, Linde had fallen head over heels in love – which came as a great surprise to her already married friends. Up until then, she had only had a few short-lived affairs, convinced that she would spend the rest of her life living with and tending to her ailing father. The roll of paper which hung from her apartment door for unexpected visitors had remained unused for years. And then, one day, when she returned home hungry and exhausted from her work, she had noticed a scribbled message. She did not recognise the handwriting, and she chewed at her thumbnail while she read. And read again. She could not believe her eyes.

Rainer was the proprietor of a pub just a few metres from the Gänseliesel fountain on the market square. And, just as he had written in his note at her door, he was waiting for her next to this fountain with three red roses in his hand the following day at precisely one in the afternoon.

"I only knew," he would later explain to her, "that I needed to meet with you privately just once."

And from that moment on they were inseparable. She dreamed of one day being a respectable landlady working at her husband's side, and he scraped together his entire savings to put a humble ring upon her finger. Linde's father was also perfectly happy. He opened a new bottle of the good schnapps every few days; he cracked one corny joke after another and always laughed the loudest. He was downright blissful. Until he struck Linde across the face one evening, after learning that Rainer was a "Half-Jew" and his only daughter was well on her way to becoming a race traitor.

Some things should not be rushed. Like hunting for an

apartment, for example. Or planning a wedding. Young couples take their time making these kinds of decisions for good reason. But other things need to happen with lightning speed. And so it was for Linde and Rainer. His German citizenship was promptly revoked. His business was confiscated. And Linde was sitting in police custody before she had had the time to ask her fiancé what a "Half-Jew" even was.

Before long, Linde grew accustomed to the knowledge that she would never again read Rainer's beautiful handwriting. The realisation, that after her time in Thirty-Seven, she would never again be suitable for marriage, came during her first month at Dora. And that – for outsiders – disconcerting stench soon became an unalterable aspect of her everyday life. She only noticed her own diminishing sense of smell from the reactions of others, like the driver of the automobile.

Maybe that was why her nose had begun to itch. She waited for the most inconspicuous moment to raise her left hand and cover her nose and mouth with her sleeve. She sneezed. The indifferent face in the window of the backseat could not possibly have heard her, and yet, in that critical moment, he looked in her direction. Something gleamed on Linde's wrist. He noticed. And she knew that he had seen. That torturous moment between recognition and punishment: It was almost worse than the torture to come because one's fantasy does not acknowledge the limits of possibility . . .

Linde's eyelids froze.
Time crawled

as slowly as
those eternal seconds
in the Ravensbrück standing cell.

As slowly as
the first minute
in which she stood there
in the filth,
in darkness.

As slowly as
the feeling of
suffocation
death from exposure
falling aslee . . .
"Are you shitting again?"
the woman to her left
crying softly
a brown river
discolouring her leg
the woman to her right
with her shoulder
in Linde's back,
a creeping death
smothering her dreams,
and this until
the morning bells chime.
The second minute—

As slow as
the first.

Eventually he turned away from her, glancing back at the pile of unsorted documents on the seat beside him – long enough for Linde to slide her hand down, bit by bit. She could only breathe again when her wrist was covered once more by her sleeve. The cold air numbed her throat. Linde stared at the ground, concentrating on the murmuring of the six-digits around her, the twittering of the birds flying overhead . . . anything to tune out the sound of her still-pounding heart. The shots from the parade grounds fell silent. Lunchtime, it seemed. The six-digits would soon be commanded to march back along the stony pathway – past the many stripes waiting with outstretched arms, their faces contorted by pain.

Moments before the vehicle shifted into first gear and the humming of the motor grew louder, Linde caught an exchange between Ada and the man on the backseat. They stared vacantly at one another, maintaining eye contact even as the driver began to accelerate. The automobile left fresh tracks in the mud behind.

"Fatty?" Linde whispered, when all traces of the vehicle had vanished from sight but for the trail of exhaust as the grey of the day began to dissipate.

"Fatty, do you know him?"

Ada's gaze remained unchanging, glassy-eyed.

"No, Cuddle Bear," she answered at length. "Not yet."

# Among the Deceived

I had summoned Lizzie – but not in the typical manner, as you might, with your shrill tongues. But I also had not summoned her through the dull sound of knocking. Lizzie was sleeping at the foot of the spiral staircase, at no great distance from the foyer, as she was wont to do whenever her mistress held her clandestine rendezvous with Mr Dickens. It would not have mattered how many times he pounded against the wooden door with the brass knocker ring I held in my mouth – Lizzie would not have heard a thing. Now it is true that she slept remarkably lightly, but on the day before, after she had served Lady Ada her breakfast, I had observed how Lizzie had departed from 37 Elm Road. Yes, even I – with my obstinate head and eyes of brass – even I could recognise her pain.

It had begun calmly, like every other day. Lizzie had drawn open the curtains of the bed chamber after setting the tray of breakfast upon her mistress's bed with a smile. Her eyes had swept the room – the flowers would soon need replacing, but otherwise things were in prime form.

Whisps of vapour still rose from the spout of the teapot, and sunlight was streaming through the open windows. Lady Ada had arisen and was nibbling absentmindedly at a bit of cheese while Lizzie buttoned her mantle.

"I'll be back promptly at luncheon tomorrow," she had winked. In order to afford Lady Ada and her "special guest" a bit of privacy, Lizzie had arranged an overnight visit to her brother.

As she was leaving, Lizzie asked, "What shall I bring along with me to cook?"

Lady Ada's response had been downright appalling. Lizzie could only stare at her mistress with open mouth – and that was saying quite a lot, considering all that they had been through together in recent times. Or had Lady Ada not newly confessed to Lizzie her considerable gambling debts? Had Lizzie not risked her own reputation more than once to pawn her mistress's most expensive pieces of jewellery? Had Lady Ada not, only the night before, confided her desperation to Lizzie in tears? Had she not permitted Lizzie to take her in her arms? Like a true friend? Had Lizzie been so deceived?

Although Lizzie had succeeded in closing her mouth again, every fibre in her body was loathe to accept the obvious. Shortly before leaving the house, Lizzie had held her index finger to her lower lip, searching in vain for a bit of nail to chew away. Instead, she had, by accident, torn off a bit of skin.

"Bollocks!"

She shook her right hand with all her might, but she was unable to cast off the miserable feeling.

I hear you asking: Could Ada really have told Lizzie

to fetch potatoes? The gracious Lady Ada? After all these years? After all the misery, the mourning, and the suffering? Unfortunately: Yes.

There could be no doubt that Ada knew about the potato blight afflicting Ireland. The reports were as omnipresent as the wretched new arrivals flooding London's streets. Children selling oranges and boys pilfering fried fish. Women with not a penny to their name sleeping in public squares, and men with the few remaining pennies waiting before the closed doors of the pubs. Bony figures, every one, dressed in tatters of skin and hair and rags.

It would have been quite easy for Ada to ignore the misery altogether. Like her Claras, Lucys and Henriettas, Ada, too, could easily have drifted from salon to salon, spending her days playing piano, writing letters or embroidering tiny flowers without taking any notice or worrying about things which would never affect her. And yet, thanks to her "special friendship" with Charles, Ada knew more than she cared to. Try as she might, she could not unhear the stories he told her. And so, she had to satisfy herself with the second-best solution: hardening her heart.

Ada knew well that Lizzie had arrived just two years before from Ireland, bringing only one large bag and one younger brother. She also knew that Lizzie's parents had been too feeble to flee to England themselves. And how could Ada have forgotten that "Ma and Pa" had starved to death in a poorhouse only a few weeks later? On the day that Lizzie had received the news, she had excused herself from her duties and tried in vain to muffle her sobs. But the thin walls had betrayed her.

And what had become of her remaining siblings? Ada

49

had not enquired at the time. In fact, neither in that moment nor in the days and weeks which followed after, had she found any words of comfort for her chambermaid. Not out of ill-will. This apparent lack of interest in the private life of her maid was not deliberate. It was simply that in 1848, Ada had not yet learned that not every problem could be solved with a mathematical formula. She had made the joke about potatoes because she had been both unable to identify as well as unable to contain the feeling of shame that was growing inside of her. It had robbed her of peaceful sleep, it gnawed at her composure, it caused her to stumble and stutter. It had even once brought her to tears in front of Lizzie. Quite bothersome, indeed! And yet, had she paused for even a single moment longer

and held her peace

it would have been clear, even to Ada, that Lizzie's suffering was immeasurably greater than her own. Ada still had a long journey ahead of her.

But it was Lizzie who left the house that morning.

While still on the front steps, she had rearranged her bonnet and cursed through her clenched teeth:

"Sure look. You're a bloody turnip, Lizzie!"

Time to go, Lizzie thought; and she went before her mistress had the chance to come up with any other wise ideas. Rushing out the front door and onto the street, looking neither to her left nor to her right, she nearly bowled over the chimneysweep.

"Oi!"

The lad had managed to maintain control over his sundry effects, all down to a single brush which teetered for several moments before toppling from his shoulder to the street.

"Oi!" he cried again. "Can ye hand me that?"

He pointed to the brush which had fallen into a heap of muck. Lizzie glanced from the brush back to the youth and snorted. She had just made up her mind to keep walking, and had not wanted to honour his flood of words with even so much as a response. But when the lad began to curse her parents – she landed a solid slap across his face with her right hand.

"Just one more word!" She wiggled her finger menacingly before his nose. "One more. Just one! I swear to you it'll be the last to ever leave that filthy little mouth of yours!"

He stumbled a full four steps backwards, glancing about himself in hopes of some assistance. But no-one was watching. Horse hooves clippity-clapped along the cobblestones. Children squabbled. Grown-ups rushed along unheeding. Rats pilfered; cats yowled. White men in charcoal-blackened faces beamed at the applause they received as they concluded their imitation of a spiritual in a street performance. Not until Lizzie had reached the next corner did the chimneysweep let loose with his curses unchecked. He leaned his assortment of brushes against a wall, muttering under his breath about the "manky Irish". The greater the distance grew between him and Lizzie, the more colourful his exclamations became.

The insults glanced off her. What more could this Englishman do to her that had not been done before? Like so many others in London who saw themselves as having been forced to flee their homelands, Lizzie already felt cheated of her humanity. One could expect no more from these – how had Ma always called them – these Sassenachs!

Tears welled in Lizzie's eyes. One could expect nothing more from them.

She would have preferred to leave Elm Road behind her once and for all. Quite understandably. And yet, I had called her back. Without a sound. I had appealed to her consciousness through a nagging sense of doubt. She should neither reappear too early nor too late, and so I first called out to her after she had arrived at Alfie's.

Lizzie's brother, named for his Pa, was scrawny as they come. It was as though his body had permanently refused to recover from the horrors of starvation which had ravaged his first life. Alfie called it his first life. But in fact, truth be told, it had not been any kind of life at all. Here and there, he could still recall a few vague memories – squatting in a field and stuffing a few handfuls of muddy grass into his mouth. But even that image came ever less readily to mind, and would – in a few short years – vanish as well.

Alfie's "second birth" occurred after a stormy crossing of the Irish Sea, when he first set foot upon south Wales. He estimated his own age to be sixteen, perhaps seventeen, but whenever he was asked, he stated his year of birth as 1845 – beginning on that icy November day in Newport, when he, covered in tears, had thanked his heavenly Father for the second chance which had been granted him and his elder sister.

All he had was Lizzie.

But since she had begun to work for Lady Ada, Lizzie spent most of her time in Ockham, a good four hours' journey from Alfie's . . . well, there was not a proper word for it. It would be impossible to describe it as his home. The

place where he lived provided something like a roof over his head, though apart from that it lacked every other component which might constitute a home. He shared "his" room with three other families, including seven grunting children and two pigs. There was no bed, not even something like a consistent corner to tuck away into. He carried the rare letters he received from his sister with him everywhere he went.

Lizzie arrived at Church Street Market as the evening sun had begun to dapple the horizon with traces of pink and orange. As they had agreed, she waited at the entry to the market, directly in front of Charlie Huckle's fish stand.

"Y'alright, Lizzie?" He grinned as he stuck his hand into the bucket of live eels.

"Could be worse, Charlie Huckle," she replied. But in truth, she felt every bit as miserable as the poor creature which he had just caught and stretched across the wooden table. Charlie Huckle – for so he was always called: never simply "Charlie" or "Huckle" – wiped his brow before swinging his cleaver down upon the table.

"Aye," he nodded. "There's few could argue with you there, love."

He removed the eel's guts and scraped them away along with its freshly separated head. The eel's mouth continued to move, as if still gasping for air.

Lizzie enjoyed watching Charlie Huckle work. It was difficult, in any case, to see other people in the market. Those more than three stalls away already began to vanish in the prevailing thickness of the yellow London fog. In Lizzie's opinion, Charlie Huckle was a bit extravagant in his choice of clothing, but she no longer mentioned it

to him. Over the years, she had grown used to the black bowler that was always balanced just to one side atop his head. His billowing hair grew ever whiter, in contrast to his apron, which was so covered in blood and entrails that it was no longer worth his while to wipe his hands on it.

Charlie Huckle sang often and gladly while he worked. Mostly for the street children. They delighted whenever he struck up their favourite tunes about cheeky lads and angry mothers. Particularly because of the hilarious changes of voice he could achieve – reaching the high notes of a screeching housewife with ease. And sometimes he spared them a fishtail or a handful of mussels. Sometimes he did not. But he was always cheerful, nonetheless.

At the moment, all his concentration was directed towards his battle to control the still wriggling eel. The children would need a moment's patie—

"For the love of God!"

Lizzie leaped from her perch on the wooden bench. From out of the blue, a slender hand had clapped down on her shoulder. She spun around and clasped at her heart: Alfie.

Alfie!

Lizzie let out a series of curses, a few so illustrative that Charlie Huckle had to pause again in his singing. The combination of her reddened face, her wide eyes, and everything he gathered from reading her lips provided Alfie with a fairly accurate impression of what she was shouting. He grinned as she shook her head, pursing her lips. And the more he grinned, the more difficult it grew for her to maintain her angry scowl. Finally, Lizzie drew her brother up in an embrace, pressing her cheek against his own, and throwing her arms around his meagre body.

It was hard to believe, but Alfie smelled even worse than he had at her last visit. He still wore the same tattered shirt, coated in coal dust on those few places which were not already rife with holes. His jacket may have provided him with a bit of shelter from the stormy days and icy-cold nights, but it was much too small, and the threadbare patches where the elbows had once been had become more a suggestion than a real covering. He had obviously inherited his "new" breeches from someone twice as wide, and he wore a frayed bit of rope for an improvised belt.

Alfie laughed and spun a pirouette before extending her a crumpled note. Her eyes grew even larger as she read it.

"*Lord King?* Are you quite certain?"

As she repeated the hand sign for "true", her fingers trembled. Alfie nodded, so slowly that Lizzie did not take notice. She tapped him on the shoulder.

"Alfie?"

He sighed, rubbing his eyes and adjusting the packet of smoked shellfish he held under his arm. He signed with his hands: "I'd recognize the bastard anywhere."

Alfie worked delivering coal, but since the beginning of the unrest in France, his boss had begun a lucrative second business in transporting desperate people. Those who could not afford to be seated in the train were not bothered by a seat atop the sacks of coal, and those who could not afford to be recognised in the train were bothered even less.

Some days, Alfie and his two colleagues would travel for hours towards Dover only to return at the end of the day with more passengers than they could safely carry. The road to London had been swarmed with migrants now

for weeks. Young and old, sick and merry, exhausted and grateful, whole families, in pairs, or solitary – all of them looked as if they had barely survived the apocalypse. And from amongst the entire hubbub, one person in particular had stuck out to Alfie. In front of a roadhouse in Maidstone: It had been impossible to mistake his pretentious airs.

"But why did he not come by train?"

Alfie shrugged, angering his sister Lizzie, since it seemed he was withholding important information. But as they exited the market, he had simply been lost in thought. Lord King had scampered from one coach to the next without any luggage. Alfie would have ignored him entirely had one of the other lads not jotted "William King – Surrey" on a scrap of paper, and shoved it under Alfie's nose.

"Surrey?"

Alfie nodded. It appeared that Lord King had assumed his wife would be in Ockham. Lizzie still had a bit of time.

"And you didn't want to give him a lift?"

Alfie laughed. "A lift? I wouldn't so much as piss on him if he were burning right in front of me eyes."

He placed a distinct emphasis on the sign for fire, dragging it out, and almost dropping his fish in the process.

"Did you see who took him with them?"

Lizzie's hand signs were not as fluid as those of her brother. In contrast to him, she hardly ever communicated by sign. As they crossed over New Road together, she wondered whether she had signed the word for "lift" properly. A lad stopped in the middle of the street, staring slack-jawed at the two siblings. Under normal circumstances his reaction might have earned him a particularly

56

crude finger gesture from Alfie, but this time Alfie merely shoved him out of the way without a word. Alfie was focused on his sister, his dark eyebrows knotted together.

"Why on earth are you so buggered about it?" he asked.

Lizzie had looked away because she was not quite sure of the answer herself. She had no idea that I was calling her. In the end, she attributed her disturbance to the fact that – despite it all – she still worried about her mistress. Should Mr Dickens yet be present when Lord King arrived, Lizzie could not imagine that Lady Ada would get out of the ensuing confrontation unscathed.

"Lord King can get himself into quite a rage."

Alfie responded to the observation with another shrug of the shoulders. It happened often when they spoke of the Kings. How Alfie despised them. Not just because they were English – although that would have been reason enough – but most of all because of their hypocrisy. As nobility they both had blood on their hands, and yet they regarded themselves as highly civilised. And acted as though there was no contradiction there. It was impossible for Lizzie to explain her unease to Alfie. She only knew that she needed to return as soon as possible.

"What about the meeting?" he asked.

Lizzie cursed. Of course, it had slipped her mind. But not mine. Everything was going according to plan.

"Please go for me," Alfie pleaded. "Our only realistic chance is to handle this strategically."

"Strategically, yes. But with the English?"

"With the *workers*," he corrected her.

Alfie stroked his sister's arm and tucked his supper into

his jacket pocket. A group of small children tottered about Portland Square. A barefoot lad with a particularly filthy mouth stopped before Alfie and waved. Lizzie shook her head.

"You're dreaming. We haven't got nowt ourselves!"

"At least we have food!"

His hands flew from chest to mouth, and the lad repeated the gesture after him. Lizzie's fingers contradicted the action.

"There's no way we're going to organise a bloody revolution in Ireland from here!"

"What in the . . . ?" Alfie's cheeks flushed as crimson as his eyes. "We've *got* to help!"

I thought they both had a point. England *had* got away with its abuse of Ireland for far too long; an uprising was long overdue. It made perfect sense to me that Alfie was thinking of the future *as well as* justice.

But Lizzie's exhaustion made a relevant counterpoint. The price they had already paid was high enough; they had to consider their own safety too. And some battles could not be won. Lizzie blinked back her tears in vain.

"No! It's not up to us to help!" she cried. "*They've* got to flee!"

An infant wailed. Lizzie glanced behind them to see a young woman glaring at her with flaming eyes, the distressed baby cradled in her arms. She turned back to Alfie:

"If Ma and Pa had done the same, they wouldn't have died in their own filth in some bloody, godforsaken Irish field!"

Balling her right hand into a fist, she drew her outstretched thumb across her throat. She regretted it

immediately. All at once, the entire swarm of tiny children began to dance about them, drawing their own balled fists and outstretched thumbs across their little throats. Alfie paused for a few moments before moving forward.

"Please go."

"Alfie . . ."

"For me. What am I supposed to do there? You and I both know the hearing only concern themselves with the hearing." He stretched out his hands towards Lizzie.

She nodded. First in exhaustion, then with determination. All she had was Alfie.

And so it was that Lizzie took part late that evening in yet another interminable meeting of the Women's Charter Association – and she stayed until each of the assembled men had commented on at least one of each other's contributions; until all arguments for and against women's suffrage had been debated and exchanged; and until a grey-haired gentleman – easily identified by his heavy accent as a German refugee – had broken the mould with an indefatigable lecture on the dehumanisation of the proletariat through Great Britain's Industrial Revolution. Even if she had wanted to, she would have been unable to fulfill Alfie's wish.

It was not until after midnight, when the meeting had finally adjourned, that she could answer my call and begin the long trek back across London to Elm Road.

· • · • ·

And so Lizzie had stood across from the house, slightly concealed, and whistled. Two times: short and shrill, as she

had agreed upon with her mistress in case of emergency. At first, it seemed to Lizzie as though she had received an immediate response. Lady Ada had cocked her head ever so slightly to the side as she approached the window, staring intently out over the grounds before her. But as Lizzie rubbed her hands together, as the tiny puffs of cloud rose from her mouth to vanish in the morning air, as she stamped impatiently with one foot and then the other, Lady Ada drifted away from the window as though there had been nothing. Had she not heard the signal? Or not understood? Or was she ignoring it entirely?

Lizzie tore at the edge of her right thumbnail with her teeth. She was just about to whistle again, this time louder and even more shrilly, and thus upset the delicate melody of the morning street, when she saw – in the nick of time – Lord King emerge from the alleyway alongside the house and approach the entryway. Good heavens, he looked haggard! Ragged and angular. Wisps of his hair hung over his cheeks, clung about his ears; his eyes seemed dull and vacant. Lizzie had never before seen him without a perfectly manicured moustache. Now it hung from his face depleted. As he dragged himself up the steps to the door, she noticed the obvious bald patch at the back of his head which he otherwise made such an effort to disguise with his remaining strands of hair. The gathering storm rumbled in the distance.

Less than thirty seconds later the front door flew open. Lizzie turned away and hurried several steps further towards the corner of the street. Why had she not arrived a few moments earlier? Why had she not come at once, directly to Elm Road? She hurled unfair accusations at

herself. She pressed the palms of both hands against her eyes.

"You bloody turnip!"

The air stank, a bitter blend of mouldering leaves and swollen clouds. As the first drops of rain began to fall, she glanced back over her shoulder. She looked at me, for the doorway was otherwise empty. Lord and Lady no longer stood on the threshold. And with that, there was no shadow of a doubt. It was high time to unearth the bracelet from its hiding place.

## Kohnstein bei Nordhausen, March 1945

For a while, Walde had been fond of shortening his name to "Al". He had long harboured a not-so-secret wish to move to the United States and begin an illustrious career there as a gangster. His greatest role model was Al Capone. Walde liked to believe that he and Capone shared certain qualities which made them kindred spirits. Soulmates if you will. For example, both had round, puffy faces, framed with slick, black hair. Thick, dark eyebrows which all but grew together, hanging over sunken eyes. They could have been twins! They had even been born on the same day, just before the turn of the century, on a bitterly cold January morning – one in New York City, the other in the restless town of Vilnius. For a while Walde had borne the name "Al" with pride, and in 1945 he would in all likelihood have continued to have done so. If there had not been this one matter which caused a nagging doubt. Because, just

like Walde himself, the entertainer Al *Jolson* was also, originally, from Lithuania. Yes, really. But Walde could not be convinced of the truth of the matter.

Walde had only been in Göttingen for about a week when he first heard the question: "Al? Like the guy from *The Jazz Singer*, right?" Back then, Walde had been toiling from dawn past dusk at the market – usually for the fishmongers – in order to secure at least one meal a day for himself. Which was why he had not yet set foot inside a cinema. He was not particularly interested in fantasy worlds, but those film posters which, in 1929, hung all around Barfüßer Straße had caught his eye nonetheless. The caricatures of the jazz singer – head raised, arms outstretched, open mouthed – were among the most recognisable impressions of the day. Walde was irritated by the consistent blackness of the man's hair and painted face, the glowing red of his lips, the beaming whiteness of his eyes, his teeth, his gloves. And all of it projected over a bright yellow-orange circular background.

The second time someone had brought up the name, Walde had been taken aback. If he had been certain that he was being ridiculed, he would have come out swinging right away. But still, his counterpart had smiled just a bit too long for Walde's taste. A bit too long to have truly meant it all innocently. Walde took it upon himself to watch the film at once, hurrying directly to the cinema after his shift. Alas, he made it to the back rows far too late, just as the screening was coming to an end. He saw a man with shiny skin; black hair; and thick, bright lips swaggering across the stage – arms outstretched, blowing a kiss to an excited woman in the front row. The audience seemed

captivated by Jolson. So musical! Such a gifted dancer! How was Walde supposed to know that the actor was not a genuine African?

From then on he no longer tolerated even the most harmless observation about his appearance. Even if he had been able to prove his Aryan heritage, the Göttingen of the 1930s would have reacted to him with ambivalence at best. Jewish people who had formerly considered themselves German spoke in hushed tones about emigration. And supposedly gullible people who continued to call themselves German pretended not to notice. And because Walde had never known the identity of his biological father, he was not willing to take any chances. Certainly not in public. Not even in his favourite pub.

Which was why the joker with the broken beer glass in his throat lay strewn across the entryway. Blood streamed out when he moved his lips. Moments before he'd thrown his arm across Walde's shoulder, singing, "Maaaaammy, maaaaammy!"

"Serves you RIGHT!" Walde screamed, giving the dying man a final kick to the gut. Upon his arrest, Walde had taken care to give his full legal time: Waldemar Jósef Zieliński.

Now he was the most feared prisoner functionary in Dora. On the same evening as the mass execution, he had brutally beaten another prisoner to death just behind Thirty-Seven. Not because he had stolen biscuits from the so-called kitchen, but because he had got caught – the jackass! It had not been Walde's intention to kill the biscuit thief, he had simply wanted to make an example out of him. And now Walde had a mathematical problem.

The week before, an opportunistic accountant had deliberately scribbled a false number into what he had thought was an unimportant record. But now it seemed the record column had not been so unimportant after all. Koçak – that was the fellow's name – had had the misfortune of his "mistake" being noticed immediately. And during roll call, Koçak had then declined to select a particularly weak-looking prisoner from the last row for execution – which is why the camp commander had strangled him.

"The numbers must add up!" the commander had barked, mid-strangulation.

Walde could remember the scene all too well, and only planned on leaving the body of the biscuit thief behind the special barrack temporarily. He stopped first at Linde's – he brought her the biscuits, and she brought him to a climax – before he went back to his own barracks. He didn't tell her where he had got the biscuits. No questions, no lies.

About an hour later Walde tore some poor wretch from his bunk and ordered him to follow him outside. They moved as quickly as the storm would allow. Above them, magnificent, swollen clouds were gathered in the night sky, their dark underbellies illuminated by searchlights from the guard towers. Below them, foul, liquid mud pooled about their calves, emitting an abominable stench.

Walde slipped, cursing in Polish, as if he did not trust the power of the German language to express the abysmal depths of his ill humour. At least the half-bottle of Kirshwasser flowing through his veins did something to dull the sharpness of the cold. When they arrived, at last, at the special barrack, Walde directed his subordinate around

the back of the building. A little light still fell from a window above, making the all-but-unidentifiable heap in the snow relatively easy for them to find. Walde kicked at it with his left foot. The corpse rolled to one side and landed on its back, face obscured by a frozen slurry of blood and filth.

"Lift!"

The prisoner approached the body slowly, gingerly taking hold beneath the arms.

"I said, LIFT!"

In the end, transporting the body became a collaborative effort, the left arm over Walde's shoulder, the right arm around the other's waist. As they began making their way over the parade grounds and back towards the barracks, Walde slipped again.

"Kurwa!"

The corpse's head tipped forward, nearly striking the window. A piteous screeching pierced Walde's ears.

"Arghh! KURWA!"

Speedy progress was nearly impossible, for the body refused to cooperate. And why should it? The approaching meeting between Linde, Ada and the SS officers would see to it that the bracelet made it to the proper place. And if things had been too easy for Walde, they would all have missed each other. The prisoners had made barely a few strides. And Walde had spat at his counterpart because he had suddenly stopped. But as soon as Walde followed his gaze, he also came to a halt, as if rooted to the snow. Their path was blocked by a group of SS officers.

*Totope, March 1459*

Afonso did not know why he had sought shelter at the first sight of the mighty raindrops. And why, of all places, with these old women? Another good question. But he abandoned the idea entirely at the sight of Senhor Guilherme sitting on the floor with another figure, apparently a woman. Standing at the edge of the village, Afonso scratched at his throat until the skin beneath his chin began to bleed. He decided to wait out the storm under a tree, for he could not predict how Senhor Guilherme would react to his sudden appearance. The countless scars which crisscrossed Afonso's back were the product of Senhor Guilherme's whip, and the consequence – or so Afonso believed – of his own actions. He had always delivered himself up to the torturous punishment of his own free will, believing – yes, indeed knowing – that he had earned these lashes. Resistance would have been futile. There was no shelter, neither mental nor physical. Senhor Guilherme was everywhere. Afonso had never even begun to question this reality. But all of this had changed upon their arrival in West Africa.

When Captain Gomes and his crew had stood on dry land again after months upon the high seas, they had soon realised that none of the assembled fishermen was this Mansa they were seeking – none seemed to be travelling with the appropriate entourage. And so, no attempt had been made then to use Afonso as an interpreter. Lucky for him.

But even had he spoken their dialect, he would not have made a sound. His mouth had hung open in astonishment

long after this first encounter. The tiny, dark ringlets on their heads were like his own! He rubbed his own hair as inconspicuously as possible with one hand. The bright eyes of the fishermen could also have been his own. Just like their gleaming skin, their bright teeth, the prominent palms of their hands. On the shoreline of a small African island, Afonso had found himself confronted with any number of incarnations of himself – only they were twenty years older and carefree, brimming with self-confidence. He had been tempted to throw himself at their feet.

Gomes had not noticed a thing. Back on board the *São Cristóvão* he took a moment to note in his logbook that the "uninhabited" island now belonged to the Kingdom of Portugal.

"São Tomé!" he bellowed, wine bottle in hand. "So it shall be called. For the glory of holy St Thomas!"

"For the glory of holy St Thomas!" the men roared in response.

The second island looked even more nondescript than the first. This time, the self-proclaimed discoverers agreed upon the name of Santo Antão – in honour of yet another European saint – without so much as pausing at the beach. And Afonso got off easy, yet again. But his luck ran out at their next landing.

Guilherme had finally convinced Gomes to anchor off the coast of the mainland. The settlement near Èkó looked promising: It was encircled by an imposing mud wall and guarded by many armed men at the gate. One could then be forgiven for the mistaken belief that the king of all of Africa was residing behind the city walls. A long, broad avenue lined by countless stands and hawkers – some

67

selling herbs and spices, others with cloth and cowrie shells and gold coins – led from the gates of the city to the house of the Oloye.

"A what?" Gomes asked.

"O-LO-YE," Guilherme repeated. "Something like a prince."

Gomes turned to Afonso, seeking confirmation in his eyes. The boy stared back, expressionless.

And so the negotiations ended as abruptly as they had begun. Because without the ability to communicate, and without the power to proceed by means of violence, Gomes and his men had had to remain standing before the gate – eventually returning to their ship empty-handed. Afonso's defining memory of the place which Gomes would later rename "Lagos" – in honour of his own place of birth – was the duration of his subsequent whipping. A punishment for his silence. "Swindler, impostor!" they had called him. And something worse which I do not care to repeat here.

The Portuguese sailed on and dropped anchor again somewhat to the east of Èkó. When Afonso was roused from his slumber the following morning by Guilherme's foot, he realised that the forthcoming exploration of the continent would not bode well for him. And for that reason Afonso had endeavoured to establish an ever-growing distance between himself and his master.

"AFOONSOOO!"

The voice was familiar, only it sounded a bit shriller than usual, almost squeaky and slightly trembling. Afonso remained standing cautiously beneath the cover of a tall plant.

Normally, had he recognised the voice as belonging

to Senhor Guilherme, he would have reacted promptly. Afonso would have hurried forward to whatever point of origin – breathless and with pounding heart. But not this time. This time, Afonso set himself against the desperation he recognized in the voice of this otherwise steely personality: Was Senhor Guilherme afraid?

The lizards hesitated. How? The wind suddenly changed direction. Can? Something rustled suspiciously in the underbrush. The? Some ants scuttled along the edge of an old bucket. All-Knowing? A particularly large raindrop plashed against the ground. Be? Afonso's left leg began to itch, just beneath the knee. Afraid? He scratched it. And just to assure himself that he was not dreaming, Afonso scratched again.

CRACK!

He spun around so quickly that he almost slipped and fell. Where had the woman come from? She stood before him, as if she had materialised out of the ether. Within a few seconds he hurriedly stammered out three Ave Marias. At the same time he recognised that if she had meant him ill, she would already have struck. She was a head shorter than he, her skin gleamed even more intensely than his own. Her fingernails were conspicuously short. In her arms she concealed three shabby, shrivelled excuses for yams. Afonso eyed them greedily, admitting to himself that – despite their poor form – he would gladly have devoured all three, skin and all. She studied his face at length, examining the scar just above his left eyebrow with particular interest.

"Damfo?"

The sound of the word burned somewhere behind his

eyes, in a hidden corner of his mind that he had locked away since childhood. Where had the moisture on her cheeks come from? Looking up, he realised his own cheeks were damp as well. Tears falling everywhere, even from the sky. She dropped her meagre rations to the ground, wrapping Afonso in her arms. She rocked with him, she laughed, she sang, she cried. The storm rain around them ceased to matter for her. She held him only tighter.

"You . . . who?"

Just those two words filled his entire body with a tangle of emotions, impulses and questions. They were the first of a few half-muddled words in a language in which he knew he often dreamed, but – to the best of his knowledge – had never spoken fluently himself. Yet he had managed to create a sentence out of these two words and force it from his mouth. A sentence he had trusted himself to make only because he had just understood every word of the song sung by the woman who was now stroking his head and back. And then she crooned something against his chest. A warmth began to spread through him, from the place where her head rested on his skin, outward towards the tips of his toenails, the corners of his mouth, the ends of his hair.

"Please . . ." he managed to exclaim. The word came more quickly to his mind than the two before it, but still much too slowly. It did not matter. Even if he would have to speak for the rest of his life in such one- or two-word sentences, he wanted only to speak this way. Her arms loosened about his neck.

"Naa Lamiley." She smiled. And then she continued speaking. There was much that he did not understand. The

words "You don't even recognise me, do you?" hit him unexpectedly, rendering him speechless once again. A jarring question. Recognise? By what means?

How could this woman act so comfortable around him? The lash of the rain must, at the very least, be just as disagreeable for her as it was for him. He helped her gather up the pathetic yams and then looked about him for a place where he could be dry and perhaps nibble at the smallest of the three. Naa Lamiley gestured with her eyes in an entirely different direction.

"Bra!"

Afonso froze. Everything in his body screamed "Away!" but his feet did not obey. Of all things, he would not follow her in the direction of where Senhor Guilherme was waiting. Unable to communicate this to her, he could only pull her back with his right hand.

"What now?" had surely been her response. But other than the raging storm and a roaring in his ears, Afonso could hear nothing. He could only recognise that her lips were still moving. Everything else grew fuzzy. His trembling hand clasped at hers in the very moment the wind began to transform the proud, towering palm trees around them into silly blades of grass. An invisible, incalculable power was in the process of ravaging the inscrutable lands, and there Afonso stood: A young man who could have carried a small horse through the streets of Lisbon, unable now to persuade a mere woman to follow his will. Naa Lamiley must have considered herself to be a man, for he could find no more plausible explanation for her overbearing actions.

The figure who had sat before Senhor Guilherme on the ground rose. Afonso had somehow felt the movement

71

rather than seeing it with his own eyes. He vanished behind the next coconut tree – a poor hiding place for him, indeed – hoping that the woman with the pitiful yams – what was her name again? – would follow suit. Or that she, at the very least – damn it all, what was her name? – would not betray him. Protected only slightly from the pelting rain by the palm fronds above, he scoured the area between himself and the huts. His eyes darted from the left – the smallest of the huts – back to the right – to the abandoned coal stove – back again to the place where the yams had just lain – and finally back to the yard. Everything now was empty. Where could they all be?

*And where the hell were his feet?!*

For an almost unbearable moment, Afonso feared that the ground beneath him would devour him. But only very slowly. If he were to be tortured to death, Senhor Guilherme would certainly see to it that Jehovah carried out the task in the utmost detail.

Afonso watched his own hands grasping for the trunk of the palm tree, even his fingernails had switched into survival mode. But how was he to escape God's righteous vengeance with a mere mortal's will? The young woman had vanished. There was not a single living person to be seen. And even if he were to die now, there was no way that he would cry out to Senhor Guilherme.

Afonso clung to the trunk of the palm tree, drawing his left foot up out of the mud – this he managed with astonishing ease. The vengeful mud, it seemed, was innocent. It only coated his feet. The ground directly beneath the tree still seemed somewhat stable. Afonso began to recite the only other prayer he knew by heart.

"Pai Nosso . . ."

"Damfo!"

There it was again. This word. The beautiful woman with the ugly yams had reappeared before him.

"Damfo . . ."

Afonso allowed the word to dance around his mouth a few times – it seemed calming to him. He would begin to collect other words now.

"Damfo." He nodded. And smiled. When had he last smiled in the past seven years?

She asked him something, and he gathered that she must be speaking about some important person. The woman by the huts? Thankfully, he remained sceptical. It was crucial for the transfer of the bracelet that Naa Lamiley did not return to Ada too quickly. Naa Lamiley rolled her eyes and pursed her lips after she asked:

"Or should he take her, too?"

Take her. These words sounded . . . no. These words *were* violent. Blurry images flickered through his mind. White men chewing, as if in slow motion. They had something harmless between their teeth. A blade of grass? A leaf? Great, yellow teeth. Fiery eyes. Men who looked like ghosts. One of the pale monsters had held a silver flask to his lips. Afonso had been forced to drink from it – it burned! He had choked, coughing with such force that he had nearly broken a rib.

"Another sip!" they'd cried. "Just one more! Come now!"

He had vomited, again and again, the sound of raucous laughter resounding around him. He no longer remembered if they had thrown him to the ground, or if he had

crumpled of his own accord. And the girl had been there. Between the many legs. High up in a palm tree. He still remembered how he had screamed for the girl, despite his ragged throat, across the stretch of beach, over the din of the sea:

"Nalamle! Naalamle!"

They had only whooped and hooted as they dragged Afonso by the arm. Had they beaten him, too? Perhaps he had been kicked? In any case, he remembered when the skin above his left eyebrow had burst open. Had they thrown him into the water? He knew only that he had soiled himself as he had clung with every fibre of his being to the back of one of those swimming demons.

Amidst the torrential storm, beneath the palm trees, Afonso held his silence for the length of a long breath. The rumbling, the burning, the distance, and the rustling, the stench and the pictures grew hazy once more. His hunger had vanished with them. Worse yet, his stomach churned. He had to choke back the bitter tasting spit again and again before he could speak.

"Namle?"

"NAA-La-M'ley." She smiled.

The boy pointed at his own chest: "DAM-fo?"

Wind howled over the trees, enraging the palm fronds and laughing in his face while everything, everything, threatened to fall apart.

74

# Among the Luckiest

*Kohnstein bei Nordhausen, March 1945*

I've said it before, and I'll say it again: If Ada had just sat down, Linde would not have got angry. That's just the way it is. And if Linde had not been angry, then Ada would not have looked out of the window. Seriously. And if Ada had not looked out of the window, none of the things which followed after would have happened to her. There is no doubt in my mind. She would not have seen the resurrection of the biscuit thief. She would not have screamed. And she would not have drawn the attention of the SS officers. We're talking about a series of unfortunate events, all of which could have been prevented if Ada had just sat down like Linde told her to.

My task was to bear witness; my four walls encompassed Ada's reality. Of course, certain things transpired for Ada outside the range of my direct observation – at least, in the form I had taken at that time. But the most consequential events did not escape my attention. For example, the inspection which took place early that morning. A certain Herr Kommandant So-and-So from high up had pointed

to the so-called special barrack with a stick. It could have meant anything: casual interest or the start of a new count, or even a command to enter and inspect. This time, however, it indicated an assignment for Officers Yes-Sir and Heil-Hitler. Of course, this order was immediately communicated to Prisoner Functionaries As-You-Wish and Very-Good:

"Vacate Block Thirty-Seven!"

I watched as the occupants of Thirty-Seven were led out. How Ada walked alongside her friend. I heard how Walde spoke to Linde during the proceedings. He described the coming mass execution in such detail – above all, with such *pleasure* – that Ada's breakfast threatened to come up. And after the execution, as the six-digits were led back across the parade grounds towards Thirty-Seven, I watched the cheery group of SS officers gathered around the gallows. One even had tears of laughter in his eyes, clapping the man to his left on the back. If at all, both officers regarded the dead men hanging over them as nothing more than a backdrop. That some of the stripes still flailed their arms and legs did not bother a single one of these cheery jokesters, nor did it distract them from their telling of jokes. The officer who stood closest to Ada looked so much like her baby's murderer that she could not swallow her food at lunch later that day.

And then, in the grey light of evening, Linde brought biscuits. Old, stale, ill-smelling potato biscuits which only moments before had cost another prisoner his life. They tasted nasty. Ada forced all three into her mouth at once. The aftertaste lingered on her tongue, on the insides of her cheeks, and on her conscience. I saw it all. Including Linde's relief that Ada had finally eaten something.

The biscuit thief lay outside before the window. As Ada dressed herself for work – fresh panties, a black bra, a white pleated skirt – her silhouette cast strange patterns over him. A snake around his neck, tinsel strewn across his face, a blanket for his legs. Linde sat on Ada's bed, massaging her right hip with both hands.

"What else can I do for you?" she asked.

But Ada was preoccupied. She puzzled over her own reflection in the window. It was not the first time that it had been interrupted by a corpse. Between her eyes, a broken nose. Between her lips, a shattered jaw.

"He can consider himself among the luckiest," Ada muttered.

"Hmm?"

Ada pointed out the window. "Him. There. Even if he's headed straight to Hell, the fire there can't burn any hotter than in Dora."

Linde glanced furtively out into the darkness and whispered: "May he rest in peace." "Peace" and "rest" in a single sentence! Linde was very much herself again.

On the other side of the closed door, the footsteps of the new functionary responsible for preparing the roll calls and maintain the records echoed. It was as if she had paced these halls for years, as if her place in the thirty-seventh barrack would be hers for all eternity. Did she know that the life of a prison scribe was as fleeting as the life of any of the other six-digits here?

She knocked at every door: The ladies needed to be ready. Their first visitor had already received his immunisation shot.

"Immunisation?" Ada laughed. "The needles alone

are probably worth more than we are. Am I right? Who gives a shit if the boys die of syphilis or work themselves to death?"

Linde nodded.

"They can replace the lot of us in less than zero seconds . . ."

A pounding at Ada's door like machine-gun fire.

"Only six visitors for you tonight!"

It was uncanny how much the disembodied voice sounded like death. In any case, Ada was able to return to a relative state of calm. This always happened when she began to disassociate. Her human-like exterior remained, as usual, in her room – ready for those who would come, while she herself began to drift outside, settling before the window. This evening, alongside the body of the biscuit thief. As Linde left her room Ada called after her: "Have a good one."

And when the evening's proceedings had come to a close, they did not flee to the common room to join the others, or take shelter in the gloom of the hallway; they both returned to me. Linde settled onto the bed while Ada paced back and forth. Seven paces from one wall to the next – so close that she nearly brushed against it with the tip of her nose – only to turn at the last second and return seven paces back in the opposite direction. Again. And again.

She had mapped her march down to the millimetre because she knew the burning between her legs became unbearable only when she sat still. Ada had already washed herself several times with the bar of lye soap, scrubbing her skin until her wrists grew sore. Blood seeped from a

tiny scratch on her forehead. As she paced, the raindrops pattered, filling the room with their polite applause. There was a consistency to that. Just like every evening, she had performed at her best. For a while she said nothing. Sometimes there is nothing to say. When she began to speak again at last, she was out of breath. Her eyelids drooped limply.

"Could the storm wash us clean?"

She sounded like a child. Curious and full of admiration.

Linde stared into the distance. It seemed poised to become another interminable night. She exhaled heavily, then patted the empty space on the bed beside her with one hand.

"Come on, Fatty, take a load off. I've—"

"I can't," Ada replied. "I'm in a hurry."

". . . brought you some white caviar."

Ada waved away the words like a bothersome fly.

"Go for it, Cuddle Bear, I'm full."

Linde patted the mattress a bit more resolutely. Each time she moved, the bedframe creaked – a sound which had grown loathsome to them both.

"Take a seat, Fatty."

"No."

Ada continued pacing. It continued to rain. If one could call it rain at all. It poured. Back and forth. It stormed. Back and forth. It thundered. Back and forth.

"Goddammit, Ada!"

Ada froze.

And blinked.

And squinted.

*What was that?*

A shrill voice began to force its way through Ada's mental mathematics –

"I. Just. Can't. Take. It. Anymore!"

*Was that Linde?*

"I can't see you like this anymore!"

Ada remained standing with her back to the window. Somehow, somewhere, something was echoing inside her. These words. They had repeated more than once over the last months. So you see it wasn't true that nothing belonged to her anymore. At the very least, Ada had retained her ability to repress. And in 1945 this had become her most valuable possession. She opened her eyes wide.

"Cuddle Bear!"

Linde threw back her head, the tears flooding her cheeks.

"I'm so sorry, Fatty," she whispered. "Please forgive me."

And as if this had just happened for the first time, Ada searched her friend's eyes for an explanation.

"What's the matter with you? You've never spoken to me this way before!"

Linde wiped both cheeks with the palms of her hands.

"It won't happen again," she said.

It took a moment for Ada to be satisfied with this answer. It was not until Linde met her own gaze with matching intensity that Ada diverted her eyes.

It would have been better for her if she had taken a seat.

When she returned to the window, Ada no longer saw the darkness of the night. She stared, instead, directly into two pale, sunken, lifeless eyes. Suddenly she lost the ability

to hear, to think, to feel: She transformed into an endless, ear-splitting scream.

Linde leaped from the bed, bowling into Ada. But the Scream swung wildly with both arms, grabbed Linde by the wrist and flung her against the wall. An SS officer, aroused by the commotion, returned the room to silence with a few blows of his fists. Ada collapsed to the ground, but he dragged her back to her feet, holding her face before his own and –

"Halt!" his commanding officer barked.

A bracelet was lying on the floor. As if out of nowhere. Good, good, I thought. Things were finally moving in the right direction.

"Where did this come from?"

Linde should have said something. This would have been the moment. But she remained silent. The cuffs of her sleeves danced around her fingernails, unable to hide her shame. And so, the two friends were led outside. Walde saw that Ada was bleeding from her head. He glanced from her to Linde to the SS officers. He could almost make out what the one officer was holding in his left hand, but the storm was unrelenting. If only he would come a little closer . . . An explosion in the sky! In the glare of the lightning, the shape of the object became somewhat clearer. A . . . hair clip?

Walde looked again at Linde. Her eyes were gleaming, but she managed to return his gaze without blinking. The SS officers were still occupied with the bracelet so they did not notice her eyes getting wider and wider. Walde wrinkled his brow, examining the object again for himself. Was it a piece of jewellery? Could it be the bracelet?! All at once,

his eyes registered the delicate curvature of each individual bead. He could smell the perspiration seeping from the officer's every pore. He heard the crashing of each drop of rain against his leather boots. He would not die today. This day was not that day. Linde would have to keep her mouth shut. Walde caught her eyes one final time. He did not need to do more.

By this point in his life Walde had seen a thing or two. Like the spectacle of a former wrestler who could hardly manage to squeak by the end of a death march. Or a medic who had snatched the last piece of bread from the lips of a dying man. Walde had once even whooped along in approval at a group of boys kicking around a ball covered with a suspicious mat of hair. Yes, he had seen a thing or two. He thought he was prepared for anything. Anything but Ada's next decision.

There had been moments of selflessness in 1945. Even behind the gates of Dora. But they were so sporadic, so fleeting, so brittle that even years later Walde would claim never to have seen them with his own eyes before that moment. And already in the first days after Ada's death he found he needed to repress this memory. Only this way could he continue to torture and murder his fellow prisoners until the end of the War without any cumbersome traces of remorse.

Only this way would he be able to report with wrinkled brow before the uniformed man one short week after Ada's death. An angular gentleman with thin hair and a dark, pointy nose, who would be seated behind a massive oaken writing desk informing him that he had recently seen two harlots at the camp's main entry gate – one of whom was

now being held in a standing cell. The air would close in thick around them as Herr Obersturmbannführer cast his eyes over the parade grounds, only to enquire in the same indifferent tone where the other one might have acquired this bracelet. Only through a violent act of dissociation would Walde manage to respond: *Which* other one?

But we're getting ahead of ourselves. The prisoners and the officers still stood opposite one another, all of them drenched by the storm rain. One of the younger officers began to tremble – whether from cold or fear, he himself could not have said. In any case, he had received his orders to detain Ada. It was only his second nightshift, and the barking of the dogs behind them seemed much too close for him. He jumped, and as he did so he loosened his feeble grip on Ada's upper arm. She tore free and had already made several strides before the SS officers could react. To Walde's great astonishment she almost made it to the electric fence, the tips of her fingers were mere millimetres from the wires. The clap of gunshots echoed through the night.

## Stratford-le-Bow, March 1848

Elm Road itself was a perfectly innocent street. The front gardens were meticulously trimmed, the hedges clipped, each wooden kennel looked identical. The Caesars and Montys obviously carried out their dirty business elsewhere, leaving no evidence upon the local footpaths. And their Lords followed suit. They wore their immaculate

vests with pride, although they knew that the cotton from which they had been made was harvested by unfree hands. Those whose business relations stretched from one end of the vast British Empire to the other considered themselves lucky. The *luckiest* of all were those who could write off the human cost against their own enormous profit margins.

Innocent and not particularly long, Elm Road was perhaps a bit too narrow, but not noticeably more so than the other streets of this outer borough of London. A bit too loud, though only during the week. Above all, the street kept no secrets – unlike Lady Ada.

Few there knew of her gambling addiction. And perhaps, because so many women of her age enjoyed trying their fortune from time to time at the horse tracks, this problem did not even become apparent to her own husband for some while. Only Lizzie knew of the threats emanating from what her Lady scornfully referred to as the "many Shylocks" who were constantly running after her debts.

Lord King, in his turn, kept secret from his wife his own flirtation with an increasingly affordable bit of property in Ireland, although he already owned – in addition to the house at 37 Elm Road – a house on Ockham Park in Surrey and a summer residence at Loch Torridon. And in her turn she said nothing of her 'special friendship' with Mr Dickens.

The tree under which Lizzie was smoking, and from where she stood gazing out over the flooded road, served as both a shelter and a convenient hiding place. She flicked away her match decisively. It glimmered and then went out in a crack between the sodden cobblestones. From her

pocket she drew the spoon which she had stolen from the Women's Charter Association.

By the time her Ma passed, Lizzie had ceased to believe in God. Pa had, perhaps, earned his own starvation – he had, after all, been the one who abandoned his family in their hour of need. But Ma? She had stayed true to her alcoholic husband for her entire life. Why had she been punished with such a miserable death? If there was a God, Lizzie thought, if there truly was a God, she would teach Him what it meant to fear! If you only knew, I thought. She broke the earth beneath the tree with her spoon.

At that halting hour of morning, only a few public houses of ill repute were already – or still – open. Even those sorrowful individuals staggering down alleyways would not have taken note of Lizzie long enough to recognise her, much less register what she was doing there, down on her knees in the mud. The storm's rage was growing. It was as if the puddles were boiling, as if the cobblestones would break apart and finally reveal the many dirty secrets hidden beneath the street. Lizzie's fingers were turning blue. She clapped both hands against her arms and recommenced her excavation work.

About three weeks before, Lady Ada had appeared late one evening in Lizzie's chamber. Lizzie had not been able to sleep anyway. In the flickering candlelight, Lady Ada's bloodshot eyes had looked terrifying. Lizzie had not understood much of her rambling, only that it was a matter of life and death.

"As quickly as you can," Lady Ada had pleaded, her voice grown shriller than Lizzie had ever heard it before.

There was no time for questions. Lizzie had simply

nodded, covering her head, while the series of instructions, caveats, warnings and requests flowed over her.

"And please take my knife with you," Lady Ada had added, handing Lizzie a pair of diamond earrings, a choker of pearls, two ruby brooches, a golden necklace and her sapphire engagement ring. Lizzie could still recall the exact moment when Lady Ada had given *it* to her – the antique bracelet with golden beads.

"M'lady," Lizzie had marvelled. "But are you quite sure? If Lord King were ever to catch word . . ."

But Lady Ada was consumed by other worries. She was still shaking from head to foot, rubbing her hands together incessantly.

"Quickly!" she had hissed. "You must be back here by midday at the latest!"

And so, Lizzie had carried out a covert operation, cloak-and-dagger: burying the bracelet under this very tree before continuing her journey onward to West London. Finding the tree again was easy, for she had carved her initials into the trunk. Her Lady's knife had come in handy, after all.

But just as she had finally freed the bracelet from the mud, she heard an explosion. Its echoes vibrated from house to house. For a moment, the sound absorbed the rustling of the weeping willow's leaves, the pounding of the storm's rain and the howling of the wind. Even the thunder held its startled peace. What had that been? It had sounded like a firecracker, but who the devil would have set it off? In this weather? At *this* hour?

Her thoughts were shattered by a cry – a cry so filled with horror and suffering that Lizzie dashed away at once.

Through the mud with her dripping shoes, around the corner and up the street . . . Perhaps it was all some kind of mistake? Perhaps the lightning had somehow played a trick on her?

She slipped, caught herself, and ran on. She had nearly reached 37 Elm Road when she saw Lady Ada rushing from the house. She wore no hat; her hair hung down around her shoulders; the buttons of her jacket were undone. She ran.

Behind Lady Ada came Lord King. He remained standing at the threshold. The thunder drowned out the words he called after her, but his intentions were spelled out by the pistol he held in one hand, aiming at her. He curled his finger around the trigger.

Only a few paces away, Lizzie waved the bracelet before him:

"Lord King!"

But he remained resolute, his eyes narrowing. Lizzie could not tell whether he was moving his index finger or not.

"Please, God!" she sobbed. "Please, please!"

She continued brandishing the bracelet, as before, but she did not dare to move another step closer. Why was he holding the gun in his left hand, she wondered. Mr Dickens was left-handed. Wasn't he? Lord King certainly was not.

In the meantime, Lady Ada had caught sight of Lizzie. She paused, glancing from Lizzie to her husband. Slowly, she raised her hands. The raindrops intermingled with her tears.

"Please, William," she seemed to say.

The bullet hissed through the air, dragging the reek of gunpowder behind it. Lady Ada fell to the ground.

Baby Kofi had been a few weeks old when the mysterious illness fell upon him, like so many others that summer. For a few weeks Oko had strolled among the houses, his chest swelled with pride. He enjoyed being commended for his skill in siring a son at his first attempt. For a few short weeks, Naa Lamiley had been "Mami Kofi". For a few weeks she had carried her firstborn on her back during the days, and he had slept on her stomach during the nights. She had hummed improvised melodies in which she had promised him eternal closeness, for he had been born much too early – just before the rainy season.

He was but a worm. And his squeaky voice! Aside from Ada, the freshly minted parents were the only ones who – without opening their eyes – could distinguish between the bleating of the goats and the cry of their baby. The first smile. The first giggle. Nothing escaped his grateful mother. He was always with her in the fields. He nursed whenever he wanted to nurse. Between the mighty green and brittle brown. He was so light, so peaceful, that she always reached for the tiny bundle in a panic, thankful that he had not fallen from the cloth slung at her back. He had been so inconspicuous, so tiny, that she had often worried she would not find him, were he to fall between the stalks and leaves.

At market he had sometimes murmured while she haggled for a better price, bringing a smile to every lip. Even recent widows would be lured for a few moments from their mourning. How he had wound his tiny hand around her finger while she fed him!

"Do you still remember?" she had asked Ada again

and again during the first painful days of mourning. Baby Kofi's arrival had been a blessing. For the marriage, but especially for Mami Kofi. She had waited so long to be a mother, even Ataa Naa Nyɔŋmɔ must have shown her mercy, for her prayers had been answered. The immense pain she had felt during delivery was nothing compared with the torture of the childless years before.

On the eighth day after his birth, they had carried him outside for the first time – out of the safety of his sleeping corner into the dawn-shrouded courtyard. At last those gathered there could admire the child! He slept through the entire outdooring ceremony. As the firstborn son of the young couple, he should have shared the name "Ayi" with Oko's deceased father. But Ada had called him "Kofi" with jubilation – for he had been born on a Friday. None of the parents complained. And this time the elders were not so strict. Ataa Ayi, a warm-hearted man who had passed on long before Oko's birth, had not thought much of these dusty traditions anyway. Warmed by palm wine and kpótomenui, all of Kofi's new mothers and fathers laughed and danced for many nights. Even weeks later they had seized every opportunity to continue the celebration spontaneously. The feeling of joy had spread like a fine spring rain over the entire settlement.

But then the baby had begun to shiver.

Oko had torn bushels of hair from his head and made wild accusations at his wife – even that she had eaten too many mangos during her pregnancy. Mango. The way he spoke the word – as though he had needed to tear it from the air with his teeth – struck Mami Kofi with far more force even than his desperate blows. She soon grew hoarse from

her endless entreaties. Her knees had long since grown ragged, but she prayed on. It was all in vain. She was not permitted to absorb Baby Kofi's suffering into her own. The cramps which had nearly broken his diminutive spine in two ceased suddenly after three delirious days and as many sleepless nights. Baby Kofi lay peacefully upon his back, his proud head turned to one side, his delicate arms and legs akimbo. As if asleep. Slumbering. Shh. Naa Lamiley sat beside him, veiled in tears; haggard yet relieved.

The burial had been modest then, for Naa Lamiley had had no idea – and had *not wanted* to know – how the ceremony could have otherwise ensued. She had been told that infants should not be remembered as "real" people because they had not yet accomplished anything in their lives. It had even been earnestly discussed – long, extensively and in heated tones – whether dead babies would return to Gbohiiajeŋ at all.

"Where else would they go?!" Naa Lamiley had screamed when she could hear no more – bringing the discussion to a close and the others to a state of astonished silence. If it had been up to Oko, the baby would not even have received a burial.

He was said to have sobbed "Papa, o! Papa!" over and again. His tortured cries of pain merging in a final "But he's afraid of the dark!" when his youngest sister had tried to convince him to surrender the baby's body to her care. She was always sent to him in delicate moments, for it was known that he could never say "no" to her, no matter the situation. But even this proven method failed then. According to her report, he had only babbled, clutching the stiff bundle still closer to his chest.

In the end one of the village elders had to take Baby Kofi's case upon herself, bringing the family conflict to a close. And so it was that the grief-stricken couple's long-desired firstborn child was buried in a location unknown to either Naa Lamiley or Oko. It was a quick and uneventful burial. Afterwards, everyone went back to their usual routines. Only Naa Lamiley still sat for a while alone in the courtyard, lost in thought. What else could Ada have done for her sister than to cook her yams, mashed and churned with palm oil?

"Special occasions require special rituals," Ada had later explained to Naa Lamiley. "Even an invented ritual is better than no ritual at all."

The golden mush was garnished with hardboiled eggs, a palm frond sufficed to ward off the chickens. When Naa Lamiley returned exhausted from market at the end of the day, her ceremonial meal was still steaming. She set the basket of tomatoes and onions at Ada's feet.

"Use your right hand!" she cautioned as Ada reached out. Ada grinned and rolled her eyes. Naa Lamiley stared back. Her smile hung weakly at the corners of her lips – for the first time since her son had stopped moving.

"Whose birthday is it?"

"Baby Kofi's . . ." Ada replied. "In Asamando."

"Asamando?"

Ada tilted her head to one side, wrinkling her brow. But Naa Lamiley said nothing more. Her sorrow returned each time his name was mentioned, choking up her throat.

"O!" Ada nodded at last. "Of course. You call it Gbohiiajeŋ."

Naa Lamiley wiped the tears from her cheeks and bent

forward to pick up the basket again. Ada pulled her gently down onto the stool beside her. She did not begin to cry until Ada took her in her arms.

"Me wiase nyinaa ne wo," Ada whispered, petting her head.

"Wiase?"

"The world. *Me wiase nyinaa* is *my whole world*."

Naa Lamiley repeated it thoughtfully. She made an effort to match the tones and melody exactly.

"*Ase* means *under*, right?"

"Yes." Ada smiled. "And *Wia* is the sun. My people say *under the sun* when we want to say Earth or the world."

"And your people live in Kuntanase . . . under the kuntan?"

Ada laughed, and her eyes shimmered.

"You're too good, o! Yes. Literally: under the kuntan trees."

"Wiase . . ." Naa Lamiley nodded after a few moments. "Me wiase nyinaa . . ."

". . . ne wo." Ada completed the phrase and kissed her on the forehead.

"My whole world is you."

They sat together until evening, when Naa Lamiley finally managed to eat a bit of the mashed yam.

For the others, the baby was soon a thing forgotten; his was only one of many deaths that summer. Naa Lamiley should not have made such a fuss. Even Oko was no longer preoccupied with things past – he had swiftly taken a second wife who was already with child. Naa Lamiley, on the other hand, had got herself a bit of red cloth to tie about her hips. She sewed a new black mark onto its hem after each lunar cycle.

The cloth now bore ninety marks. Standing beside Damfo, Naa Lamiley bound the cloth tighter around herself; she stared across the courtyard at Ada.

"Lucky thing," she murmured. "At least Ada will always know where the final resting place of *this* child will be. Nyɔŋmɔ, oyiwala doŋ."

Ada's first child, also a son, lay buried in an unmarked grave. He had been born shortly before the move, when it had been said that their community would be safer here in Totope – between the lake on one side and the sea on the other. The small city where they had lived before – and after which Ada had been named – lay a half-morning's march away. And yet, when Ada had last sought the grave of her first child, it had vanished between the heaps of rubbish and the overgrown footpaths.

At the time, Naa Lamiley had tried to convince Ada to wear a red cloth, as well:

"To keep the memories alive."

It was a beautiful cloth, this much was true. Perhaps for a different occasion. Ada had shaken her head, stared at the floor, and returned the cloth to Naa Lamiley. Why should she commemorate the death of an infant? She had not honoured the other fallen members of her family in such a way.

"Who says you cannot remember them with this too?" had been Naa Lamiley's response.

"I do."

And the fire in Ada's eyes had brought the discussion to a decisive end.

And so Naa Lamiley had been all the more overjoyed that morning – if one can speak of "joy" in such a time

– when Ada had expressed her desire for yams, after not eating so much as a crumb for days.

During the night in which Ada's second baby died, Naa Lamiley had remained awake only through the grace of God and the assistance of a great number of kola nuts. Nonetheless, she had set out happily the next morning to bring her sister the best yams back from the market.

She had been on her way back, just before the storm clouds had exploded, when she saw him. She pinched herself to be sure she had not fallen asleep on her feet. And in doing so her sad collection of yams had tumbled to the ground.

"Eh – eh!"

There he was! The crooked nose still recognisable, the protruding ears – the left still a bit more prominent than the right – and the scar over his left eyebrow. The first shadow of a moustache above his lips was new. And what a voice! Smooth as palm oil, deep as the ocean. Naa Lamiley had hardly been able to contain herself:

"Na lɛ o! Na lɛ!"

How she might have expressed this in his language did not occur to her in that moment. "Na" was something like "seeing" – look? But what was the word for "lɛ" again? He-and-she? S/he?

The last time Naa Lamiley had seen Damfo, warriors had just brought him and his sister to the coast – he had vanished into the belly of the colossal fishing boat. The rest of the children in the village had agreed: He would never return. And after a few cycles of the moon had passed since the white men had taken him away, the children told each other gruesome fairytales about the boy whose skin turned

94

white as coconut meat because he stayed too long on the other side of the great water. Later, no-one could remember that the hero of the story had not been the invention of fantasy. But even the smallest among them knew that they should only continue telling these stories when the girl whom they had all come to call Ada was out of earshot.

Could Ada bear this news today? Naa Lamiley had nearly fainted at the sight of him herself! It was as if the boy had returned from Gbohiiajeŋ.

"I was not in Asamando," he would later explain as his vocabulary grew. "But the people there, where I lived for so long, they looked like they were dead."

Naa Lamiley pulled at Damfo's shirt. She wanted to reunite him with Ada and could think of nothing else. He motioned again and again that he would not enter the courtyard at any cost. And even after the white man had carried Ada's baby away, Naa Lamiley was hard pressed to convince the boy to follow them with her at a safe distance.

At the beach, the wind was already tearing the first palm trees from the ground. A trunk crashed down directly beside the fragile fishing boat behind which Naa Lamiley and Damfo were cowering. She still clutched her pitiful yams under one arm. Her back leaned against the wooden boat, she did her best to suppress a giggle – she did not know how to explain to Damfo how much she wanted to laugh: his forehead, his mouth, the nose! Exactly like Ada's! But his grip on her hand became so tight that Naa Lamiley was forced to turn herself to see what was happening down the beach.

The fierce and pale man who had sat beside Ada in the courtyard now stood in the water. The waves raged

around him, gaping far above his head like hungry jaws that threatened to devour him. It took a great effort for him to remain upright at all. With a few steps Ada was at his side in the water, grasping at his arm. He pushed her away. She tried to hold on to him once more. He was not quite close enough. He drew something from behind his back – a stick? – and held it out to her. But it was not a stick. It shone. Naa Lamiley could not see what the white man held in his hand – not even after the heavens around him flared and a silver beam of light streamed out from him. She knew even less what he sought to accomplish with his movements. She squinted on as the stick suddenly vomited forth fire and smoke with a loud bang. In the next moment, Ada lurched forward onto her knees, then sank to the ground. Before her lifeless body hit the beach, Naa Lamiley had already begun to run . . .

# Ada

Here? At first I had no sense of the word. At least not among the toothless ones. The word should have provided an uninterrupted and clearly delineated boundary from "there". But the inclination to divide and separate one thing from another first arrived along with Those-With-The-Big-Ships. And the circumstances escalated quickly, so that soon this "here" was not merely divided spatially from the position "there", soon "here" was also elevated *above* this "there". Resources were located "there" which either already belonged to "us" or soon would. "Us" – this naturally referred to the people from "here". A simple word. A single syllable. In the end, "here" came to represent only one thing for me: alive.

How strange, I thought. It was as though I had experienced raindrops on my face for the first time; my cheeks tingled, my eyelids fluttered, my forehead felt like a drum. I recognised the movements and the shapes around the body which I had – until very recently – inhabited, but I heard nothing more. I had forgotten the sound of silence.

Those living beings with whom I had occupied this tiny piece of earth-time looked at me in fear: the woman whom they had called Ada. They all were agitated, every one. Some were without inhibition. They screamed and wailed; their hands shaking, their breaths ragged. Others buried their sorrow beneath a mixture of anger, defiance and shame; their lips drawn, pale; their eyebrows furrowed, grim. Feet which first stomped to one side and then the other. The spectacle of the storm in all its glory was paramount; I should have been afraid. And yet, within me, all was still. I simply thought: How strange. Where was the child? And my gaze drifted, for I knew that he was near me.

I had once had a son. The shiny ringlets of his hair! He had come into the world on a Friday, after such a birth – his delivery had torn me apart. His delicate little fingers! If I had died, my son would have – nothing would have become of him anyway, this much is certain – my son would have at least . . . at least borne the title of "orphan". All his life. I had mourned him simply because he had taken a piece of me with him. What do we call the mothers of dead children? As the wife of one who died, I still would have been a widow. I mourned my son, but even more I mourned the glimmering emptiness where my new title should have been. Had the prophecy been wrong?

"*A* child," they repeated.

I sat alone before the Healer in the Before Time. I looked around myself in astonishment. This was in the time the Christians called 1451. In the time when Damfo and I had

still lived with our first parents. The time before our abduction. I looked at the Healer once more. Their glowering eyes were fixed upon two different points, moved independently from one another. Their grey hair towered above their head, framing a luminous face. My all-but-inaudible stammering evaporated before their question:

"Do you know what you are?"

I knew only what *they* were: the Healer. Neither man nor woman, or: both man and woman. My gaze fell instead upon the ants on the ground. I watched them bearing out tiny specks of flesh and wondered at their strength. If only I had more of such strength myself.

I had been brought to the Healer by my first mother because my breasts had remained flat, because I had not yet bled and, above all, because – behind closed doors – all of my other mothers had already begun to conspire plans for me. But the Healer was not interested in this. They had pursed their lips austerely while I repeated myself for the third time. Then they had asked:

"Do you know what you are?"

I had shrunk down until the ants appeared as giants beside me, and I had sobbed until the Healer had rolled their eyes. Perhaps they had already known that there would soon be reason enough to cry. Perhaps they had already heard the distant battle cries of the warriors who would reach us with the violent fall of night. Perhaps they had already smelled the cold desperation and the tortured mourning which would smother our still-smouldering houses at the break of day.

In their wrinkled hand they held the bracelet. I recognised it. Now and again I had seen it dangle from the

wrist of one of the older girls. The Healer waited patiently, allowed their glance to sweep over me, and when my show came to an end they extended the bracelet to me. Whose hands shook more when I received it? I can no longer remember. The beads of the bracelet had been warm. They assumed the colour of my unshed tears. For an eternity I rolled them back and forth between my fingers.

When I had returned to my mother, she gave me an akua'ba. She said nothing as she had the wooden figure bound to my back. The bracelet *and* an akua'ba! I would have liked to know why my fertility had become so critical all of a sudden! But because we were not alone I asked her instead whether we could see each other again at the next dawn. Her head shifted and her eyes said: yes. I knew that my suggestion would please her, for my mother loved the break of day.

I could hardly wait to tell her everything – but she never learned the words of the Healer. The warriors came in the night. Just before the warriors arrived, the Healer hid me and my brother in the forest. Panting and sweating, they promised to come back for us "soon". It was the kind of promise grown-ups sometimes make to deflect further questions.

"Soon!" they hissed again, before I could begin complaining anew.

As they pushed us up a tree I clung shrieking to their hand, whereupon they began to beat me, threatening to cut my tongue from my head if I did not remain hidden with Damfo in the woods. I did not feel their blows, but I hurt everywhere.

As soon as we had smelled the roaring flames, Damfo

and I crept back towards the village. As close as possible. I would have gone even closer, but Damfo had cried and begged and pulled me back. In the end, we ran and hid ourselves in the crown of one of the nearby trees. I covered my brother's eyes and clamped my own shut tight. But my ears betrayed me. I heard what the warriors did to my mothers, and how long they did it for, until they finally slit their throats. Again and again.

The sun must have been afraid to rise between the severed remains of bodies, the victory cries and the glowing embers. It finally managed to rise, just as Damfo fell asleep – his head in my lap, his sweaty hands upon my chest, his legs wound around a branch. We were discovered when, late that afternoon, I fell asleep as well and we fell from the tree.

We were the only things from Kuntanase that the warriors did not burn down. We and the crying bracelet – of which they did not know. I could fit nothing more in my vagina. We were removed the next day and had to walk ourselves. The chains with which they bound our hands were unnecessary. Damfo and I could not have been separated anyway. And we survived the innumerable days and nights that followed because I sang him hundreds of songs. Some reminded us of the songs our mothers had sung. Some I made up as we went along. Some were a simple combination of four notes.

By the end of the march we had run out of food, and my brother collapsed. His feet were bloody, his cheeks hollow, his eyes had sunken in. He was carried then by one of the monsters – but my fingers were still wound tightly around his wrist and I did not let go. And so they had to carry us

both. I kept singing. I had nothing else to offer Damfo but my voice.

When we reached the coast, the sun lashed us with its merciless rays. My first memory of this new place was that it smelled of salt and that there had been a soothing breeze. I had still clung to Damfo, staring wide-eyed at the great, foaming water. No words left my mouth. On the same day, they named me after the coastal town: Ada Foah. But before they had given my brother a new name, they tore him away from me and sold him like a basket of fried fish. Quick as lightning. He had been at my side. Then he was gone.

For many days, I was bound to a palm tree to keep me from leaping into the sea to get my brother back. A girl who looked to be my age had cried with me. She brought me water to drink and cried with me. She took my hand in hers and cried with me. And we stuck together. Soon the mothers called us:

"Naa-Lamiley-Ada!"

I inevitably turned in her direction each time I was asked a question. Her quiet confidence comforted me. For a long time I refused to accept the ugly, foreign barking of the coastal language in my mouth. But Naa Lamiley was a patient teacher. And because she also wished to learn, I showed her how I spoke, as well. And within only a few weeks we could both speak with two tongues.

Her firstborn came into the world on a Friday and reminded me of my father, and so I called out "Kofi!" He was a wonderful child.

"*A* child?" she asked.

I nodded, but the voice had a different timbre. And the question was not directed at me. I focused on the new person until I knew when I was. It was the year 1846, of course. I could tell from her bearing. The hands always caught my eye. The fingernails were shorter than I had ever seen fingernails before. The skin beneath them was chapped, and the flesh swollen. I stared more intently at her hands, until she hid them under her sleeves. And it flooded over me. The boiling heat, the unbearable stench, above all the tugging and clamouring at my waist. It was as though a blazing rope ran down my spine, over my stomach and deep into the base of my pelvis. I vomited.

We called it Room 218. Three others were waiting in the hallway while I lay on the wooden table inside to be "treated". Three others who heard my cries and yet remained seated. Three others who were attempting to buy back a bit of their future for the price of as many shillings as they could scrape together. Three others who did not look at one another.

At some point I ran out of breath. I always thought my eyes had been closed, but I can remember her short fingernails.

"Please," the other woman in Room 218 motioned. Her cheeks were flushed, and the few thin, blonde hairs which hadn't fitted into her bun hung in her eyes. She stuck out her bottom lip and blew upwards, but the hairs fell back over her face. "It isn't stopping," she whispered. "Can you hold this for a minute?"

The roaring heat of the summer day hung over us, but we did not say a word. The punishment for "soliciting" this "service" at that time was a one-way ticket to Van

Diemen's Land, exile. A single open window could have sufficed to betray us. And so we all sweated together.

A filthy bucket was pressed into the hands of the younger woman with the tiny fingernails. A nod of the head told her where she should stand. Another scream shook through the chamber, crashing against the walls and piercing my perception. It took a while for me to realise that it came out of me.

In the meantime I have learned that it is possible to hold one's breath for sixty seconds. If I had done so then, I would most certainly have forgotten to breathe out again. Not forgotten, repressed. If I could divide my life into sixty-second morsels, this pain would not have been able to do much to me. It could not have robbed me of my vision for the future I had woven together for myself and my child. Yes, I had a future. It was born on a Friday.

I also had a past. Even if it sometimes felt that way, I had not always lived in Thirty-Seven. In 1944, I had cowered in some other godforsaken corner of the world by the name of Ravensbrück. My infant, barely five days old, lay in my arms. His frail voice was unconvincing, it barely reached my empty breast, much less my heart. There was a man named Ulmen – we will describe him here as a man. Ulmen counted the standing rows of living corpses. He saw how I sat there, surrounded by diarrhoea, vomit and dried blood. In two paces he stood at my side. And.

I had never thought about the incident again. But while eating in Dora, my thoughts drifted through the common room and landed, somehow, in the past tense – precisely in that moment when he grabbed the "vermin" by his little

leg. And. I drew a sharp breath. I let the spoon fall from my hand.

Every few seconds, a fly flew against the windowpane. It recovered, only to fly again with all its might against the glass. I made an effort to follow this process with my eyes and was not surprised that it came easily to me. That it came easily to me. That it came easily to me.

"Why?" I asked, after Linde had attempted to squash the fly. All of the other six-digits were busy with their meals. She could have just ignored the fly too. Whenever Linde was annoyed, she took a deep breath, bit her lower lip and drew her eyebrows high. She usually followed this with a question. For example:

"What do you mean, 'Why?'"

"Just let it be," I said, reaching for the last piece of bread, although I already knew I would not be able to eat it. Throat. Tight. But Linde could not just let it be. The uneven motions, the intrusive humming, the persistent suffering – it was too much for her. Linde raised her slipper again over her shoulder, concentrating on the wall. And, just like before, I closed my eyes. It echoed. Not least because Linde obviously had to repeat the motion twice more to make sure. But this hammering could not be compared to the . . . I forced myself back into the present. I opened my eyes, just as she pulled her slipper back on. A tiny, darkish mass was smeared against the wall.

Linde observed the little quiver at the corner of my mouth. That's how she was, she saw everything: Stirrings I did not recognise in myself; needs I myself was unaware of; things I did not even know I lacked. She sat down beside me without touching me. No touching! Contact with my

naked skin, regardless of by whom, always reminded me of the smell of semen, followed by a burning between my legs.

The other six-digits conversed, cleared away, cleaned up. At least two were arguing: Linde heard the clatter of the food bowls, but most of all she heard the knocking of the tears behind my eyelids. She could guess the feelings I did not trust myself to speak aloud.

"A *child*," she murmured.

My hand shook as I raised the overflowing spoon to my lips. In the end, I managed to put a bit of soup into my mouth. I put the spoon away after I had had to spit out the bits of potato again. Linde wiped the white smudge from my chin, deliberately with her cuff, deliberately with the right one.

And.

Ahhh . . . there was something. I remembered.

Shhh . . . the floor called back to me.

I moved my head from one side to the other; my head moved itself back from the other side. It grew louder, clearer, more urgent. The floor was calling. I could no longer breathe. Some of the living were trying to keep me awake. But my arms, my legs. I did not want to carry them anymore. Good night, I thought, even though it was still early. Or was I mistaken? How many hours are so expensive? I closed my eyes. It did not matter.

Everything grew light.

Everything was white . . .

An awful lot of white

And then, actually, nothing more

And that for all eternity . . .

# BETWEEN THE ORBITS

BETWEEN THE ORBITS

We were preparing for the next orbit – it was that time again. God had taken the form of a breeze. I was honestly a bit intimidated by her ability to drift so gracefully over the landscapes – but I, too, assumed the form of a breeze and followed suit. That might all sound simple, but I tell you: such transformations do not come easy. A broom, a doorknocker and a room – these are all tangible objects. They are clearly delineated, halfway consistent, and have something of a monothematic function. A breeze is entirely different.

As a breath of wind, I can neither be seen nor touched, although my effects remain perceptible. There is a certain arbitrariness to that. I can "bring something into motion" or "cause chaos". But to find a happy medium between these two positions is truly a great art. Of course, God had perfected it, her movements were calm, comforting. I . . . still needed practice.

In any case, the time had come to remind Ada that all beings – past, present and future – are connected to one

another. That we always were and always will be. This message can be overwhelming, especially if a human believes they are hearing it for the first time. And we did not want to blindside Ada with it. We already knew that she requires a bit of space for herself at the end of each life. And so, God and I set out after her – but only after she first had time to dissolve herself completely into white.

And so we swirled for the length of one earth day around the legs of yapping dogs and through the leaves of blossoming apple trees. We swirled around the edges of a city named Berlin. We swirled and we swirled, where shivering humans awoke on park benches and other humans argued over who was right.

We travelled onwards – before truly hurtful words were hurled – and played in the next moment, it was evening time, in an abandoned playground where an empty plastic bag danced. God ruffled the downy feathers of a lonely pigeon, and I borrowed a toupee from an elderly gentleman and took it along with me. I dragged it through the lawns and sandpits, but I took no particular pleasure in observing its desperate owner as he stumbled after his hairpiece. And it was not any of my business, but still I had to wonder what he was doing at the playground in the first place. He was neither without home nor with child.

"Catch yersel' on," God said. "Gie' heem bek thon thing."

I paused for just a moment – long enough for the man to collect his dignity, dust it off, and set it back upon his head. With one hand firmly on his hair, and the other clasped about his collar, he set off, while God and I gathered speed and set out on our search for Ada.

The last time we had caught up with her between the

orbits, she had stared at us wide-eyed – just like she always had, just like she always would. That had less to do with our appearance than it did with what we had wanted to say. Because in order to describe how fluid the transitions between us beings are, God had told Ada – yet again, just like the first time – about the sausage-making.

Yes, you heard that right. But it is not really about the meat itself. It is more about the form. To be more precise: about the division of a mass originating from happy, frisky animals and ending – after the necessary processing – in the form of many, individual, fine and neatly separated, chubby, little sausages. Yes. Ada usually furrows her brow at this moment, as well. But *please, bear with me.*

The filling in the sausages is divvied up somewhat arbitrarily: the one hitch in an otherwise seamless transition. And that is pretty much how it goes when you try to sort humans into different categories. Absurd? Maybe. But God has observed all of you for thousands of years in order to find a way to explain halfway convincingly to living beings how this allocation process works. There is no better analogy than a sausage.

In the realm where the recently deceased linger with the as-yet-unborn, we are all just something like sausage meat. An interminable mass of flesh made up of so many individual parts – bubbling personalities, bizarre predilections and contradictory habits. When the time comes to make mortals of us, we are all pressed together through the same machine – something like a meatgrinder. But you have got to think away the mental images of pain, constriction and blood. That is not what it is about. Just retain this simple vision: first together, then apart.

*Oh, yes.*

And even though we are all pressed through the meatgrinder from one common mass of flesh, inevitably – and irritatingly – a little piece always gets stuck in the nozzle. And right now that little piece is me. After the cards are dealt, that filling which makes it into the sausage casing becomes a brave young man who escapes from his enslavement; the jilted lover of a genius; a frightened friend who falls silent at the moment of truth – or an immortal, wandering through time and space. But all of us are also so much more; all of us are becoming. Ada has the good fortune of repeatedly being permitted to remain under the sun among the living. Ada has the misfortune of repeatedly forgetting that she cannot remain there indefinitely.

We did not have to search long for her this time. In the midst of our storm, she had been taken and spun away from the roaring and the thunder. She landed back in her childhood, right at the moment when she had first fallen with ease into the rhythm of the local language.

Will we look back over all my lives? she asked.

We'll look at the things you still must learn, I answered.

God only squawked. An imposing beak hung between his two dark eyes. He rustled his wings and turned back his head to pluck an egg from his own back:

Se wo were fi na wosan kofa a yennkyi.

. . . and, washing herself, Ada was surprised that the soap burned her eyes but nowhere else on her body. The cloud-like foam was both a fascination and a torture, but she took the punishment in her stride – because she wanted answers. For example, an answer to the question as to why

116

these men who came over the water – with their cloth and their spices – why they said that they wished to exchange their wares for land? *How should that work?* One could not capture, kill, skin and prepare sunbeams for market. Or could they? But although these water men could understand even less of the language of these coastal people than Ada, they seemed to be quite serious about their intentions. They haggled with the village elders for many days, they drank with the village elders for many nights. Quite obviously, their strategy was a successful one, for their boats were far greater than those of the local fisherfolk. But Ada could not imagine – try as she might – how such markets would look where one could trade pieces of land.

Before she went to sleep, Ada also asked herself why it was that the sun rose in fire and glory on one side of the land only to sink three meals later, pale and decrepit, on the other side at the advent of the cold. That the sun must disappear was obvious to Ada. But what about this movement? Why was it that when Ada lay down to sleep each night between Naa Odarkor and Mami Ashitey, she did not awaken in the morning on the sand by the water? Or in a dusty corner behind the fence where the hens were locked away in the evening?

Ada had discovered a few answers to her questions, but she kept these to herself because she knew that no-one else would understand. Not even the one in whom she otherwise confided. And how could she? How was Naa Lamiley supposed to believe that the sun was afraid of the dark, and so hid itself at the end of day rather than quivering alone over the great water? How should she believe that

117

the blinking lights which could only be seen in the night air were, in truth, innumerable candles? And how should Naa Lamiley believe that these candles only looked so small because they were infinitely far away? How should she believe that people would one day sail out in immense spaceships to these candles?

"Eh-eh!" she would have said. "Are you very certain, o?"

And then she would have laughed at Ada, and Ada would have pretended to laugh along because she could not condense her tender deliberations into such rigid formulations. But she actually would have thought "Of course, I am uncertain!" because the only thing in which Ada firmly believed was that nothing was certain. But she could never say this aloud because it was different for Naa Lamiley. For her, the answer to all questions was: Ataa Naa Nyɔŋmɔ – the beginning, the middle, and the end . . .

". . . of course, with the exception of mathematics," Ada always liked to say. "Mathematics can do anything."

"Anything?"

Ada nodded in agitation, seeking to catch Charles's eye.

"One day it will even permit us to fly into the cosmos!"

"Hmm?"

That was not an honest "Hmm?" from Charles. It concealed neither an open question nor a genuine interest behind it. It was more an: oh-Ada-is-dreaming-again, a patronising-condescending "Hmm". And once again Ada felt a tightness in her chest that she did not wish to grow accustomed to.

She took up her hairbrush, observing Charles as he spread himself out across her bed, his reading glasses down at the tip of his nose. He read through her notes with his eyebrows raised. One could forgive such arrogance from a Hamilton, a Bentham or a De Morgan. At least Ada's debates with these associates took place within a scientific framework. These logicians preferred glorifying their own achievements over acknowledging Ada's brilliance on even a single point. But nonetheless they had plausible mathematical results with which they could preen – no matter their mediocrity.

"Hmm?" he repeated.

Ada softly pushed Charles aside to make a bit of room for herself on the edge of her bed, then lay down next to him.

"I would like to show you the bird." She smiled, warming her feet against his calves.

"What did you just say?!"

"I was only thirteen years old when I built it. It could flap its wings."

Charles removed his reading glasses, placing one temple tip against his lips. "And? What precisely has this to do with the cosmos?"

Ada shrugged.

"I only mean, if a little girl can do such a thing – if a simple girl can even dream of flying – then conquering the cosmos ought to be child's play for the cleverest men in all of England? Oughten it?"

Charles pursed his lips, releasing three short whistles, then readjusted his reading glasses and returned to her manuscript.

"If I should write such a thing!"

"Perhaps you should," she countered him. "One day it shall take place. And then they will all wonder at your foresight!"

This time he did not look up from his reading, yet Ada observed how his eyes flashed.

"Then," he chuckled, "I shall name the novel after you, of course!"

And Ada stared out of the window while he continued to smirk . . .

. . . she had seldom seen such a glorious starry night. As usual, it stank of burning flesh. Two or three barracks down, someone was coughing so hard it sounded like he would soon disgorge his insides.

A stripe sat at the edge of her bed, maintaining an appropriate distance. He was using his fifteen minutes simply to share a bit of humanity. A daisy was wilting in his hand.

"We citizens of the Reich must stick together," he had said. Ada brushed her hair. To her it was irrelevant what some documents or record entries might have been able to prove. What was important, in the end, was what she could pass for. The silence between them did not bother him – he was somewhere else, lost in his thoughts.

"This time last year, I was still slaving away in the tunnels alongside some random Jews . . ." While he spoke, Ada put down her brush and took up her rouge. She put a little on her lips. He held his silence for a moment – watching as Ada kissed the back of her hands – before continuing:

"We toiled down there under the earth as though time had been abolished. With some effort I might have guessed

the proper month, but when we awoke – I mean, when they barked us out of sleep – I never knew what day of the week it was."

His eyes grew glassy. He had still not noticed that the flower between his fingers had fallen to the floor.

"My bunkmate, what was his name again? He kept a diary. The light scratching of his pen against the paper in the notebook lulled me to sleep despite the stench and noise. Like . . . um. Like a . . ."

He scratched his head while he struggled for the next word.

"A lullaby?" Ada said. She had finished her make-up. She sat now at the edge of the bed, hands on knees, waiting for his time to run out.

"A lullaby," he nodded, still lost in thought. "Precisely. But I first understood just how dangerous that writing was when someone else was called up for his *shoelaces*."

Ada raised her brows.

"You wouldn't think shoelaces were of critical significance for the building of rockets, would you?" He blinked. "But we were forced to stop assembling and watch as they smashed his face in. Over and over. The skin burst over his right eyebrow. And then with a truncheon – smack! – right on the nose. And again. I didn't say a thing, but still, I wondered. Why did it take so long? They hit the Jew *six times* before he finally collapsed!"

"Hmm . . ."

With a swift flick of the eye which he did not notice, Ada glanced at the door to see if they were being observed through the peephole. There was no-one there.

"While dragging the body to the main entrance –" the

stripe grinned – "I heard that it had been about *solder wire*. Do you know what solder wire is?"

Ada shook her head, but she rolled her eyes internally.

"Of course not." He nodded. "Well, it's very thin, bendable metal. You know, like bits of twine. They should have been properly disposed of. Property of the Reich."

He laughed until he cried. Until Ada could not tell whether he was truly crying or not.

"Property of the Reich! Like everything else here."

He looked away and wiped his eyes. His glance fell on the flower on the floor. He left it where it lay.

"I don't know where my neighbour pilfered that notebook and the pen. But after that, the scribbling no longer sounded . . ."

Comforting.

Later, as Ada lay at the very edge of the earth, her arms outspread, a tiny bloody circle on her left breast, she felt truly comforted. The sparkling and shimmering before her eyes did not make her feel afraid.

"No," she breathed. And she did not know why or to whom she had spoken. There were so many unfiltered sounds. She heard a female voice again, beseeching her: "Ada, please! Please stay here! Stay with me!"

"No." Ada expelled the word one final time.

. • . • .

I supposed this next orbit would really become something special because – for the first time – I had got to choose

what kind of object I would be. I was so happy I did not even ask why. I just accepted gratefully. Grateful is almost too modest a description: I was bursting with joy. Ada was less excited. As she held her cards between her fingers, they stained her hands. She read, licking her fingertips.

The smell of candyfloss was unbearable, and the message was not to her taste, either. She should become one of the living again. Ada crossed her arms, sank her head to her chest and rocked gently back and forth. It looked as though she was crying. The cards fluttered angrily but remained squeezed tightly between her right hand and her left elbow.

What kind of mother am I supposed to become, she murmured, when I don't even have one myself?

I gasped. Did she still believe that only the person who gave birth to her could be her mother? Even after all her many lives?

After all my many lives, she hissed, just once I want to have a mother WHO STAYS WITH ME. Her eyes were blazing.

Oh, oh, I thought.

She raged, she flailed about, screaming into the white emptiness. She did not want to have to live through another experience of being torn away only to be replanted somewhere new. If she could have had it her way, she wanted finally to be a finite being: one with a beginning, a middle and most importantly – most importantly – an end.

Her behaviour surprised me, for Ada had already learned that all of us have always been here and that all of us will always be here. Until that which we call "time" folds in upon itself and all but shatters. Until that which

we call "history" turns in on itself, and the so-called future begins anew. I found her forgetfulness inexplicable.

God squawked. It meant something along the lines of: You're no better yourself! Remembering and forgetting go hand in hand. How often do I have to remind you?

Until I get to be human, too, I said.

Perhaps, God answered, perhaps your life already happened. Perhaps you just slept through it . . .

Nice try, I said.

. . . or you've repressed it.

I don't think so, I said.

Because if I knew anything, it was that I had not yet lived. Of this I was certain.

I asked if the mission would be about the bracelet again. My cards were fluttering around somewhere. They were hard to hold and read without hands.

It would, God pronounced. And about Germany again.

But why, I asked (my last time in Germany had left a bit of a bad taste).

That's just how it is. But this time, you may choose your object. What would you like to be?

I knew immediately. Something that brings joy, I said.

Over the millennia, I had come to recognise what joyful beings looked like. The condition seemed contagious. And surely it would help my own progress, I thought, if I were to put more value on the affirmative. My interactions with the living had always been more productive when I'd elicited happiness in them.

I could still see the sleeping baby, lulled into comfort by yours truly: a warm bottle of milk; or the group of boys who reconciled their differences after sitting in a circle and

passing me around. In some places, it's enough for me to be a four-leafed clover. In other places, they get excited when I incarnate the number eight. A comfy blanket, a positive decision on an asylum application or top surgery suffice to evoke warmth, enthusiasm or relief.

Only love is off limits. Love is reserved for God. Which is honestly a bit of a relief for me because love is a worn-out concept anyway – and one which quickly leads to terrible decisions and even worse pop music.

I've been told that love is the greatest joy of all. I would hazard that the beings who make such claims have never been enveloped by utter silence – they have never experienced that intimate feeling of infinity. Or to be more precise: They no longer remember what it felt like.

They are like Ada.

# THE NEXT ORBITS

THE NEXT ORBITS

# Ada

## 02:59

It actually was Friday the 13th. Goodness me. Thankfully for the last time this year. My eyes were open, but being awake was something else entirely. The dream still scuttled around inside me for a while, tickling my eyelids and driving an awful pain into my neck before reluctantly retreating into the background. It lurked defiantly about my ears, knowing I would soon invite it back in.

I shoved my hot-water bottle under my left shoulder and rolled my head from side to side. It was only lukewarm, this so-called hot-water bottle. It would have been better if I'd got up and boiled myself more water. It would not have been much trouble. I told myself that I was a strong, independent woman. Come on now! Up! And in my thoughts, I was already three steps ahead – wrapped in a blanket, tiptoeing barefoot through the kitchen with a steaming kettle. Elle's kitchen. I assured myself that it would only take a minute or two, maximum – I couldn't endure longer on those cold tiles anyway. But only my spirit was willing. The flesh cuddled deeper into the

comfort of the darkened living room. On Elle's lumpy sofa.

I yawned. And the dream took this opportunity to creep back to the edge of my memory. What had I seen in my dream? It taunted me with little clues. I'd almost put it back together when something shifted in my belly. Even in the weak light which was just seeping through the curtains, I could recognise the three or four tiny bumps protruding from around my belly button. Lost in thought, I hummed the first four notes of a melody and wondered what the song was called – until the baby kicked against the upper walls of my ribcage. I had to hold my breath a moment. My hands sought to placate the little bumps and I whispered:

"Hey, hello! Quiet in there!"

Elle would have laughed. She would have said: This kid will make your life a living hell. I should be enjoying my sleep as long as I still can.

How she loved to make me feel small. As if she really believed that *she* was *my* older sister, and not the other way around. If she had been there, she would have repeated her little wisdom about sleep. And I? The thought was painful: I would have held my tongue. Just like I did last time. Exactly one week ago, on St Nicholas' Day.

By now, Saint Nick was a name that meant something to me. And, unfortunately, his naughty little helper, Knecht Ruprecht, too. Not to mention Zwarte Piet: *Black Pete?!* These Germanic traditions. But just this time last week, I had slept in blissful ignorance. A few hours later I'd been awakened by Elle. I'd tried to act as though I hadn't noticed her standing there beside me. My eyes were still closed, my

breathing deep and even, and yet my jaw had betrayed me. When she patted my head I'd clenched my teeth.

"Sankt Nikolaus was here!" she'd exclaimed, sitting down beside me on the sofa. "Sankt Nikolaus was here! Looks like you've been a good girl!"

"K'laus" and "Cash" don't sound all that similar, I know. And still, a "What?!" escaped my lips. It was a wonder I said anything at all with a frog that big in my throat. I wanted to ask when he had stopped by and why he hadn't stayed. Whether he was coming back. But my voice had only sufficed for a simple "Why? Why was *he* here?"

"Just have a look yourself," Elle had said, smiling. How she raised her eyebrows – bah! And then she'd rolled her eyes. As if I were a little kid she had been trying to surprise. She looked so pleased. *But why?* Why, of all people, should Elle be happy about Cash showing up? Since his disappearance she had hardly wasted a word on him. And even before that she hadn't spoken openly about what she really thought of him. It wouldn't have been necessary: Her facial expression had always said it all. So why this sudden change?

Luckily, last week, I had decided in the moment to say as little as possible. Slowly I had slid from the sofa, dragged myself past her, and extended my head through the doorway. I looked into my shoes; they were filled with fruits and nuts and other organic crap. I must have looked extremely confused when I turned back to Elle.

"Oh!" She'd laughed. "Do you not know about Sankt Nikolaus? Or are you just not awake yet?"

I looked away.

"Hello?!" Elle had cried.

"What?"

"Typical Ada," she had giggled. "Still savouring your sleep?"

I did my best to smile. I wasn't really successful. Since the end of June, every crooked glance – it didn't matter from whom – pierced me straight through the heart. Every sharp tone – regardless of the irony – called forth my tears. And so, I couldn't afford to answer. It was easier to just let Elle's inconsiderate bits of wisdom float right over my head. But in my fantasies I stared her right back in the eye and snorted:

"*Savouring* my sleep, you say? Have you ever been pregnant? Have you ever slept on this rubbish sofa of yours?!"

One day, I promised myself. One day I'd really let her have it. I'd give it to her good.

And, as usual for this early hour, my bladder was starting a fight with the baby. Not a chance, I thought, as my eyes began to close again. *Socks* was going to win. And then I shook my head, but it was already too late. Cash's bizarre suggestion of a "working title" for the baby clung to my brain like a bad song. And Socks floundered again against my stomach, and I hardly noticed it. Rolling cautiously to one side, I didn't even hear the crash as my lukewarm bottle tumbled to the ground.

And then I fell. I dreamed of a man who would never massage my neck.

Ashitey.

For a long time he had given me the impression that I did not even exist. During the day, he had fetched water, chopped firewood and swept the yard. In the evenings he had gone off alone – to pray in peace, or so they had said.

Normally he had returned by moonlight, and gone straight to bed. But sometimes when his eyes had not been quite so red, he had paused and stood alongside the older men. He sat beside them, nipping at their kpótomenui and coughing until they had to slap him on the back. He had observed the men precisely, mimicking their every motion. He had lacked only the stiffness of their necks. But regardless of how he had ended his day, whenever he passed me he had always concentrated on the chickens and goats. As if I were invisible. And I, on the other hand, I could have drawn a picture and mapped out every single hair on his body.

He was unusually tall, and therefore he was always punished quicker than the rest of us for the usual childhood pranks. His curls were also lighter – larger and softer – and his eyes were as changeable as the colour of the great water. The odd shade of his skin colour was a regular subject for the commentary of the toothless ones. Mami Ashitey told everyone who would listen that he was *not* a *real* Ga. His father came from a distant land. But she no longer knew what that land had been called.

"That's okay," I told him later. "My own father also came from a distant land whose name I can no longer remember."

Ashitey had been chosen for me because Naa Lamiley had tipped off the toothless ones that he reminded me of my first mother. He also had this special way of moving his head, as if the wind was blowing it back and forth. That was during the time when the men were still there. The elders with their closed eyes and open mouths, their grey-flecked hair encircled by flies, dozing away the hours in the shadows until their evening rounds of Oware. The

young men caught fish or repaired nets, they sang work songs and told jokes. And at all times they held watch against enemy encroachments and encroaching enemies. The very small children tumbled tirelessly after the fluffy chicks, stretching their plump little arms before them. They giggled until they could no longer breathe. And those who were almost young men – those who did not yet have to work – played Ampe. Although Ashitey was already much older, he still could not keep up with them. He always clapped one beat too slow, stamped first when the child across from him already had both feet back on the ground. They did not laugh in his face, but behind his back they wobbled their heads as though their necks were made of rubber.

I was torn away by a screaming boy. There was no space between the laughter of the children and the pulling on my body. Time had frozen – a yellow bolt flashed across my vision – only to begin again when Mami Ashitey's blow struck my ear.

Ashitey stayed in the yard, maintaining eye contact with me throughout, while his mother flailed at me and her wife made sounds of approval.

Whack – "That's right!"

Whack – "That's right!"

With my peaceful gaze directed at Ashitey, I must have still looked too relaxed, because after only a few blows with her fist Mami Ashitey sought out a different imple-ment. But even the flail she had fashioned out of a thin twig could not make me flinch.

Whoosh – "That's right!"

Whoosh – "That's right!"

Later, shiny welts appeared on both my legs. Ashitey brought me a gourd filled with cool water and then disappeared again, just after his finger inadvertently brushed my own. It would take a few more phases of the moon before I could speak enough Ga to thank him myself – and before I would trust myself to ask him if I could possibly . . . I had wanted to just abandon the question, but he had looked at me so beseechingly, nodded so invitingly . . . if I could hold his head between my hands? I would close my eyes then, pretending I was back with my first mother. I would not stop crying until after Ashitey and I had made love.

The men – both young and old alike – were all already away before I realised that I was pregnant. They were to explore the surrounding areas to find us a new home because our settlement had become unsafe.

"Please – take me in your arms," I had said to him before their departure. Or had I only thought it? Either way, Ashitey had not heard me. He left. I did not try again. He left with the belief that I had nothing to tell him. Who?

Charles.

He had made up his mind not to go back. And yet, with every step he took, our argument must only have confounded him the more. He could not work it out: Why was I so obsessed with the calculations? And why had I spoken of William in such detail during the preceding hours? Had there been some subtext between the lines?

I remained for a while at my bedroom window. I watched as he slowed his pace on Elm Road, how he paused and almost turned about. And how he then marched on with new resolve. I rolled my eyes. There was little difference

between him and my own husband: how obstinate they both were.

At the beginning of our courtship, William had slogged on tenaciously. He had forced himself to be my constant companion. Merriment had been a necessity: Smile! Laugh! Jokes! To every wish he had heard expressed – particularly from my dearest friends – he had always responded: "But of course!" A twinkle in his eye. He accompanied me everywhere, his coach was my coach. There would never be another man who endeavoured so heroically on my behalf.

A few weeks after the start of our acquaintance, he began turning up a little or even on occasion quite late to his other engagements because those – what had until then been pressing – matters could now be managed "on the side". Back then, nothing had been more important than to ensure the fulfilment of my happy heart's every desire: his enchanting Lady Ada. Initially I was unsettled by his singular dedication, but I reassured myself with the thought that he meant well – and that it was surely just a phase.

He asked me – sometimes several times in a single hour – whether everything was to my liking, and took the opportunity each time to lay his right hand on my back: a little too lightly for a platonic friendship, and yet a little too firmly to seem completely relaxed. How was I to appraise these contradictory feelings? I decided to keep my discomfort to myself. In order not to burden him unnecessarily.

And yet, it was still too much for him: He regularly invited me to dine with him and was then playfully offended when I so much as thought of paying. He had answers to all of my questions – even those I did not ask.

And he was at ease. The very personification of calm. Always. It was only a matter of time.

At first, I was proud to have such a handsome gentleman at my side. My gratitude was effervescent, my eyes aglow with admiration. The kind of adulation that silences all other perceptions. He was considered a good catch, indeed: My Claras, Lucys and Henriettas were all jealous; my mother was relieved. Everything would have seemed perfect to me, had it not been for his chin: as rigid as a wartime barricade. It was the chin of a man with a raging volcano inside him, and his ruthless past was catching up with him by the day. William was a broken man. A man with no future – because that tiny bit of confidence which he could muster each morning had already been expended by nightfall.

Nevertheless – or perhaps for that very reason – Charles had nothing but contempt for him. And although he tried desperately, he was unable to find any sympathy for me either. The fact that William had "done so many lovely things of late" was utterly irrelevant to Charles. Inconsequential. Insignificant. Inordinate.

"You doubted yourself," he said. "That was your mistake."

Charles, too, had answers to questions I had not asked.

"I recognised that I indeed often cut William short," I whispered. "And yet his accusations knew no end. William made assertions; often snarled; and once, verily, I had to flee and lock myself away from him in another room."

"Whatever for?"

"I had embarrassed him . . ."

"When?"

"When I gave my evaluation of the current situation

in France – and in the presence of Lord Palmerston of all people!"

I could be amused by such things, but *cher Charles*. His indignation was writ large across his face. What he would not have given to speak publicly with me about the infamous February Revolutions! Nonsense. The subject would not have mattered in the least. As long as he could speak with me.

"Soon, I'd taken to chewing over my sentences three times before I let them out," I continued. "I only felt safe when my husband could laugh with me. And so, of course, *I* was compelled to find all *his* jokes amusing."

I looked into Charles's eyes. He seemed so weary. And so vulnerable. I stroked his cheek with my fingertips. I wanted to tell him that I sometimes dreamed of being free. That I longed for a different place entirely, a realm where I could just be. A room of my own. For each day it grew clearer to me that William regarded the promise "till death do us part" with deadly earnest. But Charles would not have heard me. Nor seen me. He had closed his eyes.

Karl, I mean.

In his mind, he still sat on his granny's lap. Inhaling her unique odour – that medley of tobacco, cherry schnapps and perfume. The radio crackled, hummed and whistled out one broadcast after the other on the upcoming election of the German president. A dab of strawberry mousse ran down his chin and she licked her thumb, zeroing in on the corner of his mouth. She closed one eye to steady her aim. And although he struggled to resist Oma Gerda's arm with all his might, his body remained stiff and upright

as a candle. His brow furrowed, his jaw stiffened, he held his breath: millimetre by millimetre, he seemed poised to evade her approaching thumb. His head wobbled from side to side.

"Hold still!"

As a rule she was not a strict woman, but once she had made a decision, Gerda tolerated absolutely no objections to her will. It did not matter from whom. Her mistaken belief that her only grandson had secretly joined the resistance was truly a momentous error – in reality there were few more dedicated Hitler devotees than her Karl. But fortunately he would never learn the truth of her denunciation.

The other children in the village were every bit as blond and blue-eyed as the birthday boy. They had gathered around to sing him their long-practised serenade. The scene must have taken place precisely thirteen years ago to the day: He could remember the eight candles with the same detail that he remembered Oma's joy that Hitler had become a German citizen.

Back then, Little Karl thought he knew just what revulsion meant. He had cried bitterly as she spread a thick trail of her slobber across his cheek. His granny had only set him free after all the strawberry mousse had been removed and his little face had positively glowed with shame. The moment she loosened her grip, he had sprung down from her lap and curled himself up in the farthest corner of the room. He swore to himself then that on the day he officially became an adult his first act would be to take good care of Oma Gerda – in precisely the same manner and with the self-same lack of mercy she had shown him. And now, the long-hoped-for day was there, but his granny was not.

He opened his eyes and realised he was still standing in my room. Yes, my dear. Still. I called him Nine-Zero-Eight because he had disappeared before I could memorise the rest of his numbers. I did not know his real name. But I thought he looked like a Karl.

What might we have done for one another if he had not run away? Why do men always disappear?

## 06:48

I did not wake up when my bladder gave up the fight. I suppose my body sleepwalked to the bathroom while the rest of me remained floating in Asamando. It was there that I came to appreciate the creation of both "you" and "me". At first the new borders seemed fluid, ambiguous, and when they were no longer useful, they disappeared. They were exchanged for other borders.

My mother and I separated. I would have liked to have been like her. She knew her way around separations, and knew what it meant to be born, delivered – or perhaps better, to live the illusion of delivery. She carried me into my very first room. She set me on the forty-week journey to Wiase, then vanished again and again before I could ask her: Why?

My mother did not die in the flames.

Nor in the early morning, as she was forced to watch her only surviving children be carried off by the arsonists. My mother had disappeared in the night, just before the

attack. The Healer had hidden her by the banks of the Bro Bri under a pile of dried kuntan leaves. Her left ear was somewhat more receptive to the steady murmur of the river because the right side of her head was pressed into the ground. She no longer coughed because her tongue stuck to her gums. She drifted in the twilight between sleep and waking – as we all did that night.

My mother did not die in the flames, but she did not really live during those first four days after the massacre either.

She hummed "Mashallah" – so weakly by the fourth evening that only the ants could hear her. Zealous as they were, the ants always made time for music. And how heavenly they repeated the first notes of my mother's melody!

"Yes, we live . . ."

"O, we live!"

"But what for?"

"O, but what for?"

Their harmonies drifted about my mother and lulled her back to sleep. She dreamed of glittering fractions of raging fires and ghastly screams; of godly forges and human diamonds.

On the fifth day, two brothers who had got themselves lost in the forest stumbled over a foot. The skin, chapped and shrivelled, was covered in singing ants, lapping themselves full at her wounds. The unhappy brother who discovered the body part recoiled and retreated from the suspicious foliage. It was pure luck that he did not drop the two gourds he was carrying. He tiptoed backwards, his eyes searching the woods for the poisonous snake that had quite obviously brought its poor victim to this

agonising end. It was the boy's very first journey. His first time beyond the confines of his village. When he caught sight of the foot, the quivering thirteen-year-old clenched his butt cheeks together, contriving an urgent case with which to convince his older brother to head for home without further delay. And because his brother did not immediately react, he added: "Kodjo? Please!"

Kodjo nodded slowly, pretending that he did not notice the stench. Owusu, the younger brother, repeated his entreaty. He would have made a third attempt had he not been interrupted by a rustling. As if the stray foot had not demanded enough of him already, suddenly the pile of leaves began to move. One of his gourds came crashing to the ground.

"Aeeeeeeeee!"

Owusu did not know himself whether it was shame at his own clumsiness or his fear of the reanimated pile of leaves which brought about the scream. But it was a pity to have lost the precious wine. The white puddle soaked into the earth. Owusu hurried away, stopping to look back only from a safe distance.

Kodjo squatted beside the pile of leaves, his head tilted slightly to one side. Apart from the crickets, the forest was silent – the leopards were not yet out. Kodjo salvaged a bit of the disappearing palm wine with a shard from the broken gourd. He brushed the leaves away from my mother, and carefully lifted her head.

"Nsa fufuo . . ." he murmured, pouring a bit of the wine into her mouth drop by drop. He stroked her cheeks, her lips, her chin, until she slowly returned to something like consciousness. Only after she had weakly nodded her

consent did he wash and dry her body. He closed his eyes while he removed the mud from her breasts, and he used her own hand to wipe away the river water from between her legs.

Owusu also wanted desperately to clean the insides of his own skinny legs in the river, but his feet were tingling. Shaken, he watched as Kodjo carried my mother in his arms, her head against his neck. And when Kodjo announced that they would return to their village, there was no protest from Owusu. They travelled through the night.

Kodjo grew tired, but he did not slow his pace. And so Owusu was forced to keep up, even when he could hardly keep his own eyes open from exhaustion. When the three arrived in Pramso, morning was breaking against the horizon in scarlet flames.

A short time later, Kodjo lost his left leg in a curious accident. He left with the other men at dawn, as he did every day. After only a few work songs he lay crumpled on the floor of the mine, screaming his throat raw. No-one seemed to recall how he had fallen. And he had to be carried back to the village by six men – a feat they could accomplish only after they had beaten him unconscious.

He would never be able to work again. And so, it became his singular duty to sit in the courtyard and boast at every opportunity about how he had once, alone, carried my mother back to Pramso from the banks of the Bro Bri. Walked through the night. The wonder he awakened in the children did not take his pain away, but it provided him with a welcome distraction. Kodjo never mentioned how he *had* received some help during that night: how my

mother's breath had kept him alive. Just like his broken, useless leg, she did not fit within his hero's tale.

My mother's name was Farida.

For a long time I thought we had been separated for ever by death. But one frosty London morning, I opened my eyes and, lo and behold! She appeared like a wonder before me. I immediately recognised her scent. She smiled only with the corners of her mouth, for my birth had been difficult. Too difficult, she had said, and glared at me reproachfully, as though I had deliberately sought this out for her. I wailed. She did not take me in her arms, for she hated hearing me cry. Instead, she carefully observed how the wet nurse suckled me to sleep. And so I rarely called her "mama". Actually, only in public. Actually, only for her sake.

My mother dressed herself in flames – my upbringing: her smouldering proof that she did not need a man. Long before my time, she and my father had been bound together in a volatile love–hate relationship which reached its climax at my birth. I was only a few weeks old when my mother left our family home for good.

The porridge sat untouched in our breakfast room, the teacup still steamed and my father's tears flowed unimpeded, while outside my mother bore me to our coach. They both knew that his extreme acts of violence could not be undone. Hidden behind the windowpane, the attendants could not help but observe my father's every move. They hardly breathed. My mother, on the other hand, managed to disregard the shell that had once been her husband entirely. Instead, she concentrated on the tribulations of the wan coachman, who sat shaking his head.

"Is the wee babe ole enough, m'lady?" he grumbled. "Kirkby Mallory's a long way off, eh? A right *long* way off."

"I assume we'll be making the proper stops to rest along the way?" My mother's eyes shimmered with the hope that he would understand that her question was not a question at all. All the necessary sacrifices had already been made. More than a week before, in preparation for the journey, she had sent my wet nurse away. Those many tearful days I had suffered with my mother before she had finally managed to nurse me from her own breast would not be in vain!

The coachman nodded – less in agreement than from the sheer mental and physical overload. Never before had he undertaken such a lengthy journey with a newborn baby. He had never before witnessed so young a mother clamber aboard his carriage without a moment's hesitation, nor had he ever seen such a broken excuse for a husband – quite obviously the father of the little worm – remain behind upon the doorsill of the house. The driver hesitated, my mother's valise still in his hands, as though waiting for my father to finally take some responsibility for the matter. But we heard nothing. My father's tears flowed on. And so, the coachman stowed my mother's bag beside his seat, climbed aboard the coach himself and gathered up the reins.

He grew smaller and smaller. Flanked by two bottles of gin and the rubble of his broken marriage, my father wordlessly seemed to accept the unfolding drama. Without reinforcements, the fading echo of the horses' hooves upon the greyness of the London cobblestones would have been

intolerable. He stumbled back into the house, casting one bottle against the flagstones with a cry: a single wail from out of the very depths of his soul. It echoed in the hallway for the length of the remaining day. With his left hand he clung desperately to the second bottle. It was already a quarter gone before he reached his study.

"Papa" died during my childhood – on some battlefield or other in some distant, foreign land. And so our first parting was, indeed, our last. Although he had insisted upon the name "Ada" at my birth, in the end it did not appear that I was precious enough for him to engage in any lullabies or bouncing baby games in the weeks that followed. He was an artist, after all.

We made our first break shortly after we had crossed the Thames. The coachman introduced himself to my mother in front of a public house not far from the banks of the river. "Solomon's the name, m'lady," he said, taking another bite of his apple. "If there's anything yer in need of, just ask, m'lady. Just *ask*."

A bit of drool seeped down his jowl as he spoke. My mother was not the type of woman to suffer in silence. At that time, she had only a slight itch in her foot where the scab over the tiny wound she had received a few days before had begun to chafe. To distract herself from the irritation, she asked for the name of the man sleeping beside her in the coach.

"He's been digging at his belly for some time now, and he smells absolutely dreadful!"

"Aye, that'd be Owen," Solomon sighed. "The babe o' the fam'ly. He's et somethin' vile yesterday. Somethin' *vile* indeed."

My mother directed her gaze away from Owen with an effort, endeavouring to breathe only through her mouth in short, moaning gasps.

"Should you not awaken your brother then? To permit him to . . . relieve himself?"

She could quite vividly observe the way one thought clung to the next, chasing their way through her coachman's mind before gathering into a short conclusion. Finally it occurred to Solomon what she had intended to express by her delicate question. He chortled, slapped himself upon the thigh and choked on a remaining bit of apple in his throat. Before my mother could descend from the coach, lay me down in a safe place, and strike the coachman heartily upon the back, he was already unconscious. He lay there in the mud, one leg extended at an awful angle from the rest of his body.

My mother was afraid of nothing. When rumours began to proliferate about a possible collapse of the London government, she saw to it that enough food and provisions were stored in our home. Even the later outbreak of the Spa Fields riots could not unnerve her inner peace. Quite the contrary, she continued to host a diverse array of gatherings and meetings for prison reform at her estate. And so when Solomon collapsed, she knew just what to do. With his yellow teeth and sticky beard, the resuscitation was no doubt a revolting undertaking. But at the same time my mother knew that the alternative – to wait for salvation along the highway as a solitary woman with a squawking newborn child and two apparently dead male companions – would be less than ideal. Without a moment's hesitation, she pinched shut his nose and lay her mouth on Solomon's.

I was to become just like my mother. She raised me on a strict diet of raw indomitability and fuming rage. She sought out and selected each person who was to be responsible for some portion of my upbringing herself. The use of any texts which could in some way have sparked my own volatile disposition – in particular my father's poetry – was forbidden under pain of retribution. And ambitious as I was, I permitted my mother to awaken an early fascination for the sciences in me. I adopted her passion for mathematics, for I, too, was convinced of their infallibility and diverse applications. While other young ladies preoccupied themselves with embroidery, reading and music, I designed mechanical flying machines and cultivated acquaintanceships with cantankerous old mathematicians who were many times my age. And because my talent was so admired within these scientific circles, my mother took full responsibility for any potential damage to my reputation. And yet, in secret, I carried with me a thin, dog-eared volume of poetry at all times. Despite her every effort and to her great consternation, I remained to the bitter end my father's daughter.

My mother's name was Annabella.

We stood side by side facing our house. My mother and I. I made some effort not to look at it directly, although I already had some inkling that I would never set eyes on it again. There was something about the light. Like a sunbeam glancing from the windowpanes . . . the thick curtains which were pulled tight in all the neighbouring houses flickered and twitched now and again. I would have had to squint. And yet, had I done so, I would have

drawn too much attention to myself. My expression was to remain neutral. Our lives depended on it.

In both directions the streets were filled with marching columns, as far as I could see – whenever I dared to move my eyes. My brother and my sisters trembled along with all the other endless lines of people beside my mother and me. How much longer? I thought. I really had to pee.

I risked one glimpse in her direction. She stared motionlessly ahead. Five minutes. Fifteen minutes. Fifty minutes. Every time she drew a breath, it sounded as though she would sob. And yet, I saw only how she remained steadfast, staring straight ahead. Until she touched the skin beneath her right eye with her index finger. It was a quick movement. I almost missed it. Just look at that, I thought. Until that moment I would have laid my hand into the fire, so certain was I that she was not ashamed of anything.

Knocking back a few glasses of śliwowica on a random evening, throwing a spontaneous party and waking up the next afternoon in a puddle of drool – *that* was my mother. Sometimes she would dangle something more or less edible in front of our mouths. Sometimes she would not. The reality of raising three daughters alone from three different men and never having been married at all did not bother her in the least. Even after she had taken up with the joiner in the neighbouring village, she returned a year later and moved back in with her parents. Brwilno was a boring place, she had yawned. And Tomasz – with his absent sense of humour and strange obsession with punctuality – was in no way good enough for her and her four children (by that time she had also borne a son). She would keep looking for something better. Or not.

My mother was an awful cook, an average seamstress, and we – her four children – were always in trouble with the village elders. At some point she lost track of how often she had had to pick us up at the police station. Some parents would have withdrawn themselves from the public eye. Others would have grown abusive or violent. *She* held her head high as she walked the streets of Popłacin or played with us on the banks of the Wisła on particularly sunny days. Sometimes she decked herself out with bright scarves and delicate trinkets. Other times she wore a three-piece suit and flirted with the lonely wives of conscripted soldiers. She was hated and loved in equal measure. Of all things, it was her tears which she had endeavoured to hide during the occupation of our village.

"Crying is nothing to be ashamed of!" I had whispered: a saying I had learned from her. My hand slipped into hers – soft and warm, as always.

"Who's crying?"

She held my brother in her other arm. He laughed and wiggled his legs, for she had been telling him for months now that he was too big to be carried. She strengthened her grip on my hand, focusing her eyes on the excited man rolling up and down the street before us. I recognised him and his shoddy wheelchair. He was the owner of the antique shop which was always closed on Mondays. We did not know his real name. We called him Monday, and he called us degenerates. My mother never told us how she knew Monday, but of all the people in the village we harassed, this nasty little man was the only person mother warned us time and again to leave alone.

"Especially now," she said. "Now that Owe's not around."

I always asked who Owe was, receiving in response either a smack on the behind, or on days when she was in a better mood, the answer that I "already knew". And how would I feel if *my* own brother should die? And if she heard that we had smashed in Monday's windows again, she would dash our heads together.

Oh yes, I knew who Owe was. But I had only seen him a few times – perhaps three or four in total. Two or three years ago, he had chased us from the shop after we had tried to slash the tyres on Monday's wheelchair. I can remember Owe's swollen belly, his sallow face and his thinning hair. His gait grew ever stiffer, ever slower, until finally he gave up the ghost.

"Why did he have to die?" I once asked.

"I don't know if he *had* to die," my mother had answered. "I'm not sure if people *have* to die at all. I think more that he *wanted* to die."

"What?!"

My ice cream fell from the cone, and I did not even notice.

"Oh, come now!" She opened her eyes particularly wide with exaggeration. "At the end of the day, we all want to—"

"I don't!" I had proclaimed. How had she come up with such a bizarre idea? "I'm staying!"

It grew colder on the street before our house, and the curtains moved less frequently. I was jealous of my little brother, who had fallen asleep. His lips hung barely open, his mouth relaxed, his brow soft. My sisters no longer whispered, watching with damp eyes as family after family was loaded into the trucks. Those who were not screaming

stared into the distance, their faces void of all expression – no fear, no hate, no hunger anymore. Only blank despair upon their shadowed faces.

And then it was our turn. Up until the moment that Monday gave the order to separate us, I had believed that he did not know our real names either. But when he stopped his wheelchair before our family, he pronounced our every syllable with relish:

"Mariańska, Iwona!"

My eldest sister took one determined step forward. Monday smirked, his eyes still fixed upon Iwona.

"Mariańska, Ludwika!"

My second eldest sister was not so brave. She did not step forward herself until Monday diverted his lustful gaze from Iwona to her. Iwona quickly took Ludwika's hand in hers. I had assumed that Monday would forbid it. And he probably had the same idea. He licked his lips as he regarded their pale hands. But then he said something that I had not reckoned with. I had assumed that he would say: "Let go!" But instead, he said:

"Mariańska, Adelajda!"

My name sounded dreadful between his lips! Like a death sentence. And how I regretted then having ever stolen anything from his shop. Please, dear Lord, I prayed. I'll never do it again, never ever! I swear it! Please, forgive me, dear Lord!

"Step forward!"

I heard the order, I saw the order, I felt the order – and yet I remained, as if frozen, by my mother's side. My eyes burned. My nose ran. Urine filled my shoes. I remained standing until my mother pinched me and pushed me

forward herself. Ludwika grabbed me by the wrist. The palm of her hand was sweaty.

"Mariański, Stanisław!"

Poor little Staś. My mother had to put him on the ground to wake him up. He toddled at first, then he leaned against her, reaching up with his chubby arms. They were as heavy as his eyelids.

"Step forward!"

My mother was commanded to leave Staś on the ground, even as his screams grew louder and more desperate. And although she herself was ordered to step forward only a few seconds later, "the brat" would have to calm himself – or else remain where he lay. And although my mother's delicate figure towered over Monday, he somehow managed all the same to look down at her with his miserable eyes. This tiny bit of power oozed from his every pore. He knew that even with his wasted legs, his life remained more valuable than hers. His head tilted to one side; he stared at her with jutted chin until Staś finally whimpered his way to his feet.

My mother fanned the flames. She died. But not before taking Monday and a few others with her into the abyss. As Monday began rolling away from us with his usual denouncements of "trash!" and "criminals!" my mother counted the Nazis on her fingers against her thigh.

"When I give the signal, you run . . ." she hissed.

"What?" I whispered back.

But my mother had already broken ranks and was running towards Monday. She tore him from his wheelchair with her left hand, wrapping her right arm around his throat. She caried his still flailing body like a shield against

the first volley of bullets. Iwona had grabbed Staś and was already running, Ludwika at her heels. I would be with them now, wherever they are, had I not stopped to look behind for our mother.

"I'M STAYING!" were her last words to us, her children.

My mother's name was Ila.

## 07:45

It was Elle. She bent down so close to me that I could feel her breath against my face. So close that her hair tickled my nose. In the first moments of waking, where everything still blurred together and smelled like a sweet dream – in those first confused moments – I thought that she was Cash. But maybe even that isn't true. Maybe I already knew that it was her, maybe I only wished that it was Cash. I turned my head away.

"I'm sorry," she said. "I didn't mean to wake you."

I don't know why she always says things like that. We both know it isn't true. Her eyes bored deeper on their winding quest into my innermost thoughts. If they arrived at my secret desire for a latte, I knew I'd *never* hear the end of it.

"Hmm?"

"I didn't say anything."

"I know." She giggled. "Chamomile tea. Would you like one? It's organic!"

She held a steaming mug in front of my face. Her mug.

Her tea. I shook my head and felt a weight – like a knot in my chest – as I began to stretch.

"No, thank you," I heard myself saying. My voice was huskier than usual.

"Are you okay?"

I cleared my throat and nodded. "I think Socks is going to be a boxer."

"No, I mean – oh shit, you don't even know, do you?"

I narrowed my eyes. In the short moment it took for Elle to extend her phone to me, all kinds of possibilities for what she could have meant flashed through my mind.

"Did someone die?" I asked.

As she shook her head, a strand of hair fell over her face.

Boris fucking Johnson had won the election.

"Unbelievable, isn't it?"

I didn't even know what I should say. It wasn't unbelievable. It was catastrophic. Brexit. Before my eyes I saw myself boarding a plane back to Ghana with my now useless passport.

"I always knew he was gonna win," Elle exclaimed, "I always said so."

I didn't know any better reaction than to just hand back her phone. Why had I believed it would turn out differently? After all, it was Friday the 13th.

"I need to use the toilet," I said.

"Is it quite urgent? I wanted to tell you something else."

I held my breath. Not before my coffee, I thought. Please.

"What is it?"

"Well, I hope you won't be angry, but . . ."

I noticed how short her fingernails still were. Maybe she should just take up smoking again.

". . . but I wrote to Cash—"

I didn't say a word. My hands were itching. I needed to knit. I should have stood up and made for the door to the balcony.

"Ada?"

"What?"

"I don't wanna go getting mixed up in your relationship, but . . ."

"Hmm!"

". . . but I mean, look, you need the money."

"Not from him."

"I understand. I mean, I wouldn't want anything from him either, but—"

"Papa will send me money for the deposit."

I couldn't see the look on her face because I was facing the balcony. I pressed my lips together tightly and folded my arms.

"Yeah, okay," she said.

Even though nothing was okay. Neither of us knew how things were going to end up for me. I was angry that she'd forced me to lie to her. And it made me even angrier to know that she knew it.

Both of us fled the conversation. She went to the kitchen and switched on her radio. I pretended I was in my own apartment. Within my own four walls. Without any background noise. One of the apartment viewings today would have to work out. Please.

At the balcony door I massaged my belly with the same circular motion as the leaves eddying about in the

courtyard below. The sky was unexpectedly bright. Here and there, thin strands of swollen grey and white drifted about in slow motion. But I was still far too exhausted from the night before to forecast whether it would rain or not today. The darkest of the clouds looked like a woman spinning a pirouette on her pillow: a floating figure with pike-grey hair, candyfloss shoes and a dress of drifting blue. I had to think of my mother. Had she liked to dance? Perhaps the Kpanlogo? The waltz? Or had I inherited my two left feet *from her*? The cloud seemed to be waving to me as it floated by. I smiled and waved back.

I could have remained for some time standing on the balcony; it was brisk but not unpleasant.

"Who are you waving at?"

Through the window I could see that Elle had wrapped my bath towel around herself and was looking for something again. She shoved books to one side, picked up a pullover. It looked as though she would have ignored my answer, had I given her one.

"Have you seen my comb?"

She fumbled around inside my handbag, ignoring the fact that I had been pointing at the arm of the sofa all along. Her sofa. That was one of Cash's talents, as well. It didn't matter if the thing was right under his nose, he wouldn't be able to find it. He really wasn't the sharpest tool in the box.

"Right there," I said.

Elle looked up at me, and then in the direction I was pointing.

"A-ha!"

She waved with the comb. I bit my tongue.

I would have liked to say:

"You're welcome, by the way. And where is *your* bath towel?"

But Elle dragged her flipflops across the floor as if her feet were made of lead. She would not have heard me anyway. The bathroom door clicked shut just as I remembered that I had wanted to ask if I could use it quickly before she showered. A few moments later the sound of rushing water filled the emptiness my unasked question had left behind. I formed an "o" with my lips and exhaled as slowly as I could.

The trees around the inner courtyard remained straight and proud despite the fierceness of the wind. I shielded my eyes from the sun which was rising behind the roofs of the houses across the way and peered out. An aeroplane was piercing "my" cloud's chest.

"Well, that's a good sign," I murmured.

# Among the Luckiest

02:59

Unfortunately, the thing with the broom did not work out. I had hoped – if I could manage to save the bracelet – that I would finally be permitted to become a living being. Sort of like a reward. But already at the end of Ada's life, while she was dissolving into the white – as each particle of skin faded, each follicle to ash, each hair to dust – it became clear to me that I had failed again. I knew it because there were no images. Pictures make the difference between the unborn and the dead. Even when the dead themselves are no longer discernible in photographs, sketches or stories, it comforts them to know that the lives of their beloved still go on. The dead carry images. Those-who-have-not-yet-lived await them. Those-who-have-not-yet-lived look out only on a glistening emptiness where their past should be. As do I.

Full of expectations at first, I pored over dusty, long-forgotten documents; I leafed through books of history, diaries and old letters. I was so thorough that I pushed back even further – back to those times when water eased

the collective sorrows of the earth, singing the promise of better days to come in hushed melodies. I scrolled through broken smartphones; I perused cave paintings and subway graffiti. I read police reports and political news. Painstakingly, I appraised every thread of the Bayeux Tapestry. I scrabbled through golden medallions, along the contours of sooty mantelpieces, underneath discarded mattresses. I conducted my research from the National Gallery to *National Geographic*. I listened to innumerable stories; some were legends, others merely fables. I listened there where there was music – in the songs and through the rhythms – and found I appeared nowhere. Nowhere.

But that can't be, I thought. Guilherme had acquired the bracelet in time, hadn't he? I turned around, revolving. I reached, I stretched. But the walls closed in around me: damp and slippery. Still there was no escape. What tests had I failed?

God rolled past me as a tumbleweed.
(Just like that.)
(As if I was not even there.)
(The nerve.)

I allowed myself to be moved by everything – nɔ fɛɛ nɔ – hoping that the sensation of these occidental colours would soon wane. A breath of expectation cowered behind my hope. But I could not admit it to myself. I had wanted to leave such banal feelings far behind me. I waited.

I'm getting dizzy from so much waiting, I muttered.

Which was not entirely true, for I had never been dizzy before. And for that reason alone, I did not know that it

was impossible for the living to grow dizzy from simply hanging about.

Weary, God said.

I did not react. I had neither the patience nor the naivety needed to play along. And of course I had no compelling association with a word like "weary" anyway.

Perseverance, God suggested.

Again, I did not react. A very, very long time ago, "word associations" had been my favourite game. Until one day I realised how fleetingly scant my chances of winning against the All-Knowing really were. Something which, of course, only made the game that much more attractive for God. In the end, reason won out over temptation.

That's us now, God said, cum'on an' hae a look fer Ada.

The tumbleweed vanished and God assumed the form of a breeze before I could ask whether we had waited long enough. She was already preoccupied with examining our diverse surroundings: around, before, behind, over, under and within. I recognised that to carry on such a discussion with a breeze was doomed to fail.

While we were searching for any trace of Ada, I ruminated on my time in the form of a broom. Why exactly had it been chosen for me? I could find no illuminating answer to my quandary. I had already been any number of things by then – including a delectable crème brûlée, a winning lottery ticket and an enchantingly rosy sky at sunrise. But up until then, I had never before been such an inconsequential cleaning object. I longed for further development – God seemed to be stymieing my plans. Even during my most difficult assignment to date – in 1862 I was the

epicentre of an earthquake in Accra – even then I had been warned to keep myself under control.

And, indeed, I had really needed to pull myself together not to concentrate my efforts solely on the destruction of the European fortifications there! In the end I had to tear down every stone building in the city, just to make it look like a so-called "natural disaster" and not like the "wrath of God". It was a hard thing to do, and yet, somehow, I managed.

I had done my duty, I thought. Now I would be able to be born at last, I thought. And then I found out I was to be sent back as a broom.

That would not have been my first choice. A broom? Underwhelming. And of course I already knew that Mami Ashitey would take me in the hand to swing me at Ada. How often had I already born witness to the scene?

In the coming orbits, other living beings would also touch Ada's skin. Some with such force that she would have to ball her hands into fists, and some with such tenderness, such intimacy, that she would not be able to do more than silently melt. It would be impossible for her to determine which manner of contact was worse.

I knew then that Ada's skin – at first as frail and thin as a candle flame – would grow stronger and more immovable at every moment of contact. I knew that those who would do violence against her would be hard pressed to break her. Because her skin would persist. It would remain incorruptible. And before she could grow callous, she would settle up with those who would have her believe she should be at the mercy of each touch.

But I had not yet witnessed the scene on the coast –

Ada's last moments – from the perspective of the sea. My entry onto the coast was still far in the distant future. God blew away a bit of the eternal white to show me how Ada lay bleeding on the beach. How Damfo and Naa Lamiley bent over her. How Guilherme composed himself to swim back to the *São Cristóvão*, but allowed the baby's body to fall from his hurried hands. How he grasped desperately after it in the waves. How it evaded his fingers and almost joyously drifted away into the cool, dark waters, garnished with the pale beads. God let the corner of the white fall back again.

Oh, I see . . . I said.

There was nothing more to say. Except, perhaps, that I actually found the object I had become in 1459 suited me quite well. I was straight and clean. And useful. And in any case – in any case, I had managed to lessen just *one* of the many humiliations and abasements in Ada's many lives. And so I had great hope that I could be given another chance. To be born was the greatest aspiration of my being.

Slowly, my cards transformed into moths. They whooshed around me, the noble wings were like a crown.

Oh! Will I be a princess this time? I asked.

Then you would need a frog, God answered.

I wanted to grasp the moths, I imagined how they might feel if I had had a body. How they might graze my fingertips, how one would even land upon the palm of my hand. I would have needed to capture it with both hands to learn its secrets. And yet, I could do none of this. It was too fast. And I had no hands. Only a brazen head.

. . . . .

In 2019, I became a brand-new, shiny British passport. Burgundy with gold-coloured letters printed on my front. I found the likenesses of a lion and a unicorn reared up on their hindlegs to the left and right of a crown a bit odd. It must be part of some male fantasy, I thought, and asked no further questions. Instead, I concentrated on the joy in Ada's eyes as she clung to me with both hands, at a tender hour, shortly after the plane had landed on the only open runway of London's Heathrow Airport. It was the day on which the British government would later lose the first vote for Brexit. Tuesday, the fifteenth of January.

As the plane taxied towards the gate, she examined me. "Augusta Adanne Lamptey" was the name printed inside me. She had seldom heard it pronounced at length, and even less often had she spoken every syllable herself. She stroked my final page with one thumb, tracing the curve of her Afro in the passport picture. London, o!

Ada was by no means the only excited passenger. They all had to be warned many times to remain seated. Nevertheless, those rocking babies or hefting Bibles, those craving nicotine or chewing kola nuts, the baffled and the determined – each and every one of them wished to be among the first to stand in the way of all the others. Although the aisle was narrow, a surprising amount of hand luggage, discarded paper cups and abandoned in-flight magazines crowded between the fidgeting feet.

As Ada stepped out onto the aircraft steps, the wind had howled around the plane, robbing her of joy and slapping every side of her face at once. Yes, in Ghana Ada had also believed her face had only two sides. But the European winter would soon teach her about parts of her anatomy

she herself had never known existed before. It was as if she could feel how the cold devoured her velvety skin piece by piece, leaving only a desiccated, ashen husk in its wake. Jesus Christ! That Elle had forgotten to warn her of this explicitly was understandable. She was used to the frozen temperatures and had a white mother. But had Papa once again told only half the truth here?

Everything Ada knew of England she had had to puzzle together for herself like a detective. She had already made her first impressions from the framed black-and-white photographs which hung in their sitting room when she was a little girl. And from photo albums, of course: amazing. Otherwise the sitting room – with its plastic flowers, lace curtains and embroidered Bible verses – was to be entered only by special people on special occasions. Ada had seldom had this honour. Whenever Papa had allowed it, she had taken an album from the shelf and sat with it beside him on the sofa. Some of these tomes were twice as old as she. And so very heavy! She could tolerate the yellowed paper, but those dog-eared pages! No matter how often and how long she had tried in secret over the years to smooth them, she could never fully remove their creases.

England had left traces on Ada's father which were also impossible to smooth away, even after many decades. He was the only person, far and wide, who had ever made it overseas (known to us as "Abrotsiri"). The hope of his family and the pride of his whole community. Back then, they had all waited with bated breath for his every communication. But he had been as careless with his memories as he was with his photographs. His letters from England

(also known as "Abrotsiri") were rare, and always limited in content to the absolute necessities:

Found work.

Found apartment.

Found wife!

Daughter born!

Wife dead.

"Daughter" had been sent to his sisters in Accra directly after the funeral – like a parcel by courier. And much later, after he had endured fifteen long years in London, he brought no gripping tales with him for the welcoming committee at the Kotoka International Airport. Even his "gifts from Abrotsiri!!!" had remained – both quantitatively as well as qualitatively – limited. Five large cartons of cigarettes for the men, and two bottles of perfume for the women. To be shared. Auntie Henry had sprayed herself down amply with perfume while they were still on the runway, simultaneously smoking and laughing appreciatively. She was not one for Papa's funny rules. The others, like Ada herself, who had remained at home in Osu to await Papa's arrival were left empty-handed. "Not even a toffee?" the children had whined. "Scram!" had been his angry retort. And his walking stick had careened dangerously close to their many bottoms.

Papa's return took place in 2003, the year Ada turned seven. She called him "Papa" because she had gleaned from English lessons that fathers were called this in Abrotsiri. She had not known how to act around him on the first day. He had looked so stern and weary that the politest option had seemed to her to leave him in peace. On the second day, he was absorbed into hours-long discussions with

any number of strange businessmen. And there, too, she kept her distance. The next week he was away again. And then he fell ill. It was nothing serious, and yet he remained unapproachable all the same. And then he left to go job-hunting and was rarely home. The proper moment never came.

Why had he never called her back to live with him in London? Why had he sent her away in the first place? Why had he never visited? Why had he not sent her presents on her birthday? Or even letters? Or a card? Ada collected the many "whys" and packed them away in a tiny corner behind her heart. It was not until Elle had appeared out of the blue two years ago in Accra that Ada had even known she had a sister in Berlin. All his life, the man whom she called Papa remained as much a stranger to her as the dead mother she had never known.

And still, she tried to be a good daughter. Once, when she had brought him his lunch, she had gathered the courage to tell him about her desire to see snow. At first Papa had said nothing. Then he had warned her: "It's cold, o! Dis ting dey call winter. Eh! It's no joke, o. You don't know . . ."

On her school transcripts, Ada's English proficiency was justly evaluated as "deficient". Still, she had been impressed, frightened and fascinated by his words. As she skipped back to the pump to fetch the large plastic water bowl, she swore to herself that one day she, too, would walk the streets of London with a great satchel – not perched upon her head but actually strapped to her back. Just like the children in Papa's stories were said to do.

And because – a mere sixteen years later – Ada could still remember the dire warnings about the icy temperatures,

she had purposely brought along a second kente cloth to drape across her naked shoulder and match with her new dress. It seemed to her as though the colourful, hand-woven cloth positively exuded the words: *Abrotsiri, we are coming, o!*

But Ada did not receive a warm welcome from Europe. As she descended each step from the airplane to the run-way, she prayed that God would forgive her for her sins. She contemplated retreating back into the warmth and safety of the cabin, for she figured the machine would surely return to Ghana at some later point. But the people descending the steps around her were – in the words of the women from the marketplace – "plenty, plenty". And they had all dressed themselves appropriately for Abrotsiri – everyone but she.

Elle would later ask why the plane had not managed to dock directly at the gate.

"Normally there's a tunnel – a bridge of sorts – from the aeroplane directly into the airport terminal."

"Really?"

Ada would try to imagine what such a tunnel–bridge might look like, and in the end she was glad not to have had to crawl through such a thing.

"Normally, yes," Elle would retort. "Wasn't there some kind of announcement?"

Ada would shrug at this. She had only noticed the others' impatience in the plane. In the rows directly in front of and behind her, tired groups of parents had convened emergency meetings while disgruntled business people had tapped furiously at their phones. The cabin crew had distributed orange juice, peanuts and empty apologies.

But Ada had not known where this anger had come from.

When the doors had finally opened, it had been too late to ask. And so Ada had clenched her teeth firmly and begun her descent towards passport control. This passport control really is an ingenious invention. Sometimes I wonder how the story would have gone if the toothless ones had set up such an enterprise along the beach in Totope upon the arrival of the *São Cristóvão*. I imagine how one of the kotsa-chewing old women would have waved her shaky, gnarled left hand at Captain Gomes; he would have been forced, for lack of proper papers, to undertake the entire arduous return voyage all the way back to Portugal.

The person sitting behind the counter at Heathrow upon Ada's arrival would not have looked out of place in Totope. Black waves flowed down their head, framing an even-tempered face. With their watery eyes – which focused independently of one another on two different places at all times – they seemed to have an eye on everything at once. Had Ada met them before? In any case, Ada was delighted with their appearance.

"O, hey there!" She greeted them as if they had known each other since primary school. "Wo ho te sɛn?"

One eye on their monitor and the other on Ada, the figure remained silent. When at last they reacted, they spoke English:

"Name?"

Their voice was sonorous, and it unfolded expansively over the loudspeaker like a relentless evening service at a Presbyterian church.

"Augusta. Adanne. Lamptey."

"Where are you arriving from today, ma'am?"

The person leafed through me as though counting cedis at the market.

"Madam, I started in Ghana. Accra."

"I am not a madam," they replied.

"Forgive me," Ada said.

The person continued typing.

"Adanne is not a Ghanaian name, correct?"

"No."

"But your father's name is Lamptey? Is he from Accra?"

"Yes. A Ga. From Osu."

Ada furrowed her brow. Typically this was followed by the question as to how she came by a Nigerian first name. The light from the monitor illuminated the face of the person before her, lending them a bluish hue while they typed at their keyboard.

"Then why did you not address me in Ga?"

Ada did not know the answer to this question. Even at the smallest marketplaces in Accra, she had grown accustomed to addressing everyone in Twi. She only switched languages when haggling if it became apparent that the vendor was a local, too.

"Me ho yɛ . . ." the person said finally.

At first, Ada did not realise that they had spoken Twi. The words were correct, but the stress and melody were all over the place.

"Is that right? That's pretty much all I can say."

"Ye-es," Ada stuttered. "The response was correct. Your pronunciation is . . . excellent."

The person uttered a two-syllable noise of agreement without moving their mouth.

"You have the right passport, you know? You can enter without trying to flatter me."

A pea-sized lump developed in Ada's throat. It began to swell, revolving until it had grown to the size of a small potato. It was already painfully clear to Ada that she had inherited me through the sheer chance of birthright. On the day that Papa had given me to her, he had organised a surprise party. All of her mothers had sung and laughed and cried: "Ada, o! Ada."

The compound had been filled with plastic tables and chairs, with dancing guests and excited children, cases of beer and bottles of Fanta, with crispy legs of chicken and golden jollof rice, with great loudspeakers and screeching microphones. Papa had laughed with the other men at the edge of the compound while Ada's mothers had dashed between the kitchen and the high table to fulfill Ada's every wish. Their daughter was on her way to Abrotsiri, o! She would carry the hopes and dreams of the entire family with her.

Not even Ada's closest school friends had been invited – and this was not an oversight.

"It's time to put your childhood aside," Papa had repeated, time and again. "Think of your future now."

I was this promise. With me, everything should get better. But the question as to whether this would truly be so was suspended over Ada's head like the Sword of Damocles. Because no matter how many of the living claimed it would be so, I was not her identity. In these increasingly absurd times, I could represent only one external piece of this identity.

"Will you be staying in London, or are you travelling onwards?"

"I'm flying to Berlin."

While the person typed, Ada looked about herself. Behind the next counter, the other uniformed workers looked just as Ada had imagined the immigration control of Abrotsiri would: white and grey, white and blond, or sometimes white and bald. All of them exuded frustration, aggravation or impatience. One scornful official four counters along had just brought the entire family assembled in front of the counter to tears. Ada's gaze returned to me. My second-to-last page was being scanned.

"I'm going to college there," Ada added.

"In Germany!" The person nodded. "*Vorsprung durch Technik*, right?"

"Oh, yes, Mada— Excuse me. Yes, that's right! Vorsprung durch Technik!"

She knew the expression from Papa: "Vorsprung durch Technik!" He had always pronounced "Technik" as though it were an English word: "Teknik!" He was very proud of his limited knowledge of the German language. He had often called out "Hervorragend!" as he had walked about. He liked the way his voice sounded when he pronounced it with his Ghanaian accent, particularly with his unrolled "r" and his protracted "a": "Hevohraaaagend!"

"My papa loves everything German!" Ada laughed.

"Hmm."

Ada bit her lower lip, for she realised how euphemistic her pronouncement sounded. But it was true that Papa was obsessed with Germany. He himself had only once visited Munich for a short while, and he regretted to this day that he had not stayed longer. She of course did not know why he had been there, for how long, and why he had had to

leave early. And yet, even after many years, he still pined for the exquisite taste of Weißwurst, those divine glimpses of Mount Wendelstein, the well-ordered separation of the rubbish and, of course, the high-quality engineering. While she had still been in primary school, Ada had been deemed old enough to hazard the forty-minute walk from Osu to Cantonments alone. There she was to attend language courses at the Goethe-Institut until she was eligible to apply to university in Germany.

"I'm going to study computer science," she told the person behind the counter. "We're a fishing family, you know, but there are no more fish. So, everyone is counting on me. After my studies, I'll fly back home, and . . ."

Without a word, I was passed back into Ada's hand.

"Welcome to London!"

Ada had already moved a few paces beyond the counter when she heard: "Oh, wait a moment. Ummm . . . Akwaaba!"

Ada turned. The person was already busy examining the passport of the next passenger. At that distance they, too, now appeared white and grey. Ada would have liked to call out "Medaase!" in reply, but their look had grown hard, their forehead wrinkled, their nostrils were fluttering. Suddenly, they were all but indistinguishable from the rest of the officials. So instead Ada decided upon a whispered: "Thank you, o!"

To whomsoever.

On her way to the next gate, Ada paused before an enormous poster of the London Underground Map. She traced the meandering of the dark-blue line from Heathrow Airport all the way into central London. According to

her birth certificate, Ada's parents had lived in London in 1996. That was not *so* long ago.

Whenever the internet had been fast enough during her German courses, she had strolled virtually up and down Elm Road. And in truth Ada desired nothing more than to sometime trace her mother's footsteps along the tarmac street. But Papa had been unwilling to assist her in her aspiration. One evening, after many questions, he had asserted in a gruff tone that he no longer had any acquaintances in London. Her mother had died there in a house fire, why should he wish to be reminded of it? His eyes had returned to the television, signalling an end to their conversation. And Ada had bitten her lip.

But when she arrived in London she couldn't help crying. It was only a brief moment, in the toilet by her departure gate. The London Underground was not just some squiggly lines on Google. The Tube Map could also be acquired in a pocket-sized format – what was to prevent her from hopping aboard? Why had she not found the courage to book a hotel room and take up the search on her own? When the final call for her flight sounded over the loudspeakers, Ada wiped her cheeks and hurried to the gate.

The connecting flight from Heathrow to Tegel was uneventful. Ada fell asleep during take-off and first opened her eyes again when she was jolted awake by the landing.

In the immigration hall an elderly couple had pointed Ada towards the queue for "Non-EU Citizens" with a few staccato sounds. Ada had thanked them many times for their assistance.

"Das Gegenteil von *gut* ist *gut gemeint* – Good *intentions* aren't the same as good *results*," the customs official had

laughed forty minutes later when Ada explained why she had waited in the wrong queue. The German language still felt awkward and unauthentic in her mouth, but at least she finally understood the meaning of the idiom. It would be applicable for so many of the situations which would await her in Berlin.

· · · · ·

Now I lay pressed together with innumerable other important documents in a clear-plastic folder on a coffee table, ready for the next apartment viewing. I heard how Ada moaned and sighed – it almost sounded like melodious humming, and I did my best to reassure her. Don't worry, I thought again and again, don't worry. There will be something. Don't give up. Don't give up.

"Hey," she murmured. "Hello! Be quiet over there!"

Had I been too loud? I had been too loud. Or I had put too much emphasis on the word "worry" and startled her from her sleep. Maybe not quite, but I did regret interrupting her dream.

### 14:59

And not merely Ada. I, too, had longed for this one precious moment. Considering how long it had already taken, one might presume that a few months here or there would not make much of a difference. But even I had underestimated just how miserable a wait can be. The way it chews

into our thoughts and dances upon our self-confidence. The way it somehow manages – despite its tiny fingers – to tear away at beauty piece by piece until only a mean, befuddled kernel remains.

But the waiting would soon come to an end: Any moment now, Ada would hold it in her hands! I thought about the gold beads of the strange and beautiful bracelet. I could already see how Ada would roll them between her quivering fingers after the bracelet was handed over – intoxicated by their curious hue. Of course, Ada's mind had wandered somewhere else entirely. She was thinking about the keys which would finally grant her access to four walls of her very own. The day on which she'd move out of Elle's apartment could not come soon enough.

And while Ada had nothing but her constant prayers that somehow, sometime, her dreams would finally come true, I had the certainty that *my* vision would soon be realised. For God had promised me that I need only ensure that the bracelet return to its proper place. Of course, this depended on a good deal of cooperation between Ada and Elle, but I was confident – despite the growing tension between them – that what they had in common was still enough to bring me to my goal.

Those among the living who believed the two sisters did not look alike were focusing on the wrong things. Yes, Elle lived chaotically. Most days began – as this one had – with Elle seeking frantically for something she had left in a "safe" place. Her head tipped slightly to one side, her tongue between her teeth, her eyes watching God. She didn't take the concept of personal property too seriously, anyway.

"Life's too short for that," she always said. She never hesitated to make use of other people's things, but she also bought a lot (even if most of her purchases were second-hand). She shared without hesitation. Perhaps she would get her beloved books, CDs, or clothing back in the not-too-distant future. And perhaps not. It did not matter to Elle.

Ada, on the other hand, had brought only the bare necessities with her to Germany at the beginning of the year. And for this reason she kept her every possession organised in neat little piles (assuming they had not already vanished between the heaps of Elle's clothes). Clean, ironed and meticulously folded, or else freshly laundered and hung out to dry on the line. And as for my humble self, immediately after her arrival in Tegel Ada had acquired a clear-plastic folder to stow me in. As one of the very last British passports to bear the inscription EUROPEAN UNION, my appearance was to be preserved like new for a very long time.

Although she was three years younger, Elle was taller than Ada, a good deal more elegant and quite proud of the mid-sized beauty mark beneath her left nostril. Ada had a gap between her front teeth and a scar on her forehead – in Accra it had often been assumed that her skin had purposely been so marked in childhood.

Elle was vegan. She worked part-time in an organic supermarket, wore shoes made of hemp and frequently took to the street to protest against factory farming. And although she already knew better, from time to time Elle still offered to cook jollof rice with smoked tofu for Ada.

"It tastes –" she nodded – "just as good as with meat! Maybe even better!"

177

Awkwardly, this conversation often took place in the kitchen when Ada was in the process of mincing beef. The pounding of the blade against the wooden cutting board then resounded through the apartment like fired bullets. Typically Ada would remain silent until the situation resolved itself. Otherwise she loved to talk. In contrast to Elle.

Their bodies conformed to the ideals of the families in which they had grown up. Elle was slim and satisfied with the privileges her classic beauty afforded her in Germany. Ada was curvy and plump and every bit as satisfied with her body as her sister. Elle had inherited her unusual green eyes from her mother. Ada's eyes were dark and sparkled a luscious brown. Shoulder-length "blow in the wind" curls cascaded effortlessly from Elle's head, while Ada's tiny black braids required hours of painstaking work and the weaving in of at least three packets of extensions.

But those who did not permit themselves to be distracted by such external things soon recognised the two sisters' shared sense of humour. And the deep, warm belly laugh capable of infecting almost anyone around them. It could have been endearing had they both not also had a nasty inclination towards schadenfreude. Any number of unfortunate situations were sparked by one sister's ill-fated attempt (and failure) to ignore the insolent grin of the other.

During more harmless occasions – like, for example, at the supermarket or the post office – they always managed to get off with a cursory apology. But in more sensitive situations – such as police checkpoints or the registry office – this could have truly dire ramifications. Once, Elle had

even resolved to wait outside in the corridor, knowing that even the most well-intended questions about Ada's homeland or the most creative attempts to pronounce her name would have been more than she could bear with a straight face.

Whenever the two laughed together, they became very much their father's daughters. He, too, closed his eyes, held both hands over his stomach and pursed his lips. He, too, began almost inaudibly, and then – after drawing a deep breath – let out a tremendous guffaw:

"Haaaaaaa!"

The three of them were together when they first discovered this. It had been almost two and a half years earlier, on that fateful day when Elle had appeared in Accra and turned Ada's life upside down within a matter of minutes. I had not yet assumed the form of a passport – Ada had not yet even known that she possessed British citizenship. I'd cast about as a breeze over the vaulted roofs and alongside frantic taxis, among the dancing flags and between rustling leaves, among the burning waste piles and behind the doctored radios.

When Elle had appeared, Papa had refused to so much as take a step outside. Even in the sitting room, even with the air conditioner turned up to its highest setting, he claimed he was sweating like a fountain. But Ada had not seen a wet spot on his grey undershirt, and the freshly laundered handkerchief that lay by his side had looked dry as a bone. Although his forehead had seemed a bit shiny, that little bit of sweat did not deserve a mention.

From her bedroom window Ada had watched a petite woman walk the final paces along the chicken-wire fence

to the front gate. Innumerable children marched behind her in a column, laughing and pushing one another along. They had stumbled over rocks, and the red dust swirled up to settle on the freshly painted white walls. Now they milled about at the entrance to Papa's property, singing:

"*Blɔfono, how are you . . . ?*"

Until then, even the oldest among them had never had the opportunity to try out their few words of English on a real, genuine blɔfono. They clapped with joy.

". . . I am fine, tank you!" the smallest sang along enthusiastically. It did not matter to them that they could hardly pronounce the mechanic sounds of the language. All that mattered was that they kept rhythm.

She was new here. Ada had squinted at her, peering through the blinds. The woman was certainly not from Accra, else she would have shushed the children at once. What did she want? People from Abrotsiri seldom strayed into this neighbourhood. There were nightclubs and bars on the main streets of Osu, but even one block off the main thoroughfares, the most spectacular articles of clothing were more likely to hang from washing lines than young bodies. The latest track from Beyoncé did not blast from a DJ's turntable, it echoed as a ringtone through the alleyways. In the backyards of Osu, men like Papa lay about on sofas panting like dogs. And what sightseer would seek out such a thing of their own free will?

Something about the way the young woman moved fascinated Ada. It was a bit like watching a mirror image of herself. When the children began their song again, Papa lost his composure.

"What is this? Ada?!"

Ada slipped into her flipflops and ran.

"I'm coming . . ."

In the meantime Papa had propped his busted leg onto a chair. Ada ran through the living room, past her father and out onto the patio. The young woman had already entered their property, quite possibly to put a bit of distance between herself and the singing children. She clung to her backpack with one hand; in the other she held a note. It was bright outside, but that was not the primary reason why Ada narrowed her eyes. Something wasn't right. Who was this woman? Why was she holding out a note to Ada?

Ada stopped a few paces before her, deliberating whether or not she should take the piece of paper.

"I'm looking for this man," the woman said, fluttering the paper. She did not come across as demanding. More sheepish.

Her skin was dry, almost grey, and her hair had collected much dust between the curls. She had obviously already undertaken a long journey that day.

"Who's looking for him?" Ada demanded.

*"Blɔfono, how are you . . . ?"*

This time the children sang so loudly that even my concentration was broken. I blew a few discarded plastic bags from one corner of the property to the other and could not remember what I had wanted to do with them. And how those little rascals laughed! One over-eager boy had pulled his shirt up over his head to imitate the long, flowing hair of the blɔfono. While he sang, he swung his head about from left to right seductively. A deep and unforgiving voice drove the children's laughter away at once:

"GET OUT OF HERE!"

Papa limped behind his voice. Walking stick in hand, he had been prepared to send a few good curses in their wake, but he stumbled on the patio. The conclusion to his furious appearance was sealed by a few dusty plastic bags about his feet. That was a good place for them, I thought.

"I am his daughter," the young woman answered after Ada had helped Papa back to his feet.

Papa furrowed his brow.

"Whose daughter?" he grumbled, still squinting after the children.

Ada passed the note to him: "Yours."

It was so quiet one could have heard the sound of a mosquito's bite. Even I paused my eddying. No cars passed by in the street, no mobiles rang. Even the rustling of the plastic bags grew still.

The silence was broken by another child who ran past the gate, a stick in one hand. "Gitoutta-HARE!" the girl squealed, before tumbling with great theatrical gestures to the ground.

Ada closed her eyes and turned her head away. Her body was already quivering so severely, she thought she couldn't breathe. But when she opened her eyes she saw both Elle and Papa holding their stomachs with both hands. And then, as if on cue, all three erupted in a mighty:

"Haaaaaaa!"

That was all so long ago . . .

Now there were few occasions for shared laughter. Ada had always known that one day she would become a mother; she had longed for this special feeling of intimacy. But neither she nor Cash had been prepared for such an early pregnancy. They argued the most – at least to all

appearances – over the fact that, while she wanted to get married, he found marriage both unnecessary and outdated. That useless scrap of paper had not kept his parents from making each other's lives hell.

"Let's just move in together," he always said. "Then we can see. Let's not rush things."

"If you don't want to commit, I might as well just stay alone!" Ada would retort.

And even after he had offered to fly to Ghana to meet her family, even after he had offered to buy her an engagement ring, even after he had finally offered to settle with her on a date for their wedding – even then she found holes in his statements and picked apart his words. He could not say anything right. Her anger could not be assuaged.

Just leave me in peace, she thought.

But the apartment hunt was even more difficult even than Elle had imagined.

"Mitte is an expensive neighbourhood," she had said at first. "But people move in and out like there's no tomorrow. We'll find something for you! Twelve weeks is more than enough time."

Ada went to student services, and with just a few signatures she had cancelled her housing contract for the end of September. I could have told her that this was a mistake, but she did not listen to her gut feeling.

It was the dog days of summer. The once-luminous golden lilies in the flower beds along the tree-lined streets wilted in the July sun; the dried-out patches of lawn yearned for rain. Each blade of grass slowly transformed into straw. Tired Rottweilers panted at the limp end of their leashes, their tongues lolling from despondent jaws. Children cried

incessantly, their ice creams melted after just three licks and their parents teetered at the brink of desperation. It would have been unbearable for Ada without copious amounts of water and constant naps during the day. The weeks dissolved into a spiral of nausea, exhaustion and lukewarm vegetable broth – the only thing she could consume without immediately vomiting. August did not bring the longed-for respite. Those who had not escaped Berlin's heatwave slunk about sweating in the shadows of the city, exhibiting no desire to move.

And so, by mid-August, Elle and Ada were still in search of an apartment. In the meantime they had extended their search to include one-bedroom apartments, studios and rooms in shared apartments – even in the less desirable districts of the city.

"Tiergarten's easy to get to with public transport," Elle said, scanning through the latest listings. Ada smiled in exhaustion. By that time her sister had already written hundreds of emails and posted innumerable messages on social media. She'd registered with any number of property managers, and even encouraged her sister to hang fliers on lamp posts and billboards.

And still, despite her every effort, Ada was only ever invited to view an apartment when she used Elle's last name on her application. And then every apartment which had been available for "Frau Hückel" suddenly became unavailable as soon as Ada made an appearance. It was no longer on the market, or someone else had just now signed the lease. Sometimes there were far less fanciful excuses.

"Of course we know," one frightened-looking woman had said, standing in her doorway towards the end of

August. "We know there's discrimination on the job market. Discrimination against women. And then with a child . . . *And* a foreign passport."

A foreign passport? *Foreign passport?* She meant me!

"My sister is British," Elle had retorted. "They're still in the EU."

Back then, there had yet been a small hope that the whole Brexit thing would blow over. It felt like all of Europe was crossing its fingers.

"Well, yes," the jittery woman had said, wringing her hands with great urgency. "But how will she pay the rent after her parental allowance is up if she still hasn't found a job?"

Ada tried to make eye contact with the woman. If she would only look at me, Ada thought. If she would only *see* me – surely she wouldn't just send me away if she got to know me? But the landlady made a concerted effort to direct her attention at everything else – at Elle, at children skipping on the street, even at a dead fly lying on the stairway – at anything but the person standing directly before her eyes. Ada was both grateful and annoyed that Elle managed to maintain a friendly tone throughout their conversation.

"Well, she'll continue with her studies at first," Elle replied. "Even students with children need a place to live."

The woman wrung her hands even harder.

"Well, yes. Of course . . ."

There was much sympathetic nodding. The blond ringlets bobbed gently about the landlady's shoulders. She was the textbook image of innocence.

". . . Certainly. Indeed. Naturally. But *afterwards*?"

185

A familiar medley of fear, shame and regret gathered in her eyes. Ada took Elle by the arm, squeezing only as long as it took for Elle to turn away at last. And so the question in which the woman had disguised her excuse remained unanswered.

To the untrained eye this behaviour might have appeared submissive. And I must admit it even took me a few rounds before I could recognise the power behind Ada's action.

In Ghana, Ada had been many things: a daughter, a student, a beloved friend. She was ambitious, tenacious and reliable. Sometimes she had been moody, sometimes even annoying, but she was always fair. When it came to mathematics, Ada was an intolerable smartarse. And yet her academic success had only been possible because at a young age she had learned the most important lesson of all: Never take up too much space.

Ada wasn't even sure whether she could still yell, for she had not tried to do so for many years. At some point she'd realised that she always held her knees together, but she could not remember when this had begun. What had become of her childhood? It seemed like only yesterday she had been racing against the boys on Labadi Beach. Until they all collapsed laughing in the sand. And hadn't she played football in the street opposite the stadium just the day before that? How quickly the days had passed! After a certain point, style had become more important than swimming, cooking more important than climbing, and fashion a great deal more important than beating others at Ludo. In Ghana, Ada had tiptoed her way to womanhood and scarcely noticed the transition. In

Germany, Ada had suddenly become Black, and she felt it immediately.

To listen in silence to a conversation in which she should by rights be the lead actor was nothing new to her. Ada already knew the bitter taste of swallowed pride. At times she could even laugh about it. But the kind of denigration she had experienced in Ghana had a different quality. It had been lighter, more bearable. In Accra Ada was still a woman, but she had also been valued and loved as a human being. In Berlin she was seldom appreciated outside the immediate confines of her world. Far too often her body betrayed her before she could even open her mouth. And each time the pain she felt in her throat cost her a bit more of her precious strength. Each time, the cut dug a little deeper, and always in the same place. And after a certain point it was too much. Withdrawing herself from humiliating situations was not submission for Ada. It was resistance.

At the beginning of October, she dragged her suitcase to Elle's apartment, and left all of Cash's attempts to contact her unanswered. Shortly thereafter Ada came up with her idea for the "racism credit check". Elle was immediately in agreement, for she too had grown weary of the long-winded, offhand excuses exhaled before some fast-closing apartment door. By the end of November Elle was so good at it that she could manage in a single, pointed phone call to acquire not only all the pertinent information about the apartment, but also to reject those people who might represent an insult to Ada's dignity. She often concluded her calls with the words:

"This is grounds for a lawsuit. Be prepared to hear from my lawyer!"

But now and again there were also good people on the other end of the line. The "good people" were those who expressed no preconceptions about Ada's pregnancy, or who did not ask whether Ada wore a hijab. Of course, it happened all too frequently that these individuals could not refrain from sharing every detail with Elle about some holiday they'd taken in Tanzania. Nevertheless, Ada and Elle remained optimistic about the three forthcoming appointments that afternoon.

Elle had even rescheduled her work shift so that she could be present for the viewings. She held a glowing, hand-rolled cigarette between her lips and, smartphone in left hand, caressed the screen with the tip of her right index finger.

"Yes," she murmured. "I must have made a mistake. I'm sorry. We're half an hour early."

Elle put away her phone, removed the cigarette from her mouth and exhaled. The cloud of smoke drifted over Ada's face. Elle seemed not to notice. Ada pulled her coat – Elle's coat – more tightly around her body and rubbed her hands. Shivering, Elle pointed at the café across the street.

"We can have a tea first."

The last time Ada had walked down this street – perhaps two months ago, when she had still been able to button Elle's coat around her waist – the café had been a shabby bicycle-repair shop. Now, the floor-to-ceiling windows were framed with a sleek, artless shade of green through which she could observe customers typing at their MacBooks while sipping on lattes. They shimmered and glowed through the window like an advertisement for a dating app.

Ada made a noise without opening her lips. I knew that this was less a sound of agreement than something to the effect of: "Yeah? With whose money?"

She could have said much more, but chewed on her tongue instead. It itched.

"Let's just ring the doorbell," Ada said finally. For a few moments she thought Elle had not heard her, and was about to repeat herself. But Elle shook her head.

"No, that's a shitty thing to do."

How typical of Elle. She would rather freeze to death on the street than show up one minute early. But Ada could not complain. She was wearing Elle's only winter coat. Elle would have to survive the whole winter with only an old hoodie and a denim jacket.

"If this –" Ada glanced at her phone and read the name – "Alfons, if he's not home, then we can go to the café as far as I'm concerned. But if he opens the door of his own accord . . ."

Ada wanted to end the sentence with "what can be wrong with that?", but after one look at Elle's face she decided to allow doubt into her voice. She certainly didn't want to appear aggressive.

"Maybe he's waiting for someone else," Elle countered. "Maybe he's taking a shower. How should I know?"

"Would that be so bad?"

Elle's hands were shivering as she rolled her next cigarette.

"You ring," she sighed, stepping aside.

Ada stared at the names by the doorbells. Some were taped over. Some of the buzzers had no name at all. Elle pressed one at the top right. Ada frowned.

"Müller?"

"Alfons is his first name."

And you're only telling me this now, the voice in Ada's head screamed – so loudly that I was surprised Elle couldn't hear it. Ada pulled the coat tighter around her body and took one deep breath in and out. It would hopefully be a matter of days. A couple of weeks at most. But then she would have her own apartment.

The graffiti-smeared wooden door buzzed. Elle pushed it open, letting Ada slip past her to enter the building first. As soon as they had entered the stairwell, Ada realised that the house had no elevator. And by the time they had reached the third floor and still seen no sign of a "Müller", Ada knew that this would not be the apartment for her.

"Let's at least take a look," Elle murmured, winding her arm around her sister's elbow.

"It's not worth it," Ada panted. That slight cramp she'd already felt in her side on the second floor was becoming torturous. "How am I supposed to do this with Socks? With a buggy and shopping? I'm already half dead."

She would not have thought it possible, but the next two floors were even worse. By the time she'd made it up the final steps, the pain in her hips had become unbearable. It felt as though the baby could have just slipped out.

"Good heavens!" Ada puffed, holding her belly. "If there really is a God, please help me now!"

If you only knew, I thought.

"Just ten more steps," Elle whispered. "Just nine . . . eight . . ."

Ada had to take two more breaks before she finally

reached the sixth floor. The view from the window would have been enchanting – to the left she could have seen the impressive red-brick construction of the Church of the Holy Cross, to the right, tiny figures who still dared to brave the elements huddled drinking their coffees under blankets outside Marheineke Market Hall. But Ada could see only stars before her eyes and could barely breathe. She searched her pockets in vain for a water bottle.

A cheery-sounding voice disguised in words Ada couldn't at first understand drifted into the stairwell.

"Should we take off our shoes?" Elle called back.

But there was no answer. Ada followed her sister into the studio apartment. Just as the listing's description had promised, the size was "manageable". Like so many other things in Germany, it was also functional, durable and clean. But it was lacking a certain warmth which the marigolds on the windowsill could not replace – no matter how much their colour reminded Ada of sunbeams. To the right, someone was balancing on a wooden chair, unscrewing a curtain rod. A tattoo ran down his neck and disappeared under his tight-fitting pullover. His shoulder-length blond hair was bound together in a loose bun. And his trousers hung down a bit too low, so that Ada could see his underwear. She looked away.

After so many months of unsuccessful apartment hunting, her eyes were trained to take in the important details within the first thirty seconds: stove and sink in the back left corner, the white door opposite was probably the bathroom. Otherwise, the room was filled with nothing but moving boxes of various sizes. Some were half empty, others were full, but none were packed shut. Elle squeezed

herself expertly between the boxes to reach the kitchen nook in only a few paces. While she examined the stove, the blond man climbed down from the chair. The curtain rod still hung above the window.

"Guess I'll do it later," he said in English, laughing as he extended his hand to Ada.

He had to have been in his late twenties, maybe early thirties. He looked exhausted. He did not seem annoyed, but he didn't look like someone with limitless time on his hands either. As he extended his hand to Ada, she noticed the scar over his left eyebrow.

"Alfons." He grinned.

Ada would have liked to answer, but she was still panting for breath. Her hands were back on her belly, the fingers massaging it in tiny circles. Gradually he let his hand drop, acting as though his leg had suddenly begun to itch. Ada was still struggling to speak. He squinted.

"Água?" he asked.

"A-da," she finally managed. "My name is Ada."

Languages, I thought, internally rolling my non-existent eyes.

"No," Alfons groaned. "Água . . . um . . . Wasser? Water?"

He pointed to her, then spun his finger in a circle and pretended to drink.

Elle appeared at his side and held out a glass.

"I hope that was okay," she said to him, handing Ada the water.

He gestured with his hand as if to say, "No problem at all."

For a few seconds it was completely silent in the apartment. They stared shyly at one another. When Ada had

finished drinking, she nodded slowly, her eyes scanning the room.

"Well," she began.

Elle coughed. Ada decided – despite the severity of the look – to continue speaking. She turned to Alfons with an artificial smile.

"I think, unfortunately, I'm going to have to say that it won't—"

Instantly, Elle pointed to the floor.

"Is this real wood?"

Alfons stared in confusion from Ada to Elle.

"Sorry, what?"

"Wood." Elle repeated her question in English, "Real wood?"

"Oh yes." He nodded. "From oak. I think in German you say Eiche? Yes? Very strong. Stark. Massiv."

Elle shrugged as Ada stared at her, her mouth agape. Alfons grinned.

"Where do you come from?"

He had spoken to Elle, but she acted as though she hadn't heard. She turned away and walked back towards the kitchen. He then turned to Ada, smiling with expectation.

"Ghana." She sighed. Her hope that they could keep the visit short had been shattered and now lay in a million splinters on the wooden floor. Stark. Massiv.

"Ghana!" The blond man beamed. "I thought so! I have been there last year!"

Ada formed an "o" with her mouth and exhaled slowly.

"I was many days in Obuasi," he beamed. "Making a film."

He scanned frantically through his phone while Ada raised her eyebrows.

"Obuasi?"

Alfons grinned. "My grandfather's father was born there."

Ada squinted. There was nothing about his appearance that indicated Ghanaian ancestry. She searched among his freckles for a clue.

"You know Obuasi?" he continued in English.

Ada nipped at her water glass. The quicker she could flee the apartment, the better, she thought.

"And how much did you want for the furniture?" Elle called from the kitchen. She stood at the stove, opening the doors to the nearby cupboards. Perhaps she even closed the cupboard doors a little louder than necessary. Alfons looked a bit gutted. For of course he would've liked to continue his conversation with Ada. Eventually he turned his attention back to Elle. On his way into the kitchen, he pushed several moving boxes to one side.

Ada couldn't follow the discussion between Elle and Alfons, but when she heard the indignation in Elle's voice ("three thousand Euros?"), she knew it would not be much longer now. It was no surprise, she thought, that he had not found someone to rent the apartment to. At the same time she knew that he would not have to forego a single Euro. It just wouldn't be a quick transaction. The soft murmur of their negotiations was interrupted when Elle called out: "Hey, Ada, do you even want these cupboards?"

Ada exhaled slowly. She scratched an itch on her forehead.

"Ada?"

"Ye-es. Just a moment!"

Ada squeezed herself between the numerous half-

packed boxes, doing her best to glide through, but inevitably her belly collided with a particularly over-filled crate. Which, in turn, collided with another. That knocked into yet another . . . the full domino effect. Books, brochures, loose sheets of paper and envelopes cascaded to the floor. The slow-motion image of the falling objects reminded Ada of one of those senseless, artsy Berlin performances.

"I'm so sorry, o!"

She bent her knees ever so slightly, but a sharp pain shot through the base of her pelvis. There was nothing close by for her to hold on to – the other boxes were far too unstable.

"It's okay," Alfons laughed.

He was already beside her, gathering up the strewn documents from the floor. Elle kneeled next to him, piling books into another upright box. Ada rubbed her belly with one hand.

"I'm really very sorry . . ."

"Forget it." Alfons smiled.

He waved a giant roll of packing tape in one hand.

"This time, I will tape them shut!"

Ada could only watch while he taped up the re-packed boxes. If she had tried to lift something herself, Alfons and Elle would have ended up having to rescue both her and the documents she had already scattered. Good intentions, Ada recollected, aren't the same as good results.

"What's this?"

Elle held a glossy catalogue in her hands, leafing through its pages. Alfons turned to her.

"Hmm?"

"What is this?" Elle repeated.

"No idea," he said, stowing the packing tape away. "I *accidentally* took it from some Canadian." He made air quotes as he emphasised the word "accidentally".

"What?" Ada asked.

"He said he nicked it off someone from Canada . . ."

"No." Ada held her hand out for the catalogue. "What is it?"

Elle stood up, holding out the pamphlet to Ada. It was a catalogue for a special exhibition.

"Pre-colonial West Africa," Ada murmured, reading the title aloud. The catalogue had been artfully made. Innumerable colour photographs of artefacts shone beside detailed descriptions.

"And? You like it?"

Ada nodded, switching the glass from her right hand to her left in what appeared to be a highly complex manoeuvre before taking the exhibition catalogue from her sister.

"It's so funny, this left-hand thing," Alfons grinned, waiting expectantly for a follow-up question about what he meant by that. It didn't come. Ada tried to concentrate on her reading, but she still had the misfortune of hearing all too well as Alfons explained with great animation just why he found it funny that Ada had avoided using her left hand. How could he manage to miss how narrow Elle's eyes grew as he mused on "traditional customs".

"You know, they have toilet paper in Ghana too these days, if that's your question!" Elle hissed eventually.

"Please . . . ?" he stammered. "I don't—"

"You're saying Ghanaians use their left hand to clean themselves? I'm saying they have toilet paper there, too!"

Alfons's face exploded in crimson.

"Oh. Sure. Of course! I . . ."

Elle turned away from him abruptly, fixing her eyes on Ada.

"Wɔ te," she said. Ada nodded. Finally.

· ● · ● · ● ·

To get back to Elle's apartment by the quickest route, they could have taken the U7 from Gneisenaustraße to Hermannplatz, and then changed to the U8 towards Wittenau. The quickest route, but hardly the most scenic. The entire journey took place in subterranean tunnels, and the subway was often packed to bursting. Uncomfortable in winter, unbearable in summer. But at least the escalators at Hermannplatz were usually in working order. This time, neither Elle nor Ada was in a hurry. The next apartment viewing – which would have been right around the corner from Elle – had been cancelled at the last minute.

"Ah, too bad!" Ada exclaimed. "Why?"

"No idea," Elle grumbled. "Am I a mind reader?"

And so, judging by the way Elle glared at everyone in her path on the stairs at the U-Bahn station, Ada decided it would be better to just follow her in silence. In answer to her question as to why they were waiting at the wrong platform, Elle had hissed "Hermannplatz reeks of piss!" And she had not been wrong. Ada raised an eyebrow. At least piss is organic, she'd thought, as she sat down beside her sister.

The ride to Mehringdamm was short and uneventful. It was as if all the other passengers knew to avoid any kind of

contact with Elle. Even the Elvis impersonator who spoke to everyone else on the train passed Elle by without a word as he went about the car collecting tips. Elle glared at her phone as Ada tossed a fifty-cent piece into his hat.

Ada didn't dare speak to Elle again until they were seated in the U6 and had already arrived at the station at Kochstraße.

"Of all the Ga expressions I've taught you," she said. "Is *wɔ te* really the only thing you remember?"

Elle glanced up from her phone.

"Why? It does mean 'We're going'. Right?"

Elle's tone had become conciliatory. Her face looked more relaxed; her eyes were soft again. And so Ada dared to smile again as well.

"Of course," she said, nodding. "That's totally right. But all the same. Since when do you speak Ga with me?"

Elle's answer was barely audible between the snippets of conversation from the teenagers around them and the muffled announcements over the station loudspeaker. And although Ada had to bend closer and strain with every bit of her body to capture Elle's words, she was still relieved that Elle was talking to her again.

"I know more than you think." Elle grinned. "I only speak German for you."

"For Papa, actually."

Elle shrugged, and Ada stared out of the window. Although she could see nothing in the darkness besides the occasional strip of tunnel lights, she preferred this to looking at the people standing directly in front of her. The woman with the bags, for example. She just looked so tired. She leaned with a sagging back against the yellow

handrail and peered about herself in the train. Her bulging backpack tugged at her shoulders; her overstuffed shopping bags tugged at her arms. Ada would have liked to offer up her seat. But whenever Ada had this impulse, she had to remind herself of the time she'd been sitting on the bus with Cash. It had been the exact same situation.

Ada had stood up and pointed to her seat. The woman had smiled at first, and had already begun redistributing the weight of her bags from shoulder to hand, nodding at Ada. Then she had registered who she would have had to sit beside. How she'd grimaced then! It was as if Ada could not have paid her a greater insult. Ada had stood gaping at the empty seat while it slowly dawned on her. Cash was not the least bit surprised. On the contrary. His stony expression had remained unchanged throughout the entire interaction. Ada bit her lower lip, trying to think of something else.

"How cool would it be," she said to Elle as the U-Bahn began to brake, "if we had Ga as our secret language?"

Elle arched her eyebrows.

"Don't you know anything about Germany, Ada? They've tried to kill off all the multilingual people here once before."

The woman standing opposite Ada stared wide-eyed at Elle. Her skin flushed, becoming mottled. Elle seemed not to notice.

"I don't know why I'm even speaking in the past tense," she muttered. "To be honest they're still doing it today . . ."

"Except for the English speakers," Ada said.

Elle stared back at her phone. "If push comes to shove, they won't be safe here either."

When the train stopped at Stadtmitte, a troop of kinder-garteners boarded their car. Two children collided on the same seat giggling, only to decide a few moments later that it was big enough for both of them. Three others tried, with outstretched arms, to maintain their balance as the train jerked away from the station. Their squealing hurt Ada's ears. She removed the catalogue from her bag.

"Ahh," Elle marvelled. "You took that with you?"

Ada shrugged.

"That guy didn't want it anymore," she said. "And I wanted to show you something."

She ruffled through the pamphlet until she found the page. "Here. Did you see this?"

She leaned towards Elle, holding out the catalogue. At that moment a child began to wail in one formidably long, single note of grief. Elle looked over the pages in confusion, staring at both of them at once.

"No, here," Ada pointed. "Supposedly people from Portugal had already set foot on the Gold Coast much earlier than the Ga!"

"Wait, what?!"

Elle took the catalogue from Ada's hands and continued reading.

"The Ga come originally from Nigeria?"

"From the place we call Nigeria today . . ." Ada nodded.

Elle stared back at her, puzzled.

"Did you know that?"

"No!"

Elle's lips moved slightly as she continued reading. Ada watched her so intently that she hardly noticed the U-Bahn had already arrived at Französische Straße. The

mass of excited children were herded from the train by their already exhausted-looking teachers. It was only after the doors had closed that Ada noticed that the woman who had stared at Elle in such horror had departed as well.

"How awful," Elle whispered, pointing to a passage of text.

"The boy they abducted?" Ada nodded again. "He couldn't have been more than eight years old."

Elle stroked with one finger over a baroque painting of a frightened child at the royal court.

"Poor Afonso," she murmured.

"Afonso? Like Alfons just now?"

"Yeah, but without the 'l'. They named him after the king."

"They probably," Ada began, "probably thought it was particularly funny to give a kid like that that kind of name."

Elle nodded sadly.

"They toy with us," she said slowly and so quietly that Ada could barely hear. Ada stared back at her sister, studying her face. The furrowed brow, the lowered eyelids, the stiff lips. It all seemed so familiar to Ada.

"Elle, what's wrong?"

Elle glanced quickly at Ada, fleetingly, then immediately looked away. She pressed her lips together and only began speaking again after the announcement in the U-Bahn was over.

"Why did you answer him?"

Her voice was quiet, she kept it even with an effort, but it was seething under the surface. Ada knew she had to take care how she proceeded.

"When?"

"When he asked you where you come from?"

It grew tight again around Ada's waist. The discussion was threatening to escalate, and Ada didn't have the energy for it. She searched her mind for the sentence that would keep things short.

"Oh that," she lied. "I didn't really think about it."

The train rattled along towards Friedrichstraße. Ada stared out of the window again, trying to organise her thoughts.

"You have no idea how shitty that question is for me, do you?"

Ada rolled her eyes internally and silently counted to ten. Whenever Elle got like this, Ada found it best not to answer.

"I live here. I was never anywhere else. I was always the only Black person in my family. Everyone always told me 'We are the same!' but I could see with my own eyes it wasn't true. Do you know what a shitty feeling that is? To know that everyone is always lying to you?"

Ada stared at the floor. Elle was talking too loudly. And for much too long.

"To be the only person in class or at work or just when I go out with friends – to be the only person who gets asked where I come from. Just like that. At a party. On the street. In the shops. My whole life's like one long fucking ID check . . ."

The part about the ID check was new. ID check. Really? Ada rolled her eyes again, internally.

"You don't have to stare like that," Elle hissed. "I know there are worse things. But it still feels like shit. And at least you had Papa."

The passengers opposite them stared conspicuously in the other direction. Ada rubbed her belly, remaining silent for a few moments.

"I'm very sorry," she said finally. "It's just that sometimes I get the feeling that they're genuinely interested."

"Interested?!"

Those who didn't know Elle better might have thought she was about to laugh. But Ada knew there was no joy in her voice.

"Then why is it never about what we *do*? Or what we're studying or what kind of job we have? What our favourite TV show is? Our favourite colour? Do you know how I know it's not about me at all?"

Ada shook her head, even though she knew it was a rhetorical question.

"Because the answer doesn't matter. As long as I say somewhere between South America and South Africa, then it's not about me anymore. It's about football. Or food. Or holidays."

Ada reached for Elle's hand, but Elle pulled it away, staring into space.

"Elle . . ."

They sat together in silence all the way to Oranienburger Tor. Elle was chewing at her thumbnail. When the doors clanged shut again, Ada began to speak.

"I'm sorry, Elle. Really. I get asked so often where I come from that I –" she made a passing hand gesture – "I don't even think about it anymore."

"It might be a harmless question for you," Elle answered. "You *did* grow up somewhere else."

"Yeah," Ada said, nodding. "But you know what? It

was different this time. Alfons said his great-grandfather came from Obuasi."

Elle's eyebrows clashed together like lightning in the middle of her forehead.

"It's not about Alfons for me!" she groaned. "It's about the pigeonholing. Just one time, just once I'd like to enter a room and just be myself: Elle. You know?"

Ada nodded.

"In Ghana the kids yelled 'blɔfono!' at me. Do you remember? And in Germany they treat me like a foreigner. I mean, what is that?"

Ada nodded again. She wanted to make a joke about Germans being potatoes, but the timing wasn't right. Elle continued silently flipping through the pages of the catalogue. The picture of an extraordinary bracelet hovered momentarily before Ada's eyes.

"What kind of beads are those?"

But Elle was lost in thought and had already turned several more pages before she realised that Ada was talking to her.

"What?"

"Just a moment," Ada said, thumbing back.

"Here."

Ada pointed with her index finger at the jewellery.

"Thirty-three beads. Is that a symbolic number?"

"In some religions, maybe." Elle shrugged. "What kind of bracelet is it?"

"The description says: Fertility beads. Fifteenth century, West Africa. From a private collection." Ada looked up from the page. "How does a bracelet like that end up in a German exhibition?"

Elle shook her head slowly. Almost as if, in doing so, she was not just answering Ada's question, but passing judgment over the entire exhibition.

Ada read on, searching in vain for some sort of additional footnote or reference. She frowned.

"What were the museum people thinking?" Ada asked. "And who even gets to see it anyway?"

The train lurched to a halt. Elle returned the catalogue to her sister and stood up.

"Probably only the luckiest," she said.

# Among the Deceived

*06:48*

Early that morning Ada had known nothing about a strange exhibition catalogue, not to mention the bracelet displayed so prominently on page 37. Things were off to a quiet start – dark and moody. Still half asleep, there was something she found disconcerting about that, although she could not say why.

Be that as it may, *I* had a good feeling. As a British passport, I now had certain opportunities I had only dreamed of before. Had Ada had the kind of freedom of travel in the nineteenth century which she now possessed through me, she would most certainly have immediately left her husband. Of that I am quite sure. What am I saying? She would never have married him in the first place . . .

My thoughts were interrupted by a sound: Ahem! God drifted down in the form of an old man – long flowing robes; an imposing, shoulder-length mane of hair; glowing eyes; slightly wrinkled skin; a sumptuous beard. Everything white. A piercing white. Yet whiter still. Blinding.

What a cliché, I exclaimed. How boring.

Opera, God said, pacing back and forth and tugging at his chin and beard as though trying to remember something.

What, I said.

If I'd had eyebrows, I would have scowled.

Yeeeooooo, God cried, clapping His hands which quickly disintegrated. Shattered like broken glass. The tinkling of his finger shards on the wooden floor: soft as summer rain.

Bah, I said, please no word associations. No associations at all! If at all possible, I'd like to discuss the *bracelet*.

Hmm, droned God. What about it?

I tried to be patient. Don't get angry! So far, so good. God sprawled across the room, stretching out His right arm as if He were about to touch something with His index finger. His white gown was a bit too tight around the chest and short enough that I could see His knees.

Everything, I countered.

I wanted to know where the bracelet was. I wanted to know who was supposed to get it this time. (I wanted to know if God could maybe wear a different dress.) I wanted to know if I would get another chance if the handover didn't work out this time either. Because despite my optimism, I still had a touch of doubt. I felt like certain walls were closing in around me – pressing in particularly on that place where I formed my thoughts. I could turn only with a great effort. I started to get downright queasy, wondering whether I would only have animal cards to choose from when the next orbit came around. I wasn't into that at all. Who on earth would choose to be a beast of their own free will? Or an insect? To be a fly? To get

squashed by Mami Ashitey already in the second chapter? No way.

Thanks.

But the day is still young, God said. There's no reason to worry about that yet.

But then, I countered, but then there'll be a sudden storm and Ada will dissolve in white, and in the end – wonder of wonders – I'll have failed again. I know how that goes. In 1848 the bracelet never so much as touched William's hands!

God shrugged. Psh.

Psh?

Psh! Then what good would another hundred chances be? How are you going to do it better when you don't even know why it didn't work before?

Tiny wheels activated somewhere in the realm of my imagination. They whirred and hummed. Was God trying to pull a fast one on me? His face was hard to read. A mixture of boredom and surprise.

Isn't it obvious, I said finally, isn't it obvious why it didn't work?

God shrugged again. Not for me.

My irritation subsided only when I saw a faint smile flicker across His face.

Look, I said. I failed miserably in London. A total flop. It had been so blatant, in fact, that in the end I had been the only one to mourn the loss of the lion's head.

And that was not an exaggeration. Shortly after his wife's funeral, William sold the house on Elm Road at auction. Murder – even inadvertent murder – was expensive. And due to the financial losses accrued through the costs

of his legal defence, the house needed to be sold quickly. The otherwise estimable Lord King was forced to accept a rather humble offer.

The wife of the new owner, an elderly dame with grey hair, grey eyes, grey teeth and an inexplicable predilection for East London, thought "the gruesome door knocker" a bad omen and demanded my immediate removal from the entryway. Of course, the honorable Mrs Widdecombe had completely misread the cause of Ada's untimely death – and certainly overestimated my role in the proceedings. At first, I was tickled by her belief that I had had so much influence in the matter. Then I recalled that the living are always in search of others upon whom to cast the blame – preferably those who lack the ability to defend themselves.

Even if William had made the effort to offer me to her, Lizzie would not have been interested. Unemployed and without any financial reserves to speak of, Lizzie had other more immediate concerns. What should I do with a door-knocker, she would have said, when I haven't even got a door?

Only a few weeks after the keys had been handed over, William found himself seated in a rickety coach, lurching along Elm Road. As they rattled past the house he glanced out upon the red bricks, the casement windows and the ivy-encrusted walls of the façade. I was no longer occupying my place of honour at the entrance – and this was a good thing.

God's arm began to droop. It seemed as though he was no longer reacting to me, as though He had completely lost interest in our conversation. But my impression was deceptive. For He was whirring and humming, too.

And why was this good, He asked after a moment.

Stay cool! Don't let Him upset you! I allowed the question to hover in the air between us, perhaps even a moment too long. It began to fade after a while. I spoke only when my answer had sufficiently matured.

I hadn't kept my promise at all. I had neither demonstrated strength nor had I held power. Ada literally bled to death before my eyes; where was my promise of protection? I had not lived up to my end of the deal!

And the feeling that was taking hold of me was likely what the living call "doubt".

God shook His head. Strand by strand, His hair assumed a darker tone. Almost like ebony. At first only on some of the tips.

You don't know, God said, whether William was even supposed to receive the bracelet.

The walls were closing in around me again. The line between comfort and pressure is razor thin. Over long decades, the thought had never so much as occurred to me that the bracelet was not meant to go to William. That had always – ever and again – been my goal. So why all of a sudden this? I . . .

Then again.

Hadn't William given his wife the bracelet in the first place? Why then *precisely* should it go back to him? That made no sense either.

Think about it for a moment, God continued. Silver orbs blossomed on the ends of His arms, black curls of hair bounced lightly about His face. His wrinkled skin had vanished.

If Lizzie had not retained the bracelet, she would not have been able to sell it to Charlie Huckle.

Charlie Huckle? I repeated. The fishmonger?

God nodded.

Otherwise, she would have ended up on the street, destitute and alone, He continued. But in this way she could rescue both herself and her brother. See for yourself. Charlie Huckle gave her his entire day's earnings for it: cash in hand. Not even half the bracelet's value, but still a good deal more dough than Lizzie had ever had before.

Alfie got new clothes, I murmured.

That's right, God beamed. And it was like Christmas and Easter rolled into one for Charlie Huckle. The very next morning, he traded the bracelet again for a substantial quantity of fish and a choice selection of lobster tails: *Win win win!*

In the meantime, God's eyelashes had grown to an enviable length. The silver orbs at the ends of His arms had grown thinner, transforming before my eyes into two palms – each with five elegant fingers.

I said: Oh, I see. Because it sounded somewhat like the right thing to say. But in reality these three simple words by no means sufficed to express the breadth and depth of my feelings. I was trembling on the inside. Then what the hell had I been doing all this time?

God marvelled at His own shimmering hands, bending one joint after the other, brushed one tiny curl of hair away from His eyes and then pointed with His right index finger at me.

What were you?

I was a doorknocker.

Yes, that's right!

Huh, I said. And that's supposed to be some big

211

accomplishment? What did I achieve as a doorknocker? Other than now and then letting Lizzie know a visitor had arrived?

God pointed with both index fingers at me: And?

I was getting angry at His questions, had I not already said that I had accomplished nothing of value during my paltry time as a doorknocker?

And, I groaned, *one time* in his entire life, William knocked upon the door himself. And Lizzie was not there. Okay. And so one time I also let *Ada* know a visitor had arrived.

And then?

And then nothing! What else could there be? Ada let William in. Although it would have been better for her if she had not.

You see!

See what?

I was feeling so claustrophobic now that I could hardly think. God continued his monologue and His silver hands fluttered up and down, emphasising certain syllables as He spoke, underscoring the illuminating words. Encompassing entire thoughts.

Ada didn't have one single possession of her own, God explained. Everything belonged to William. Even she belonged to William. Of course, he had open access to her!

But I let it happen, I screamed.

You let her *know*. William could just as easily have broken into the house by force. The fact that Ada opened the door herself was by no means an indication that he was welcome there. She could not have kept him out anyway. And he knew this, too. You simply ended the charade.

Hmm, I sighed. And what did that accomplish?

God dropped His hands. They vanished into His billowing, white robes.

That's a really good question, God said. Let me know when you've come up with a good answer.

· · · · ·

I enjoyed being a passport. A part of Ada. Some people even said I was the noblest part of her. Ada had got so used to sharing her body with the baby that this morning the idea of having it all to herself again had seemed like a bad joke. Where did such an idea even come from anyway? She could hardly remember a time when she had existed without heartburn.

Ada was convinced that she would never bend over again, never again be able to lie on her stomach or run to catch a bus. Reluctantly, I had to think of God. The joker must have planted these ideas in her head. Because despite everything – her packed hospital bags which had sat ready in the entryway of the apartment since the beginning of November; the dresser in Elle's living room stuffed with gifts like baby pyjamas, second-hand swaddling wraps, at least three tiny jackets and a home-made knitted cap (she had also nearly finished knitting a matching wool blanket); not to mention Elle's amassed collection of organic cloth nappies – despite everything, Ada still could not reconcile the feeling of the movement in her belly with the notion that she would soon hold an infant in her arms. One was self-evidently her body: the pain in her back, her full bladder. The other was something different entirely: the

shadowy outline of an autonomous human being – with its own back and its own bladder – whom she was yet to meet and get to know.

At the beginning, I found it strange to receive so much acknowledgment from Ada. I was a good passport, to be sure. But not better than a human being? Socks was just as much a part of her as I! But after a while I began to sense her own growing fears during the quietest hours of the day. For example, her misgivings that after the baby's birth she would never be as close to Socks again. Or her worry that she would not feel motherly love. Or the creeping fear that the child would not survive its birth at all. Ada preferred to repress such thoughts entirely, to concentrate on the here and now. But the most treacherous thing about sleep – at least, so I have been told – is that it permits such thoughts to run free and uninhibited.

And as Ada – returning from the bathroom and still hovering between dreams – endeavoured to lie down in the most comfortable position she could find, the framed portrait of her mother flickered before her eyes. It hung alongside Jesus in her father's sitting room. The portrait. Black and white puzzle pieces of the image drifted back and forth behind her eyelids: the snug head-covering she wore, her perfectly formed eyebrows, her graceful eyelashes, the high cheekbones, the painted lips. For years now, Ada's mother had gazed only to one side. Her stare was earnest, decidedly not merry, but also neither angry nor sad. Perhaps thoughtful? Would she have been happy to know that she would soon become a grandmother? Had Cash told his parents that an heir was on its way?

Ada placed one hand on each side of her belly and

marvelled at its supple curves. The little bumps rippled once more. Socks was probably trying to stretch his arms. For a short moment, the eerie quiet of the living room was broken by Ada's giggle. To have a "working title" for a baby was an absurd idea. And then to call it Socks?

"Yeah, well," Cash had argued. "With that baby on your arm, you're gonna feel as safe and cosy as a foot in one of your handknit socks. Right?"

Ada's smile vanished as she was overcome by something akin to a pre-emptive feeling of loneliness. Cash could stay lost. Tough shit for him. But she would miss Socks. Had her mother felt that way, as well?

When at all, Papa had spoken sparingly about his time in London, and he had never so much as uttered a word about his wife. Ada had got used to never mentioning her name in his presence. She couldn't bear to see the way the tiny muscles in the corner of his mouth twitched, as though the taste of sorrow would only be manageable so long as his lips remained tightly pressed together. In those moments she was certain that her papa had forgotten how love worked. He hadn't practised it in so long.

What Ada would never hear from him, however, was just how far from the truth she really was. In reality he had moved heaven and earth to ensure that his Augusta would not grow up the daughter of an African janitor in a cold, foreign country. But rather that she grew up surrounded by the warmth of his homeland. Why have no mother at all when she could, instead, have many? He had observed very closely how the children of his contemporaries had grown up in London. Hopeless and destitute. Without belief in themselves. Without respect for their elders. His daughter

would not, under any circumstances, live that way. She should be valued; she should be loved. His Augusta.

In England he had undertaken occupations so atrocious and so demeaning that he would never so much as dream of doing them in Ghana. He had scrubbed and polished hundreds of toilets and thousands of floors. He had accepted every insult and every deprecation without a word. Everything for her. And in memory of her mother who had died before her time.

The bits and pieces Ada had learned of her had been stitched together from scraps and shreds of other people's words, and even much of this was still mere fantasy. All of which I found completely appropriate. After all: What is the past, but a project of the imagination?

"She was so slender, o!" they had repeated over and over again. "Thin as a needle. *Shwɛ!*"

That was the day before Ada's departure. Just before the storm. Ada had mentioned that she would need to change planes in London. Papa's sisters had begun quite spontaneously to discuss his time in London among themselves, and eventually had come to speak of Ada's deceased mother. That is, to speak of the only existing photograph of Ada's mother.

"As though she'd had no money for food!"

"Eh-eh!"

"If your father had only brought her home just once, we could have plumped her up!"

They laughed and howled, and certainly their words were well intended, but Ada's stomach had twisted in a knot. Where had they suddenly found their tongues? Surrounded by plucked feathers and half-dissected chickens,

Auntie Clara had twirled a knife in one hand while she held the feet of a struggling hen in the other. Auntie Lucy and Auntie Henry were actually supposed to be cooking, but they had dropped their yams, shaking with laughter. Ada squinted, turning her gaze to the evening sky. A smouldering crimson melted its way across the horizon, soon to be replaced by the sinking interplay of violet and indigo.

As long as she could remember, the topic had been off-limits throughout her childhood. But why? Had someone enquired, all of her mothers would have replied that they had wanted only to protect Ada. But protect her from what exactly? Had someone enquired again, all of her mothers would have replied: something. And, with their eyebrows arched high, they would have appeared so determined that it was clear there was nothing more to say.

But this "something" hung like a discarded scent over the hearth, the market stands, the meals. Every place where they sat together and otherwise shared everything with Ada. This "something" hurt. This "something" prevented Ada from overcoming the fantasy that one day a stranger would stop her on the street and say: "I knew your mother, o!"

Ada would overwhelm this stranger with a thousand questions: Where had she lived? Where had she worked? Did she have other children? How had she and Papa met? What had been her favourite food? What kind of music had she listened to? Was there a second photograph of her? And was she smiling in this second photograph?

But where should Ada have encountered this wonderous stranger? Someone who had known her mother so well that they would recognise Ada only by the curve of her

nose or the shape of her mouth?

A few minutes after she had finally arranged herself comfortably on Elle's sofa, Ada fell asleep. Her breathing slowed. It grew deeper, transitioning into a soft snore. She spoke out, shortly before she sank into a deeper slumber.

"My mother," she whispered. "My mother's name was Ijemma."

## 18:48

The rent was unbeatable, and that was the deciding factor for her. For me, as always, it was about the bracelet. The room – or at least its viewing – was a step in the right direction. I could feel that I was close to my goal.

You're not close. You're obsessed.

God again. I decided not to dignify this comment with a response.

Ada remained reasonable. It's not ideal, she said to herself, but it's a start. Still, you and Socks won't have to sleep on Elle's lumpy sofa anymore. And who knows whether you'll find something suitable in time. Twenty square metres is a good amount of space. And at this price, you won't have to worry about the money – maybe you can even save a bit each month. That's the kind of thing she told herself. And all of it was right. Yet still, Ada's heart grumbled at this solution: But . . . Charlottenburg?

So far away. So conservative. So many Krauts. Even the multiple variations of the names at the doorbell – "Mayer", "Mayr", "Meyer", "Maier" *and* "Meier" – appeared more

diverse than the people who actually lived there. As they entered the building together, Elle interpreted Ada's silence correctly.

"I know," she said, nodding. "I know. But at least you will only have *women* for flatmates, right?"

Ada narrowed her eyes. If I'd been her, I would have done the same. How often in the last months had Elle deleted a text message in disgust, proclaiming how she could never – absolutely *never* – live in a shared apartment? That she would rather work three jobs than deal with shared expenses and a mind-numbing cleaning plan. That Ada should stay with her until she had found the perfect apartment. Why this sudden change?

It had to be the due date. It was swiftly approaching, but the home they had envisioned for Ada and her child had not materialised. And all of a sudden there were no more disparaging comments from Elle, no matter how expensive, how tiny or how far away the apartment was. It seemed to Ada as though Elle wanted to be rid of her as quickly as possible. A look here, a hand gesture there, nothing conclusive. But it hung in the air, on the tongue, in the throat, in the gut. Ada had become far too used to holding her silence. She simply should have asked Elle.

And so, they stood awkwardly side by side in a strange hallway. Squeaky clean, and yet somehow uninviting. Ada took a deep breath, readying herself to say something just as Elle pressed the button on the lift.

"If it goes really well," she grinned, "they'll even help you out from time to time with Socks!"

And then she rubbed Ada's belly. Just like that. It was no doubt well intended, but good intentions aren't the

same as . . . well, you know. Ada clenched her teeth. All her thoughts, her insecurities, her fears began to dissipate. There remained only one question for her: Was the lift broken? Because nothing was happening. Elle's hand was still touching Ada's belly. But nothing else was happening. Where was the fucking lift?

Ada pressed the button as well, staring stubbornly at the number panel above the door.

"I already pressed it," Elle said.

Ada did not react; which is why what sounded like a "Hmm" appeared to come from her ears. Elle removed her hand from Ada's belly, pulled the collar of her hoodie up over her nose and exhaled deeply. Finally, the number above the lift door shifted from ten to nine. The lift's downward journey matched the sinking feeling Ada had been carrying inside her for at least an hour. Since her phone call with Papa.

Ada scratched her wrist and went over everything in her head again. She inhaled deeply, formed an "o" with her lips, and exhaled even more slowly. She wasn't doing well. She hadn't been for a long time. To be honest, not since that fateful moment when the second bar had appeared on her pregnancy test.

Nine, eight.

Ever since the discovery that she would be a mother, Ada had been formulating a detailed message to the future grandpa. At least once a week. It had been unusually slow work: typing out each overthought expression and carefully avoiding the use of emojis whenever possible. The messages were always perfect. Not too long, not too short. Upbeat without showing any disrespect. Optimistic

without appearing naïve. And even after five revisions, they still remained very, very good. At a certain point her finger needed only to move to the little green symbol. Just press one more time, and then the message would be sent.

Seven.

Sometimes immediately, sometimes after a short pause, Ada had always decided against it. No matter how long the process of drafting, the act of deletion still always felt right. A relief.

Six.

Back in July, Ada had even briefly considered writing an old-fashioned letter. Truly detailed, multi-page, with all the bells and whistles. Not some two-line wonder like Papa had written her before.

It was more than twenty minutes' walk to the nearest post office. Ada had braved the heat, the stench, the noise, the rubbish. She had suffered through nausea which always threatened to rise up in the back of her throat. She had believed that only there – on Torstraße, only a few steps from Rosenthaler Platz – only there could one find the special envelopes for airmail.

Five, four.

But when she had returned home with an entire packet of pearly white envelopes – and without the special envelope which, truth be told, had not existed in Germany for many years – she had been unable to put anything down on paper. In the end, Ada had known the eternal wait for his reply would have been the death of her.

Three.

Ada would have preferred to go and visit him in person and say: "Congratulations! You're going to be a

grandfather!" The occasion surely warranted such an effort. But at first she'd lacked the courage, and then she'd lacked the funds. And at some point she'd just been too far along in her pregnancy to travel.

Since then, Ada had convinced herself that no matter how the joyful message arrived, Papa would probably, initially, be unnerved. Perhaps he would not find the proper words, at first. In fact, he probably would not find any words at all. But in the end, chest swollen with pride, he would run up and down the streets of Osu, waiting to be congratulated for his skill in finally acquiring a grandchild. Assuming this news ever reached his ears.

"You're so quiet," Elle said.

Two.

An hour ago, while Elle had smoked a secret cigarette on her balcony, Ada had made a secret call. His scathing words still echoed in her ears.

"Yes," Ada nodded at Elle. "I'm praying one of these next apartments will work out."

"Really?"

The lift door finally rattled open. Ada would have liked to act as though she hadn't heard the question. But they were facing an enormous mirror. And so, she watched as both Elles repeated their question.

"What?" Ada said. "Praying? Yes, really."

With a jerk, the lift rattled into gear, climbing slowly to the fifth floor. Ada rustled through her purse. But it was all in vain, for the furrows in Elle's brow did not vanish so easily.

"You really believe in God?"

I feel sick every time I hear this question. This time, a

corner of one of my pages curled over. Believe in God? Who else would the living call upon when something unbelievable transpires? Or when they must give thanks? To whom would they turn in fear? Whose name do they cry out right before an orgasm?

"It's not my concern," God said at some point, while my questions fluttered about the room. "It's absolutely none of my business whether they believe in me or not!"

The number five began to blink on the screen.

"Hmm?" Ada said.

For a moment nothing happened. Ada chewed her lower lip. Maybe they'd be trapped inside the lift. Maybe she'd be forced to spend the rest of the evening evading Elle's questions.

"Do you really believe in God?" Elle repeated.

The door finally began to open.

"For me," Ada responded as they exited the lift together, "the more interesting question is: Does God really believe in us?"

The light was blinding, but the otherwise neutral colour scheme of the hallway – beige walls and a grey floor – was calming. And it somehow smelled yellow. At least that was Ada's first association. It neither smelled like lemon slices nor freshly picked daffodils. It did not smell of polished amber. Ada sniffed again. It was disappointment. Perhaps resignation, with a slight hint of coarse rage.

The first apartment door on the right was open, just a crack. And yet the smell seemed to emanate from there, colliding with the walls of the stairwell in its hurry towards the lift. Freedom at last.

A short length of metal chain prevented them from

pushing the door open any further, and so the voice which came from the other side was difficult to place at first.

"Who's there?"

Elle stood closest to the open door and found herself examined critically by a wizened eye peering from the other side. The eye measured her at length, before she finally introduced itself.

"My name is Frau Hückel."

"What's that?"

"Frau. Hück. El."

The eye did not react. Elle cast a fleeting glance at her sister, who nodded encouragingly. Elle turned back to face the eye.

"After we spoke on the telephone, I sent you an email . . ."

"What's that?"

"I sent you an email."

"A what?"

"An email. E. Mail."

"I don't read emails."

"I see."

Elle turned briefly again to Ada, staring in exasperation. Ada rolled her eyes.

"Well, anyway," Elle said, staring back directly into the peering eye. "My sister and I wanted to have a look at the room. Is it still available?"

At this, the door was promptly slammed shut. Perhaps slammed is not the proper word. It was not particularly loud. And yet the noise echoed down the hallway, just as the lift door also lurched shut. Elle turned again to her sister and raised one eyebrow. Ada asked herself whether it

was time to move on to the next viewing, but before she could find a fitting expression they heard the metal chain tinkling against the doorframe. A moment later the door swung open again.

The woman standing before Elle looked even older than Auntie Clara. She must have been in her late seventies. Her hair was tightly bound up in a bright, patterned headscarf, but a few kinks of her grey Afro peeked out from beneath the fabric. A few others sprouted from her chin. Her back was slightly bowed as she shuffled away amiably down the hall.

"Should we take off our shoes?" Elle called after her.

The question drifted off, vanishing without an answer. The old woman ducked into a room on the left at the end of the hallway from which they could hear the sound of a television game show with its canned laughter and applause.

"I'll help you," Elle whispered to Ada as she untied her sneakers. But with her close-cut fingernails, she struggled with the knots on Ada's shoes. Whenever Ada was upset she knotted her laces extra tight.

The sound of clapping and laughter came again from the living room, along with the cry: "Where did you two get to?"

"Excuse us," Elle said, as she arrived at the threshold of the living room. "We're right here."

All at once, Ada was reminded of the room in Papa's house. Although the colours were different, everything else was there: the bold patterns on the sofas compliment-ed by tiny, crocheted doilies, faded Bible quotes framed on the walls, and the obligatory wooden statue of a slender

woman with a water jug balanced on her head. Two dusty artificial plants and greying lace curtains. The only thing missing was the eternal whir of the fan. And Papa, himself.

"Come in, come in!" the old woman laughed.

"Come take a peep!"

As she followed Elle into the room, Ada pretended to cough. In doing so, she managed to wipe her eyes discreetly with her handkerchief. An equally ancient woman stood before the television, pointing at the sofa.

"Come, come," she clucked. "Come and have a seat."

Her cackling reminded Ada of her mothers, but the woman's eyes were surprisingly light. As she peered closer, Ada realised that her pupils were a milky-yellow hue. The woman also wore a scarf around her head, though its pattern was less daring than that of the other woman. Nevertheless, it was clearly a West African design. She scratched herself behind one ear and took a seat in a chair opposite the couch.

"Would you like something to drink?" the first woman asked, as Elle settled down beside her. Ada nodded, opening her mouth, but because she had sat down behind Elle, her sister didn't notice.

"Actually, we only wanted to look at the room," Elle said. She tapped nervously with her fingers in her lap.

"Eh-eh!" the woman beside her answered. "Just in and then back out? Like the Germans?"

"We have another appointment . . ."

"Hmm. Just like the Germans."

Elle pursed her lips so tightly that they almost disappeared. The tip of her nose was turning red.

"Maybe," she whispered. "Maybe because I'm German,

too?"

The old woman beside her leaned in closer to Elle, cupping one hand behind her ear.

"Gịnị ka o kwuru?"

The other woman made a few attempts before she brought the sentence to a close:

"O kwuru na," she crowed. "O kwuru na ọ bụ onye . . ." And then shaking her head, ". . . ọ bụ onye German!"

At this, the only word that all four understood, both women threw back their heads in laughter.

"My dear, o," sighed the woman closest to Elle while she wiped her eyes. "People like us: We will never be German. Never."

Elle crossed her arms and glared out of the window. Even I could sense the fire of her wrath, though Ada had stowed me deep within her handbag. Ada was burning too, but for another reason entirely. She glanced back and forth between Elle and the woman who sat opposite her. She began to tremble slightly.

"Excuse me, please," she said at last. "But were you two just speaking Igbo?"

The woman seated beside Elle clapped her hands, leaning back and gesticulating with a motion that seemed to signify something like:

"You see? I told you so!"

A loud oohing and ahhing erupted from the television. The woman in the chair leaned towards the sofa, bending forward and squinting at Ada. Seconds passed which felt like long hours. She remained squinting at Ada for so long that Ada began to wonder whether she was waiting for the answer to a question she had somehow missed. The

woman with the yellow pupils made several noises of approval.

"I really have to stare at you," she said at last. "Of the two of us, I'm the one whose eyesight is poorest."

After a few more hour-long seconds, she said: "Augusta?"

"Only on paper," came the delayed response. "Everyone calls me Ada, actually."

The woman opposite her nodded, as if all of this was already known to her. The other woman – of the two, the one whose hearing was poorest – called out, again cupping one hand behind her ear:

"Gịnị ka o kwuru?"

"Ada. Aaa-daa!"

"Eh-eh!"

Elle tapped Ada on the shoulder.

"What's happening right now?"

But before she could react, the woman beside Elle began to wag one finger in Ada's direction.

"You are the daughter of Ijemma. Am I right?"

Everything inside Ada tightened into a knot. She had never honestly believed she would hear these words spoken. She drew a deep breath.

"You knew my mother?" Ada whispered.

"No."

"No?"

Ada stared from one woman to the other. They were both smiling.

"We were in London once to visit our sister," said the woman opposite her. The one whose eyesight was poorest. She squinted again, nodding, lost in thought. And then

both women spoke at once. It bubbled out, from zero to one hundred:

"We only met Ijemma two or three times when we were there."

"*She* was a friend of our sister."

"Eh, eh!"

"Ijemma, o!"

Applause from the television. Socks turned a somersault. Elle grabbed Ada's hand, squeezing it tightly. Too tightly. Ada could not smile. Her mouth had grown so dry that the inside of her cheeks stuck to her teeth. And her hand hurt.

"Do you also know my father?" she managed to squeak.

"No." "No, o!"

Both women continued speaking at once. And yet it was easy to follow their words. As if they could be understood only in tandem.

"That was before his time."

"But we heard that they were married. Was that six months later?"

"A Ghanaian!"

"Hmm! These Ghanaians!" one repeated in English.

"And we also knew Ijemma had had a child."

"A daughter!"

"Eh, eh!"

"Ijemma, o!"

"This can't be real," Ada murmured. "All my life I dreamed I would meet people who had known my mother. But I never thought that it would happen here. In Germany of all places!"

"What's it got to do with Germany?" asked the woman

seated opposite Ada.

"You've got to admit," Elle replied, "that it's a strange coincidence."

"I don't think so."

The woman whose eyesight was poorest measured Elle for a few moments. More applause came from the television.

"Are you really not thirsty?"

The woman seated beside Elle struggled to raise herself from the sofa.

"I'll fetch us something to drink."

The woman on the chair clapped her hands.

"Yes, bring the kpótomenui! It's a celebration."

"What's that?" asked Ada, as the woman whose hearing was poorest left the room.

"You must know it, of course," the other woman nodded. "The bottle we have is from Ghana!"

Her hands moved to her head and she pulled the scarf a bit more snugly together.

"No," Ada said, after Elle had also shrugged. "I have no idea."

"No idea?" the old woman stammered. "Eh-eh! Is your father a pastor?"

In the meantime the first woman had returned carrying a tray. On it she had arranged four glasses and a small, inconspicuous bottle with no label.

"You probably call it Akpeteshie," she said, placing the tray onto the coffee table.

"Akpeteshie?!" Elle exclaimed. "That poison? I'll never drink it again!" She waved her finger in Ada's face. "And Socks doesn't need it either!"

"Nonsense!" the first woman cried. She had taken her

seat beside Elle once more. "Kpótomenui is good for your health! It makes the blood flow!"

"Why do you call it kpótomenui?" Ada grinned.

"Because that's its *proper* name . . . !"

While she spoke, the other woman made a few noises in affirmation.

". . . When white men came to West Africa, they outlawed the making of our own traditional alcohol. Yes!"

"White men!"

The old woman opposite Ada barred her arms over her chest and shook her head.

"Just so they could peddle their gin or schnapps or whatever else it was."

"Eh-eh!"

"But we made our own anyway. We just gave it a new name: Akpe-te-shie means something like 'Hide yourself'. But we don't do that anymore!"

She opened the bottle.

"Hey, Madam Ijemma," she cried. "Your Ada is here, o!"

The other woman leaned back and closed her eyes. A smile spread across her lips. Dimples formed in her cheeks, and her warm face was lit by the harsh light of the television.

"Augusta Adanne Lamptey." She sighed. "Your mother was a beautiful lady . . ."

For the first time since she had entered the apartment, Ada laughed. A shy laughter, but it came from the heart.

". . . How strange that you two don't look anything alike."

And for the first time since she had entered the

apartment, Elle laughed. But she so quickly managed to disguise it as a cough that Ada probably didn't notice.

"We never saw the baby," the old woman spoke again. "Only in pictures. But we knew that Frank . . ."

Her eyes were closed again, a deep wrinkle formed across her brow.

"It is Frank, right?"

"Francis," Ada said.

"Francis. Of course. We knew that he wanted to give his child an English name . . ."

She shook her head and continued.

". . . and we knew he thought the name Augusta was stylish. That's what our sister said."

"Why Augusta?" Elle asked.

She opened her eyes.

"Dreadful, isn't it? I don't know myself. But you don't hear the name Augusta every day. When you called about the room we were reminded at once of the London days. And then, with the second name, Adanne, we had no more doubt."

"Do you know what your name means?"

The woman beside Elle spoke as she poured the alcohol into their four glasses. Her hand quivered such that Ada was amazed she didn't spill a drop. Ada nodded, her eyes fixed on the bottle.

"Well, then tell your sister."

"I know what Ada means: The *first daughter*, of course!"

"Not Ada. *Adanne.*"

"Her mother's daughter! I'm not completely clueless."

Both women laughed again. Luckily, all four glasses were already full and the bottle had been returned to the

tray.

"You see?!" The woman with the yellow pupils pointed at Elle. "And that's why you'll never be German. Who of them would know such a thing?"

She lifted one of the glasses and squinted at Ada.

"And how is Frank?"

"My papa? Francis."

"Yes . . . Francis. How is he? How is his leg?"

"His leg?"

Ada stared at Elle, who simply shrugged. Ada was not used to Elle having no answers.

"We heard," said the woman, "two or three years after the fire, the arson attack—"

"What attack? Arson!"

The question was clearly not one that should be asked at an apartment viewing. But even before their silence fell, the answer had been clear. And even the woman whose hearing was poorest understood what had just happened.

Elle again took Ada's hand. But this time as if it were made of fragile glass.

"I'm so sorry," she murmured.

Ada maintained her composure, as if they were discussing some utterly unimportant thing. As if she had not longed her entire life to find out more about her mother's death.

"Who did it?" she asked.

The woman whose eyesight was poorest shook her head.

"Yes, who would do such a thing?"

Ada closed her eyes. Yes, what now, she asked herself. Just how had she imagined it? The words "house fire" had

not had the same effect as "arson attack". Ijemma had died in a fire which had *purposely* been set? But why had she been at home alone? Where had Ada been? Where had Papa been?

"They never found them."

"What?"

Ada opened her eyes. The woman seated opposite her was leaning forward.

"The people who started this fire."

"And . . ." Ada searched for the right words. Shreds of thought. What had they been talking about before? "And the foot? I mean, my father's leg?"

"The leg. We heard a few years later that he had a bad accident at work."

"He almost lost his leg!"

Ada was still gaping at the two women. In all the time since he had returned to Ghana, her father had not mentioned it.

"He was in Germany when it happened. Actually, we were supposed to meet. My sister told him to visit us here. But after the accident he had to return to London at once."

"But what happened?"

"We do not know. An accident at work."

"What kind of work was he doing?"

"All I know is that he wanted to study some kind of mechanical engineering. He'd started working for BMW."

Both women were now holding a glass. The woman opposite Ada continued:

"We heard that he would never walk again."

"He walks," Ada said slowly. "Always with a cane. But

he can walk."

Elle cleared her throat. The others turned to her expectantly.

Elle needed to swallow a few times before she could ask her question.

"Was that sometime around 1999?"

The woman whose hearing was poorest handed Elle and Ada each a glass.

"Yes, I believe so," she said.

"Then that was around the time he met my mother."

Elle's voice was so quiet that it was almost drowned out by applause from the television.

"You are also Frank's child?" the woman opposite asked.

"Yes, but we've only known each other for two years."

"Frank has *two* children?" asked the woman seated beside Elle.

"That he knows of. Yes."

The woman beside Elle raised her glass.

"Well then," she cried. "To Frank!"

It was amazing how quickly the old women drained their glasses. Ada and Elle could only gasp. They placed their still-full glasses back on the table. The woman with the yellow pupils fixed her eyes again on Ada.

"How long is it until you are due?"

"Two or three weeks?"

"And where is the father? Why are you not looking for an apartment together?"

Ada scratched her head. It occurred to her that although she had been expected to divulge all manner of information during all these long weeks of visiting apartments, no-

one had ever asked her about Cash.

"That's a good question," she said.

"Where is he?"

Ada swallowed. There had just been such a cosy feeling in the room. A commercial for laundry detergent blared from the television.

"I don't know where he is," she whispered, gazing out of the window. "He's gone. He doesn't call. And it's better that way."

Elle shook her head.

"Yes, well . . ."

Ada turned to her and scowled.

"He did try to . . ." Elle said, as if entering a minefield, ". . . you've got to admit."

"I haven't heard from him since the *middle of October*!"

"Yeah. And that isn't cool. But you also stopped responding to his messages."

"Yes, and he knows why!"

Ada wiped her eyes with her right index finger. The old woman leaned in to her.

"My daughter," she said, and waited. And waited. Until Ada had heard her fill of "hygienically clean laundry through and through" and "radiant colours", and until she had memorised the pattern on the rug so carefully that she could have drawn it in her sleep. Until she could look at the old woman again.

The woman's voice grew as soft and deep as her yellowed eyes. "I would just like to say one thing." She nodded. "I don't know what happened between you. But I can see that he hurt you—"

"You can say that again!"

"Forgive him."

For a moment, Ada could not form any sound in her throat. Who was she to say such a thing? What did she know of her relationship with Cash? Nothing! Why should Ada forgive him? If she only knew the mess he'd made!

"I-I can't," Ada stammered. Her lower lip began to tremble and she struggled to maintain a steady voice.

"Forgive him," the woman repeated.

"Why *me*?"

"Because you can."

"Ha!"

Ada stared out of the window. Tears streamed down her face while she swallowed. Elle held her hand again. The woman waited until Ada looked at her once more.

"My daughter," she nodded. "Listen to me. These things he did to you – I know that they did not come from him. He only passed them down. Forgive him."

Ada rubbed her belly. Then she whispered, "I can't do it."

"We have to let go of this pain, my daughter. It doesn't matter whether you will ever see him again or not. Forgive him."

"Gịnị ka o kwuru?" said the woman whose hearing was poorest. Elle answered, handing Ada a tissue: "She says she can't do it."

The woman removed her hand from behind her ear.

"Do you know what you are?" she asked Ada.

"*What* I am?"

"You are Adanne. You are your mother's daughter. You *can* do it."

And then, for a long time, they sat in silence. Credits

scrolled on the television.

"Can we see the room?" Elle asked at last.

"Of course!" the woman whose eyesight was poorest answered her in English. "Come along, I will show it to you."

She struggled to rise from the chair. Ada was not quick enough to help her, but before she could say anything, Elle was at her side.

"Is that okay?"

The old woman nodded as Elle took her arm.

"Thank you, my dear," she said, smiling.

They walked to the room together, while the sound of clapping and cheering poured out once more from the television.

The room was directly across the hall. The woman gestured for Ada and Elle to enter first.

"As you can see, we've wanted a baby in the house for a long time. Not just since yesterday!"

Ada stared at the wooden cradle, the brightly coloured curtains, the hundreds of stuffed animals – bunnies, teddy bears and ducklings.

"Wow!" She laughed, stroking a baby blanket with one hand. It smelled of lavender.

"What a beautiful room. It's lovely!"

Ada picked up a tiny knitted frog.

"How many children do you have?"

The old woman leaned against the door frame. She smiled back, less brightly than before.

"None, sadly. And no nieces or nephews either. No bonus children of any kind. For a very long time I wanted nothing more than a baby. But it never worked out. If only

I'd had the fertility beads then!"

"Fertility beads?"

Elle glanced at Ada, and Ada reached into her hand-bag. For a moment I was overjoyed, for I thought that Ada would finally take me out. But she was only reaching for the catalogue from the museum.

"Like these here?"

The woman took the catalogue from Ada's hand and held it so close to her face that the pages brushed against the tip of her nose.

"Eh-eh! It's that exhibition!"

"Yes, exactly," Elle said, nodding. "Have you been to it? Or are you planning to go?"

"Who, me? No! I won't pay money to look at my own property."

"The bracelet belongs to you?"

"Not me: *us*. To you and me. And to my sisters. And mothers. And their mothers before them."

The woman whose hearing was poorest had shuffled over to them and was now examining the page too.

"Did you know," she said, "that this bracelet originally came from Kuntanase?"

"Kuntanase?" Ada exclaimed. "By Obuasi?"

"Gịnị ka o kwuru?"

"Obuasi," Ada repeated.

"Yes, precisely!" the old woman answered. She still held one hand cupped behind her ear.

"But then why is it here?" Elle asked.

"My dear. What can I say? We were cheated."

The woman whose eyesight was poorest nodded, spreading her arms wide: "They tried to destroy us. But

here we are!"

"But for how much longer," Elle said in a quavering voice. "Our planet is destroyed. We should all be living completely differently. But we aren't."

"Many are doing their best—"

"Really?" Elle scowled. "All this driving around in cars. Eating meat. Popping out babies . . ."

Ada was glaring at her sister, and Elle grew quiet. The old woman who still held one hand behind her ear locked eyes with Elle.

"You do know that you, too, will be a mother, yes?"

"Who, me?" Elle shook her head vehemently. "Never."

"Do not say this. The child of your sister will also be your child."

The four of them stood in silence while the weight of these words settled in the room.

"It's lovely," Ada said after a pause. "It's really lovely. But it will be too small for us in the long term."

Both of the women nodded. Elle glanced purposefully at Ada and cleared her throat.

"We've really got to be going to our next viewing," she said.

"Oh, no!"

"But we're already going to be late . . ."

The woman whose eyesight was poorest placed her hand on Ada's arm.

"You can come again." She smiled. "The room will always be here for you."

Ada nodded, forcing a smile to her lips. But how bitter was the taste. She still had so many questions. And at the same time she knew that the next viewing was perhaps her

last chance to find an apartment before the end of the year. Unfortunately, Elle was right – like always.

"Thank you, thank—" Ada began to stutter.

"Bring more time with you," the other woman continued. "We can tell you stories. And show you pictures."

Ada could only nod. She would have liked to cry: "Yes, please!" or "That would be lovely!" But her voice was not cooperating. It remained deep within her throat, containing an explosion yet to come.

The sisters left the house without a word. But as Elle attempted to hurry across the street as the light changed, Ada remained standing on the pavement.

"What did you mean by 'popping out babies'?"

Elle shook her head.

"Please, Ada. Forget it," she said. "It just slipped out."

"What are you trying to say?"

"Nothing, Ada. Please. We're already running late."

Ada did not budge.

"Do you mean that I shouldn't have got pregnant, or what?"

Ada could see how Elle struggled with her answer. How the wrinkles in her forehead deepened.

"I just wanted to say . . . there's always . . . there's almost always a choice."

Ada narrowed her eyes.

"And what do you know about why I got pregnant?"

Elle shook her head again.

"I never said that I—"

"That's pretty low, Elle."

"I'm just afraid, Ada. Okay? The whole world is

crumbling. Everything is happening *now*. I'm sorry if I—"

"You aren't!"

"All I wanted to say was that as long as *I* have the choice, I won't be bringing any kids into this world. That's all I wanted to say. Forget it."

Elle wiped both hands over her face and shrugged.

"And so, I shouldn't have got myself pregnant?"

"That's not what I said!"

"Or I shouldn't have *stayed* pregnant?"

"Ada—"

"Leave me alone!"

In her head Ada could hear the way her mothers in Accra would cry out:

"Eh-eh!"

"Ada! Be careful, o!"

But Ada didn't care. About anything. Her heart was hammering against her ribcage. A boy who had been waiting to cross the street was gaping at her, open-mouthed. Normally she would have ignored him. He was certainly not the first, nor would he be the last child to stare at her. So many people had already told her she needed to be understanding of white children. They were only curious. Or interested. Maybe surprised. Possibly even afraid. But only because they hadn't seen that many real Black people before. Ada shouldn't take it personally. It wasn't their fault. But no matter how furtively she'd press her lips together in such situations, she still always had to swallow. Quietly. But she'd already swallowed enough today. Now was the time to throw it all back up!

Ada leaned down so close to the boy that their noses almost touched. His eyes were bulging out of his

head.

"Piss off!" she hissed.

She didn't need to say it a second time. He yelped, and took to his heels.

And Elle walked past Ada.

Ada did not call after her.

# Among the Toothless

## 07:45

I never want to be a concentration-camp barrack room again. Believe me, I know expressions like "never again" are bandied about far too easily. But I'm serious. I've seen first-hand how . . .

Or perhaps it would be better to say: I can bear witness that . . .

Ehh.

Okay, let us put it this way: Every time Ada separated herself from her body was a disaster. Every time. And not merely for her. But the fact that she felt compelled to do so was . . .

You already know.

And every time it was more difficult to put her scattered pieces back together again. Every time, the glue that held them together grew weaker.

And.

And her dissolution blew a hole in the façade of her tormenters – including those proverbial "good guys" who claimed to have done nothing.

And.

And because I, too, had done nothing to stop it, I felt that I was implicated. I complained, of course. By now you all know how it is with God and me. This has nothing to do with justice, I said. I'm completely innocent, I couldn't even choose my form back then. Who would do such a thing? God grinned. It looked like a flash of lightning, and I was filled with an indescribable rapture.

What could I have done?! I thundered. I couldn't do anything! As a doorknocker, at least I could make sounds! In 1945 I was a fucking room!

God's answer spread like a beam of white light across the heavens: Blabla is no excuse. No excuse for a crime.

Blabla . . . ?!

In other words: You always have a choice.

I blustered and rattled until the heavens seemed poised to collapse.

The saying is, I roared: Ignorance is no excuse!

That's right.

IGNORANCE!

Yep. Thanks.

But ignorance wasn't my problem!

Then what was it?

I was *a room*. What could I have done?

Alone? Not much, I admit.

The wiry shafts of light which accompanied God's answers vanished nearly as quickly as they appeared. Continually leaving me in the dark.

That's what I said, I grumbled.

But still, He said.

Still what?

You always have a choice.

God dropped the mic and vanished, and I drifted aimlessly through world history, searching for a new assignment. With the exception of my short interlude as a breakfast egg which had refused to become hard-boiled, my existence had mostly been uneventful. Until I chose to assume the form of a passport. A form I am still proud of. But the reason why it had been both fitting and important for me to have been a room in a concentration-camp barrack only made sense after Ada had confronted her own trauma.

Only then did I notice that it had been Friday the 13th. Which is actually a good thing. Otherwise, I would not have been able to resist the urge to do something which I would no doubt have found amusing, but which I would later have regretted. On that morning, Ada's memories of Cash were swirling together – sometimes quite tangibly, other times, ephemeral. A few weeks earlier she could have drawn a perfect portrait of his face from memory: Every lock of hair, the curve of his eyebrows, the soft indentations of his cheek, the chaos of his beard. She could have immortalised it all in a few carefully chosen pencil strokes. But these times were past. And Ada had become a different person entirely – at least, so she told herself.

Ada's first thought after Elle had mentioned Cash this morning was both wonderful and terrible at once: *Is he coming?* How could it be that *this* was her first reaction? Still? She didn't want to think about him at all. But. Elle's knack for stowing things away so well that they were never found again was also a great talent of his. He spent a great deal of his life searching for lost keys. Or his wallet. Or his phone.

Everything seemed to remind her of him. Definitely her knitting. But also: tea candles. Strawberry mousse. Vests. Even an innocent shake of the head. Her finger now moved automatically to the skip button after the first four notes of "Redemption Song". She avoided the smell of burnt toast because Cash – clown that he was – possessed neither a toaster nor an adequate concept of time.

Even I nearly sufficed to drive Ada to tears. And that's saying a lot, since Ada was not the kind of person to cry for no reason. But yesterday evening – it was the end of a long and stressful day, after another round of hopeless apartment viewings – her belly was stretched to bursting and her temples throbbed. It would still be many hours until they announced the final results of the Brexit vote. Yesterday evening she had begun to put together new application documents, fearing the inevitable, and she had taken me up in one hand. By chance, she thumbed open the photo page.

No matter how long she stared at the picture, she could not figure out what Cash had found so attractive in her. She brooded over her hair, counted her pimples, and dissected her facial features until she could no longer bear it. She put me away, deciding that Cash must have been lying to her all along. And then she grew even more frustrated with the realisation that so much of her feeling of self-worth still depended on this asshole.

Ada could usually distract herself: blood tests and wire transfers don't cease to exist for a broken heart. But whenever she found herself thinking of him, she always counted silently to ten. Or she wrote herself little notes on a tiny pink notepad:

"Crying is nothing to be ashamed of!" or "This candle burns on." These she taped onto her other notebooks and binders and into her maternity journal. She no longer cried herself to sleep. She painted her fingernails red. She couldn't reach her toenails anymore, but with the last money in her bank account she purchased the latest pair of overpriced trainers to admire in their shoebox until she would return them in the new year.

Ada was preparing herself for a bright future: A future which consisted solely of yoga classes for young mothers, freshly squeezed organic juices and amusing stories on Instagram. (Not that she had followed her plan to the last detail, but) Ada had fought her way through each of the fifty-seven days since his last message with the thought that, soon enough, all this pain would go away. And she could have managed it today, as well. It would not have been a problem. If it hadn't been for Elle.

Across the many loops and orbits, I had learned that the living often maintain a difficult relationship with their own pasts. If they maintain any relationship with it at all. This has always puzzled me, for to be honest I can think of nothing lovelier than one day having a story of my own. How I would love to dance the Kecak in Bali alongside my playful granddaughters. How lovely it would be to pass on everything I know – everything my grandmothers knew – to them through the rhythmic motion of our chanting bodies.

How I would love to lie with fever in a sickbed in Kilkenny. How comforting, to listen to the lullabies of my worried mother:

*". . . your brothers have all gone to find work in England*
*the house is so empty and sad*
*the crop of potatoes is sorely infected*
*a third to a half of them bad . . ."*

But of course, in need, I could also do without such pleasant things entirely. I could also get on fine in places where holidays were celebrated that glorified despots and conquerors. Commonwealth Day? Columbus Day? No problem. The Day of German Reunification? Bring it on! Better a dolled-up take on history, I say, than no history at all. But in Berlin very few people enjoyed being reminded of the past. It was no different with Ada. And so, when Elle made the mistake of mentioning Cash, tidal waves of suppressed memories began to wash over her. The first wave left Ada sweaty and breathless behind the counter of a café near Oranienplatz.

Had that been March, or had it already been April? In any case, Ada had just completed her language exam and was waiting for the start of the semester. And she had got lucky. Although she had only come in to hand over her CV, the manager had told her that she could do a trial shift that very day.

"Mazel tov!" the manager had cried out, tossing Ada an apron. "Just go ahead and put it on!"

Later, after the chaos of midday was over, she had extended Ada her hand and said:

"Friede."

"And also with you," Ada had said in halting German, mistaking her boss's name for the German word for peace. And Friede had roared with laughter until her sides had

ached. She had still been giggling when the next customer entered the café. He was unmistakably a German. The leather sandals he proudly sported over his long socks had been a dead giveaway. No young Ghanaian had worn such things since Papa had moved to England in the late '80s. And even back then they had not exactly been fashionable.

The young man walked straight to the refrigerator near the entrance. He had tried to compensate for his Germanness by wearing a brightly coloured T-shirt. But Ada could tell at a distance that the material wasn't real Kente. He probably hadn't bought the thing in Ghana at all. His haircut was more Boney M than Burna Boy. Ada would never have addressed him first in English, not in a million years. But Ada's boss lacked her employee's powers of observation.

"Cash!" she had called out from behind the coffee machine, as the young man had tried to pay for his Club Mate with a card. And the name had stuck.

Her arms crossed, Ada had measured him slowly from head to toe as he searched about in his bum bag for spare change. Eventually he arranged three Euros' worth of coins along the countertop.

"That's all I've got," he'd grinned. His eyes had awakened a warm, faint memory in Ada which she could not identify. But the vexation she had felt simultaneously had been clearer, and more suitable for the occasion anyway. Ada had shaken her head, kissing her teeth. And then she had taken fifty cents from her own pocket. Just like that.

When the second wave of memories washed over her, Ada found herself walking beside Cash on their way to the

U-Bahn station. It was the end of her fifth day at work, and the sun hung low in the sky – tired and full behind the shadow of the linden trees. The young leaves whispered in the breeze, glad of the growing warmth which the hint of approaching spring had carried with it. Cash had been pushing his bicycle with his left hand while gesticulating with his right. He jerked his head from time to time, and each time this happened Ada had to look away. A dull feeling of shame had crowded in amongst the faint sadness that had enveloped her, and she did not know why. He was talking very quickly. Ada could only half-follow his words. But his lips looked like velvet. And then he had turned to her, as if awaiting an answer. How pretty his eyes were.

"Sorry." She shook her head a bit too vigorously. "Come again?"

"I asked if you wanna get somethin' to eat?"

She frowned. Had he heard her stomach growling?

"I want no bread," she said in German.

"Actually, it's 'I *don't* want bread.'"

She rolled her eyes. But he didn't notice because he was busy searching his pockets for his wallet.

"I don't want bread," she repeated.

"What are you talking about? It's not all bread here!"

"Here." Ada pointed to a kebab shop. "Flat bread. And next door they have . . . what do you call it . . . Fo-kosh-ya? And look here: naan, right? And everywhere else it's sandwiches, wraps and hotdogs."

They stopped walking for a moment. Ada squinted at the innumerable cafés, shops and restaurants with their useless food, lining both sides of Oranienstraße as far as she could see.

"I don't want any of it. I want some real food."

"What about pasta?"

"Do you mean spaghetti?" Ada snorted. "More bread: finely chopped and stretched to length. I said I wanted *real* food."

Ada pulled her jacket in tighter about the waist, ignoring Cash's grin. They continued a few steps side by side in silence.

"And what would you like to eat then?" he asked when they stopped at the next crossroads. "What's your favourite dish?"

"Dish?"

He laughed again. "Don't worry. I just mean what's your favourite meal?"

But Ada's eyebrows remained raised, her mouth in a frown.

"What's my favourite dish?" she repeated, as they crossed the street together.

"I mean, what do you miss most about Ghana? Probably everything . . ."

"No, not everything. Only the food."

"Seriously?"

She shrugged.

"What else would I miss? I've got Spotify and YouTube for music. I already brought everything I need for my hair from home. And I don't need more clothes."

"And what about your father?"

Ada grew quiet. She did miss her papa, but it wasn't as if living in Ghana again would help.

"No," she said at length. "Though I do miss my mothers. But we've got our WhatsApp group chat. I talk to them

often enough."

"Mothers?"

". . . Yes?"

"You've got more than one?"

"But those are the women who raised me. What else should I call them?"

Of course, she knew that her father's sisters were her aunts. She had learned this in the first month of German classes. She also had learned that the correct term for Elle was actually "half-sister". But she had neither time nor patience for such constructs.

"Why half-sister?" she had asked her teacher then. "Elle is a whole person. She's my whole sister!"

And Ada had not let up, even when she repeatedly lost points on her assignments for this. The sisters of her father were her mothers. And when she needed to distinguish between them – for example, if she needed to call only one of them – then she used her first name. And *then* always together with "Auntie". Out of respect.

Cash stroked his head with his free hand. He had no answer. His hands were very pretty, too. "You know," Ada continued, "you know what I miss most? The smell of simmering palm nut soup."

Her eyes grew misty.

"And the taste of freshly mashed fufu. And the feeling of your belly stuffed full of Red Red and crispy-fried plantains."

"I don't know about any of that," Cash said, laughing.

"Well, I'm not surprised. Everything in Germany tastes so brooding . . ."

". . . *boring*?"

"Yes, that, too." Ada nodded.

Elle had once brought Ada home some chips. An act of kindness to make her sister happy. That had been in the first weeks, when Ada had not yet learned to use her poker face. Fried hunks of potato. With salt. Nothing more. Not even so much as a decent hot sauce.

"I mean, come on: Spices. Is that even a concept here?"

"Of course." Cash grinned again. "Salt. And sometimes some black pepper."

"I said, SPICES!"

They had both laughed as they approached the U-Bahn station at Moritzplatz. Ada had quickly buttoned up her jacket at the top of the stairs, not noticing until she had finished that she had fastened the buttons crookedly.

"Wait," Cash had said, leaning his bicycle against a streetlamp. Just before his fingers touched her jacket he had paused: "May I?"

And the way he had asked her this, and the way the evening sunlight had fallen on his face at that moment so that he'd needed to squint to look in her direction, and the way he'd smelled – a mix of strong coffee and mint chewing gum – she had been unable to do anything more than nod her head sheepishly.

Ada watched his slender fingers encircling the buttons on her jacket. And as he had unfastened and refastened them one by one, he kissed her. First on the cheek, and then on the forehead.

"I'll cook something for you," he said. "But only if you'd like that."

"With spices?"

"Of course."

"And without any bread?"

254

"I promise."

Ada had nodded again.

"I'd like that."

The third wave rose suddenly, nearly crashing over her head and tumbling Ada breathlessly into a small venue where she had sat waiting now for hours for Cash's performance to begin. Ada looked about herself. It was a tight and stuffy room, but still big enough for thirty chairs arranged into three rows. The stage which lay directly before her was empty but for a single microphone standing beneath the spotlight. To her left stood a shaky wooden table – someone no doubt considered it an antique – piled carelessly with a handful of books beside a hand-scribbled sign. To her right sat Cash, tapping his feet and moving his lips as he bobbed his head.

They had officially been a couple for three weeks now, and Ada always brought something with her when they went out. She could not concentrate on reading, and drawing had always attracted too many nosy, amateur art critics. And so she spent the time during Cash's many sound-checks teaching herself to knit. She had woven together her feelings for him out bits of old wool. Wool because the beginning of the year had been so bitter cold. But also because Elle had once stumbled over her words after giving Ada a particularly portentous glance, warning her that Cash *wool* try to leave Germany as quickly as he could.

Inspired by Bob Marley, he had taken to calling it "Babylon" here. Most of his lyrics were angry, and critical – in both senses of the word. Ada never asked why he still lived in Germany. She just continued with her handiwork, counting her stitches and taking care not to drop

them. Concentration was everything. Three months later she gave him her first home-made knitted pullover. She had chosen blue because it matched his mood, and green to give him some hope.

Cash really only ever came alive on stage. Only there did he feel truly free. And always, just before he began, Ada could observe how the heavy clouds of stress lifted from his shoulders, how they dissolved into the air. He cleared his throat. He closed his eyes. And:

*Babylon!*

The word echoed through the room. And at the same time a piercing tone resonated through the ears of his audience, for he had held the microphone too close. But he did not allow himself to be distracted by the hecklers.

*A land without prospects.*

*A street.*

*One way – and no-one at the helm!*

Ada carried on with her knitting, ignoring the whispers from the corner.

*A stench – bird shit!*

*And The Third Path should be outlawed.*

*The Second Path, just for education?*

*Then only one path. And no deposit.*

Cash opened his eyes, nodding intently at his audience. Ada knew he was particularly proud of this line. The Poetry Slammers in the corner stopped their whispering, but all three now stared intently at their phones.

*Plastic bottles but no fish. We cannot live from them – not even for a day.*

The woman standing behind the mixers shook her head. Ada hoped this scepticism was directed at the sound

quality. Knit one, drop one.

*Teach the people* tolerance *instead.*

*People, folx! Heads or tails?*

*Are we seriously talking about a piece of cloth*

*While our sisters still cry*

*Equal pay for equal work?!*

He followed this with a well-intended line about the female scientist who had "photographed" the Black Hole and the female athlete whose body supposedly "produced" too much testosterone:

*Maybe she should be a cathedral in Paris?*

*We call her "Notre Dame", but we watch her burn!*

Ada had begun to hum quietly. That song by Bob Marley, what was it called again? It was a total earworm: "Redemption Song!" Cash played it on repeat every time she visited him. But now his own voice was growing louder, growing more urgent. He was interrupting the fine melody in her head!

*And colonialism is such a dirty word,*

*everything was better before and some bullshit about the Autobahn.*

*Why can't we get back to our*

*Place in the sun? You miss it? #MeToo!*

The sound tech woman shook her head again. Ada smiled at Cash, hoping he wouldn't notice how stiffly her cheeks were stretched.

*And women were happier without feminism.*

*The roots of all evil end in -ism*

*Except maybe for prism . . .*

The Poetry Slammers in the corner cackled. Ada concentrated on her hands. Knit one, drop one. She realised

too late that his performance had come to an end. Along with the rest of his audience. Because there had been so many other lengthy pauses during his reading, Cash stood silently at the microphone for a good ten seconds before the sound tech began to clap.

That was during the time in which the days still stuck together and she could separate them only with great effort.

"Super," she had nodded.

"Super shitty, maybe," Cash had laughed. "But it's an awesome feeling either way!"

Later, Cash told Ada that he couldn't understand why she had moved to Berlin. Back then Ada had still believed that her German was too poor, that this was why she constantly misunderstood him. He sat beside her in that little room, staring at her as if in disappointment.

Ada was still waiting for resolution: a "just joking" or perhaps an "okay, sorry".

"We have actual Nazis in our government!" he exclaimed.

And it was true. But Ada didn't know where else she could have moved.

"Do you know what's happening in England right now?" she had countered.

Her ball of yarn fell to the floor. And despite her attempts to rescue it, it rolled away into a dusty corner. The blue faded to grey. For Cash's sake she quickly gathered it up, brushing away as much dirt as she could.

"Ah, you don't understand," he had said.

But even back then Ada had understood a lot. Much more than Cash had realised. Just because she hadn't possessed the vocabulary to read the signs, it did not mean

that she had not recognised them . . .

And then the greatest wave of all crashed over her and left her lying on his bed, shaking. It was the beginning of May.

"It's not going to hurt," he'd assured her. "It's just a little pressure. For a minute or so. And then it will be over." She had said she didn't want to. That she was scared.

"There's no reason to be scared."

But I am, she thought. He kissed her on the cheek and then the forehead.

He had always kissed her this way.

And she had always felt safe. But this time was different. Had he said it would be like a little operation?

She lay on her back and watched him as though she were not with him in his room, in his bed, under his blanket, but somewhere very far away. Back in Osu? Or at Elle's? Even here, just outside the door, would have been better.

He had risen and pulled the curtains shut. And to drown out the slowly creeping feeling of being trapped, she had thought about the cinema. He wasn't standing by the window but on a screen. She watched as he removed his T-shirt. It was yellow. He had not been wearing anything else. And that had surprised her. She could not remember him taking off his trousers.

He lay down on top of her. She concentrated on the imaginary screen.

"There's no reason to be scared."

But Ada wasn't listening. She focused on the curve of his back, how he moved up and down. She smelled the sweat on his skin. She was gone. She lay her hands on his

hips. She hoped that if she could help his movements it would end more quickly. He had to be almost finished? He moaned, and she turned up the soundtrack in the back of her mind. But no matter how loudly the music played, she could not drown out the little voice inside her head. Single words pierced the fog of movement [It.] and rocking [Serves.] and the squeezing [You.] and the pressure [Right.].

At first the pain had been a single point. A minute point. Tiny and red like a fresh pinprick. The point – no bigger than the prick of a needle – yawned and opened itself wider. It became a gunshot wound, and stretched still wider. It became a stream. Thin as a piece of thread, winding down the inside of her leg; past her knee; gathering along her heel. The stream became a conspicuous puddle. Ada could not say how quickly the pool formed, for she had lost her sense of time. She had not wondered at the appearance of the blood, for blood was nothing new to her. But she grew nervous from the sheer quantity. The thread grew deeper, darker, broader. Soon her whole leg was covered, as though she were wearing a wine-red stocking. And strangely: only on one leg. Perhaps because her other foot was not touching the floor.

She had gone to the bathroom and the bleeding wouldn't stop. Ada had cried, but quietly enough that Cash had not heard her. She didn't want to wake him. And so, Ada cried and mopped the floor. She cried and lathered herself with soap in the shower. She cried and washed her underwear. And after everything was clean again and she had put on a white T-shirt and clean panties, she lay back down beside him. She watched his breathing and wondered at

his peace.

In March of 1945, as a room in a concentration-camp barrack, I had been unable to prevent anything. But I witnessed everything. Ada's truth was burned into my walls. And all the others who were there had seen it, too. The recordings, the diaries, various objects – entire museums and memorials: afterwards all this became a part of the German experience. And I contributed to this. But in May of 2019, it was only Ada and Cash. Her word and his. I lay in some bag or pocket, nothing more than a few bound-together pages which were about to lose their meaning anyway. This time, I did not even have the ability to see. And yet I still bear witness. And that is, perhaps, the greatest proof of love . . .

Ada was cold. Not only physically, though this was a big part of her discomfort. Elle's voice tore her from her thoughts.

"Ada?"

"What?"

Ada was standing by the balcony door without even having realised that she'd stood up. Elle was still sitting on the sofa. Her sofa.

## 19:45

Towards the end of my time as a passport, I saw something that at first I had difficulty identifying. I saw a twisted hand, an open mouth and a furrowed brow. Was the figure

bending forward? Were they falling? Neither, nor. They were running – their legs draped in orange, in yellow, in blistering white and riotous black. The right foot ready to spring, the left still anchored to the ground. I shifted forward, watching. The smoking hair. The crying eyes. If they could only run a little faster, I thought, they might escape the brutal waves engulfing their upper body, licking mischievously about their throat. Run, run, I thought. It was unbearable. And then the image vanished.

• • • •

It grew cold. But Ada could not force her body to move any quicker. Every centimetre ached. Doggedly, she set one foot before the other, merely trusting that she was still making progress. One moment, her left foot was resting on a crack in the cobblestones, the next, her toes were scuffing through stray weeds.

"Just a little bit further . . ." she murmured. Luckily for her, the last apartment viewing was not so far away. Only about a ten minutes' walk. "Just a little bit further."

But as she turned down Ulmenallee, she discovered a bench to her right beside a small neighbourhood playground. Everything in her body screamed: "Stop!"

"Just a little bit further . . ." she murmured again, sinking onto the bench. Memories of her conversation with Papa ran uninhibited through her mind. She had not expected so much anger. Yes, the family was counting on her. But her life was far from ruined. Ada would not be the first computer scientist with a child. But what had got into her? She closed her eyes.

From behind her eyelids, she could still make out the silhouettes of the leafless branches spread out above. The trees were bare, but they did not cry. When trees cry their tears are not borne externally like those of clouds. They flow beneath the surface of the bark. Trees breathe, they grow, they flourish – and then a human comes along and they find themselves completely helpless.

Ada heard footsteps. And wheezing. And the sound of flowing water. She opened her eyes and saw an elderly man watering a tree. He had only a small can with him. When he had emptied its contents, he put it aside and – placing both hands on his lower back – he stretched. He gazed so lovingly at the tree that Ada wondered whether he was in fact watching some tiny baby animal hidden among its branches.

A breath of wind scattered withered leaves across the playground, swirling them about with an old, discarded plastic bag and stealing the toupee from the old man's head. His cheeks shone and his fingers splayed as he hurried after it, the hairpiece dancing always a few millimetres beyond his grasp.

"Catch yersel' on," a voice in her head pronounced. "Gie' heem bek thon thing."

Ada blinked in amazement when the breeze immediately ceased, leaving the toupee lying on the ground. A stillness settled over the playground. The hush nestled between the empty beer bottles and the merry-go-round, winding itself around the squeaking swings. The calm lay warily over each and every grain of sand that was not currently being disturbed by plastic buckets or tiny beach spades. The old man took the opportunity to bend down.

Grasping for his hairpiece, he snatched it up and dusted it off. The involuntary shaking of his head kindled a rapid succession of black-and-white images in Ada's mind.

"Do you know what you are?"

Ada glanced to her left. There was no-one there besides the elderly man who was now departing hastily from the playground, still adjusting his toupee. But the deep, sonorous voice was as clear and present as though someone were seated beside her on the bench. Ada scratched at her right wrist. A few ants wound around the sidewalk past her foot. "Why, Ada, o?" cried the voice inside her head. "Why do you no longer know? Why have you forgotten yourself?"

·  ·  ·  ·  ·

Ada had forgotten what would happen if even a single being forgot to do its homework. Otherwise, we would all have been practically ready. Almost all of us. All of us, but Wilhelm. He was the rascal who was determined to misunderstand the meaning of his earthly mission.

When he had held the cards in his hands, they had stained his fingers. He read, licking his fingertips. Yuck! This candyfloss smell! He tried to remove as much as possible. He did not appreciate the pink colour any more than the message it conveyed. His skin grew wrinkled and dry before his own eyes. The veins wound like rivers across the backs of his hands. Here and there, a liver spot blossomed.

Reading glasses, please! he said.

I lay myself across the bridge of his nose, watching as

264

he read and licked his fingertips once more.

Bitter, he muttered again and again. Given the far-reaching consequences of the assignment he had been given, Wilhelm was having a hard time remaining still. And he was not alone in this. In 2019, there were many people living in Germany who spoke again and again of the past – particularly after the terror attack in Halle – discussing it as though this history was something which could be overcome as quickly as possible. Although Wilhelm's past offered ample grounds for collective mourning.

In the previous orbit, his meeting with Ada had appeared incidental. He had been surveying the condition of the innumerable trees from the window of his freshly polished Mercedes Benz.

Proud rows of European beech looming over the horizon – trees which he had personally rescued from the threat of deforestation. It remains a great mystery to me how these uniformed men had committed themselves so much to the preservation of these landscapes and not to the preservation of human lives. But anyway.

SS-Obersturmbannführer Helmut Wilhelm – lieutenant colonel of the SS, senior executive officer, leader of diverse branches of the State Police, commander of Task Force I of the Special Ops Unit IV in German-occupied Poland and counterintelligence representative tasked with the production of the V2 Rocket in Mittelbau-Dora concentration camp – had not been interested in the six-digits at first. He was a man fascinated by trees. And yet, before the inspection of his vehicle had ended, his eyes had caught a glint of colour from the bracelet. It flashed like a spark of hope out of the desolation; it stopped him in his tracks.

And because – even many hours later – the thought robbed him of his peace, he decided not to delegate the investigation of this theft to a lower-ranking officer, but to determine himself how such an exquisite piece of jewellery could have landed in a filthy pit like Dora.

After "interviewing" a number of prisoners, SS-Obersturmbannführer Helmut Wilhelm took the brace-let home with him. He had wanted to have it inspected more closely, but history caught up with him. Before he knew it, the glory of the Third Reich lay strewn among the rubble and ashes. Only yesterday he had worn his SS insignia with pride. Today, he found himself stowing it hastily away in an inconspicuous chest and hiding this behind a pile of his tools. Helmut Wilhelm died shortly before the end of the War. He did not live long enough to hear that his wife was pregnant. And she never knew that, with this chest in the cellar, she had basically kept a skeleton in the closet.

This will never work, God cursed.

I diverted my eyes awkwardly as the cards were collected once again.

We've got to give it another go! What realm should it be this time?

The voice of the being who would become the son of Obersturmbannführer Helmut Wilhelm grew deeper, and he sat resolutely, his legs spread wide.

It doesn't matter much to me! he said, but I'd like to be surrounded by other men!

By men? God asked.

Yeah.

By *real men*?

Yes!

Suddenly, a diverse array of male figures was displayed upon the cards: some with beards and some without, some with turbans and some without; some of the men were covered in muscles and as tall as fir trees; others flounced about with polished fingernails, as skinny as grasshoppers. Men with thick skin, and men with thin. Some in Western-style business suits, some in snowsuits, others in bathing suits and still others in their birthday suits. Men with penises, men with vaginas . . .

Okay, okay.

What's that?

I want to be surrounded by other men *like me*.

By men from Abrotsiri? God asked.

What?

I could no longer hold my peace.

Tell me, I mocked. How is this supposed to work? Only surrounded by other people like you when you don't even know what kind of person you are?

Wilhelm gaped. His eyes rolled back and forth: from me to God and back again to me.

You don't even know whether Abrotsiri means something positive or negative, do you?

I tumbled from his nose in indignation.

In any case, among the many cards Wilhelm had been dealt were "no children" and "no pets". He inherited his love for trees from his father. The wife selected for him was even-tempered. He accepted all of these things gratefully, and led a mostly honorable life. He even received a few extra bonuses from time to time: a favourable tax bracket, an autobahn without speed limits, and an effortless and

unquestioned mastery of mainstream German culture. But all that was for the birds. This time, his past wound up in a museum.

He even looked proud as he began telling God about it.

I found this chest full of Nazi memorabilia in my cellar. Of course, I wanted to have it removed at once.

Have it auctioned, I corrected.

Fortunately, a colleague of mine gave me the idea of having the bracelet valued, since it was obvious that it was far older than the rest of the stuff . . .

Far more valuable, I corrected.

And because this magnificent piece of jewellery is a part of our cultural heritage, I consented to having it displayed in a museum . . .

For a modest sum? I asked.

Open to the public, he nodded. At this, God quite literally cast his toys out of the buggy. A little wooden wagon whizzed past Wilhelm, narrowly missing his head by a millimetre.

You've *deliberately* misunderstood your assignment!

No, no! he cried, cowering.

Open to the public?! What do you know of public relations? Did you even consider *which* public it should be made available to?

Well, I mean, all the people, of course!

All the people in Spandau? All the people in Germany?

From Asia, from Africa, Wilhelm stretched out his arms. From all over the world!

Those! People! Who! Have! Been! Denied! Entry! To! Europe!

The sound of rumbling came from behind the sun.

Should they take a little jaunt, a little stroll to Berlin then, or what?

Until then, Wilhelm had never moved in circles in which "a little jaunt to Berlin" would not have been possible. Now, while the wrath of God thundered around him, the tip of his nose turned red. He remained frozen in place but for the movement of his eyes within their sockets, shifting left to right. And so Ada was sent to him – from Ghana via a number of detours – to Germany.

· · · · ·

Fifteen minutes. She was not that late when she arrived at the house at Ulmenallee 37. The streetlamps cast their regular spots of light along the cobbled street. They looked inviting, calming – quite the opposite of the voice that crackled from the speaker at the door.

"Who's there?"

"Ada Lamptey," she wheezed.

"Who?"

"I'm the sister of Elle Hückel."

"Well, finally."

The door buzzed open. I knew that we had come to the right place. I felt a warmth streaming through me – later I learned that this feeling was called "joy". Ada was happy too. To her great relief she found the apartment located on an elevated ground floor.

The elderly man from the playground stood at the door.

"You've come too late."

He tapped at his thigh with his right hand as though he were playing the piano. Ada stepped into the doorway. He held a clipboard in his left hand.

"Is the apartment already taken then?" she gasped.

"I'm referring to the time."

Ada found the way he rolled his "r" impressive, but also a bit menacing.

"Ah, I see." She nodded. "That's true. But I've learned that in Germany there's such a thing as an academic quarter? The important things always begin fifteen minutes past the hour."

It was a bold move, to be sure. But she had wanted to lighten the mood and thought the joke was harmless.

"Not. For. Me." came the curt answer.

Ada nodded again.

"I apologise."

"If anything," he continued, "you should be saying: 'I beg your pardon!'"

His moustache twitched up and down, but he remained otherwise immovable. Ada would have to crank up "the good immigrant", or she would find herself thrown out of the apartment immediately. She folded her hands together and smiled. She fluttered her eyelids.

"You're absolutely right . . ."

"I already know that!"

". . . and I beg you, formally, for your pardon."

The deep creases in his brow smoothed almost imperceptibly. He growled something that sounded like "accepted" and turned on his heels. Ada followed him into the room, closing the front door behind her. He waved at her with his clipboard.

"Have a look around then," he said. "Here: bathroom. Kitchen. Everything freshly painted. Renovated. Tiptop."

Ada nodded.

"And here –" he pushed another door open opposite the bathroom – "the room. Have a look, have a look. I'll wait here in the hall."

Ada poked her head inside the door. Except for a single candle burning in the back left corner, the room was empty. The flame danced to its own quiet rhythm, casting shadows on the walls which accompanied Ada as she entered the room. Take a seat, take a seat, creaked the floor. I'm here for you.

I was positively overjoyed when Ada kneeled down. I can be here, she thought. This feels right. Her body was stiff and sore, and it took her a moment to make it down onto the floor. The floorboards shimmered in the candle-light. Just lie down, the window sang, the sky is beautiful, indigo embroidered with diamonds. Enchanting.

From her position on the floor, Ada could see a sliver of moonlight reflecting off the windowsill. When she turned her head to the right angle she could also see the edges of grey clouds, but only just. She lay at first on her side, then she rolled onto her back to better admire the stars. She felt cradled by the floor; it had not made a promise it couldn't keep. The floor felt solid and secure, a floor for the ages. Deep in thought, she didn't notice that she was no longer alone.

"What are you doing down there?"

Ada looked up. The old man stood in the doorway, squinting down at her. He did not seem pleased by what

he saw.

"I'm sorry." Ada grinned. "I know it looks strange, but I had to lie down."

"*What* did you have to do?"

"Just for a moment. I'm so exhausted, you see."

The old man grumbled. His moustache continued to dance about.

"Now listen. You're not to give birth here, is that understood? Otherwise you'll have to pay the cleaning fees."

Ada began to laugh. From the bottom of her heart. It erupted from deep inside her, and it did her good.

"I . . . I beg your pardon again." She giggled. "Everything is fine. I'd like to have the apartment."

"Yes?"

With an effort Ada sat up. "Yes. Where do I need to sign, Herr . . . ?"

"Wilhelm's the name. Do you have all the necessary documents at hand?"

Ada dumped the contents of her bag onto the floor. She still didn't know how she would manage to pay the rent. Tomorrow, she thought, I'll have to patch things up with Elle. She'll help me out. We'll find some kind of solution. Despite its protective covering, one page of her passport had somehow folded over. But she did not let this bother her.

"Here's my passport . . . and my bank statements . . . Now, what am I forgetting?"

He did not answer. Ada looked up at him. The exhibition catalogue lay open beside her bag. He stared wordlessly at the picture of the bracelet, as if he no longer realised that he had been mid-conversation. It was not until Ada

had repeated his name for the third time that he slowly returned his gaze to her. All the colour drained from his face. He fell . . . as if in slow motion.

"Herr Wilhelm!"

He did not land directly on Ada but tumbled backwards onto his outstretched hands and, unable to land properly, continued to fall until he lay collapsed on the floor. The dull thud startled even me. In that moment I realised that I could not see anything . . .

"Be careful, Herr Wilhelm!" Ada exclaimed.

I recognised her voice, but it sounded like a great water had grown between us.

"I've always been careful," he murmured.

"What's that?"

"He ran!"

"What did you say?"

"And how he ran! Because the next one was already standing at the door. A great man, with a misshapen face and a hard look. He was clearly only thinking one thing: get in quick!"

"And then?" she asked.

What's she doing, I thought. And in the next moment – why don't I know what she's doing? And why can't I see anything?

"And then?" she asked again.

"There was nearly a collision," he said. "The next one came in. And just in time Nine-Zero-Eight-Dot-Dot-Dot leaped to one side. Right out of Thirty-Seven, down the steps and quickly out of sight of the place. And onward. Although everything was black before his eyes. Onward. His rope belt cut into him, his trousers staining red around

the hips. Onward. In the midst of the parade grounds he stopped and vomited. Again. The golden spittle dripped down the length of his body, hung from his lips in sticky threads, clung to the back of his hands. Again. Again! AGAIN! The next one in line, the naked whore and the nothing."

He stumbled over his words.

"Did you know her?" Ada asked.

"I never saw her! I never saw her!"

"Is that true?"

"I am SS-Obersturmbannführer Helmut Wilhelm. I never lie!"

"Never?"

"They. Vanished. With the bracelet."

"Is that true, Helmut?"

"I don't have it anymore."

"Is that true?"

"AFFIRMATIVE!"

"Then how did you get the bracelet?"

"Get the bracelet?" he stuttered.

"*How?*"

"They wanted to bring it to the warehouse. If I hadn't taken it, someone else would have. The swine!"

"What?"

"The swine! They were far worse than I! *Far* worse. I only took the bracelet."

He propped himself up like a jack-in-the-box. His eyes wide, he took Ada's face in his hands.

"I was careful," he whispered, stroking her across both cheeks. "Do you believe me?"

Ada grew quiet. I could hear her heart pounding. But

the sound was strange. Muffled and echoey.

"Do you believe me?" he demanded.

"Of course . . ."

"All the same. The baby fell into the water."

"The *baby*?"

"It was already dead! And a dead baby doesn't need a bracelet anymore. Right? I had almost got it off him, and then you came along. You! You wanted to take the bracelet away from me!"

"Who are you now?"

"Guilherme. Fernandes. Zarco."

"Why did a baby have the bracelet?"

"A waste! You people have no idea! In Europe, we know what fine art is!"

"And where is it now?"

"The baby? It fell into the water."

"I mean the bracelet."

"Oh. I killed you. I beg your pardon."

"No big deal."

Her voice was calm.

"They tried to rescue you. Your people. But I went under. Looking for the baby's corpse. In vain. It was already gone."

"And where is the bracelet now?"

He grew quiet.

"Guilherme?"

"Nenhuma idéia. I've been dead for more than five hundred years. What do you want from me?"

"The bracelet."

"I don't have it anymore."

"But you *did* have it?"

"Yes. The lads found the baby. They were in the sea on their way back to the ship when the baby drifted past them. They took the bracelet off him. And as soon as I found out, I gave them all a lashing. With my right hand tied behind my back! After all, I'd seen it first!"

"But it did not belong to you!"

"Easy come, easy go!"

Ada's heartbeat quickened, but her voice retained its composure: "And then?"

"Then I sold it."

"Where?"

"In Lisbon. I was able to pay off all my debts and never go back to Africa again."

"Who bought the bracelet?"

"Never again!" He laughed.

"*Who?*"

"A King. I can't remember his first name anymore."

"A king? Of what country?"

"No. A man. Named King."

He struggled to collect the shards of his concentration, scattered across the centuries.

"King . . . A king . . ."

"What's that?"

"A king," he wheezed. "He forbade the final banquet."

"What are you talking about . . . ?"

"Banquet. Banquet! A great company at table. You know what food is, right? Four francs for a dry hunk of bread, some dried codfish and an absurd little sip of red wine. Downright absurd."

"And why was it forbidden?"

"That's what I'm saying. The knave!" He waved his

hands about. "If he had only let the banquet happen, he could at least have prevented the protests. And all of Paris shuttered up. All because he wouldn't listen."

"Who? King?"

"*The* king! Louis Philippe. Roi des Français. Louis, I said. Louis, Louis, Louis. Just a bit of social reform – even just the pretence of it – that had already worked wonders in London! That's what I told him. William, he said to me, they want to be rid of me. And even with a ban on public gatherings, they're still meeting up around the table. All the time, William! He was really worried. The Campagne des banquets? Let them go on, I said. There's no cause to be alarmed. *Pas besoin!* That was the whole reason they invited me to France. To advise the king."

"How long were you away?"

"Why? Were you worried?"

"Maybe . . . ?"

He grunted. "Preposterous!"

"William . . ."

"Lying does not become you, my love."

"I should say not. So why would I start now?"

"I didn't want to hurt you, Ada. I was simply tired. After the long carriage ride from Paris, you know? And I shot with my left hand."

Ada stared at him.

"Oh?" she said at last.

"I'd struck my right hand bloody against the wall. I didn't mean to hurt you. It should only have been a warning shot."

"But why on Earth would you want to warn me with a gunshot?"

277

"I don't know anymore."

"Where is the bracelet?"

"I don't know that anymore either."

Ada nodded slowly, as if trying to decide what she should say next.

"We want the bracelet back," she said at last. Her voice was calm, her hands rubbing her belly.

"You can't have it. It's ours now."

"But you know we'll get it back. It won't take long now."

"You will not. I'm not afraid of any of you. You have no teeth."

"We are many things," she countered. "But we are never toothless. Never."

# Ada

"Here!"

Considering how the cramp in Herr Wilhelm's chest was worsening, my voice was surprisingly composed – even if it did sound loud and urgent. I was completely in control of my faculties, an unusual feeling. The people gathering at the entrance of the apartment were quite the opposite and growing ever more anxious. High and low voices mingled with one another before drifting in my direction. I remained seated on the floor beside Herr Wilhelm, and called back to them once more:

"Here!"

I lay my hand on his.

"See, Herr Wilhelm, my sister was right. Like always . . ."

Dull footsteps echoed in the hallway.

". . . she said it wouldn't take long, didn't she? And can you hear? They're already here, the paramedics . . ."

One of them sounded hoarse, clearing their throat again and again before they spoke. I remained seated on the floor.

"Here!" I called once more.

Herr Wilhelm's lips had acquired a greyish hue. The first time I called Elle, they had not looked that way. But the intermittent spasms were there. She told me I had nothing to worry about. She had nothing but good experiences with emergency workers.

"It won't be long now, inshallah," she wrote after I had called them. Her message still illuminated my screen.

"They're here, Herr Wilhelm," I whispered.

Already, figures were moving about us in the room. I hardly paid them any attention – my gaze remained directed at him. By the time they'd covered his mouth with a plastic oxygen mask, his lips had parted just a little. I thought I could detect a smile. But it all happened so quickly.

They kept asking me over and over:

"What happened?" Or:

"What is happening?" Sometimes they asked:

"How did it happen?" Or sometimes only:

"Are you sure?" But each time

s l o w l y and with *e m p h a s i s*.

Their words stretched out like bubble gum in my ears, they whirled around inside my head. Gradually, time began to stick together. I no longer knew how long it had been before he came into the room. I thought he hadn't been in pain at first, but now I could not be sure. My tongue stuck to my gums, I was sweating and I felt a little dizzy. I didn't trust myself to tell them this. Other than repeating their questions, they didn't really talk to me. And when they did they sounded gruff and angry. I formed my lips into an "o" and exhaled slowly.

They asked me more questions in the ambulance. They

took notes. They sighed. When we arrived at the hospital, they typed as well and squinted at their screens, shaking their heads. Again, I was asked to repeat my story from the beginning.

"Nenhuma idéia," I muttered, rubbing my eyes when it all became too much for me. The words felt pleasant in my mouth.

I forgot with whom I had already spoken. I was no longer paying attention to name tags or uniforms. There were too many. It was loud and glaring in the hallway. The dried-out pretzel sticks beside me were meant to be a snack. I left them on the paper plate, hoping no-one would take it personally. The plastic cup beside it had long stood as empty as I now felt.

"Someone comin' to pick you up?"

Finally, a different question. I looked away from my cup as a group of white coats swept past me. The voice who had asked was already fading away.

Had I answered? Had the question been directed at me at all? Strange people, I thought. My gaze went back to my phone.

Of course I had answered. I had produced a quiet "yes", for Elle had written seconds before that, according to Google Maps, she was about seven minutes away. And where was I, exactly? I had looked up and said "Yes," and my word had ended with a comma because I had actually wanted to ask whether . . . but the person was already gone.

I let my head fall backwards. It seemed like the wall did not want me to feel welcome. It was cold and white. And hard. Mostly just hard. Maybe, I thought, maybe I

can . . . just close my eyes . . . But then my phone vibrated again:

"Room number? Ward?"

I left the message unanswered and laid my phone back in my lap. To my left I saw a group of white people standing around a white counter and talking animatedly with one another. The documents they held were white, their stockings were white, even their shoes. I saw a white bucket and the corresponding mop standing abandoned in the white hallway. A narrow cart with many little white drawers filled with tiny bottles stood nearby. It was a very tiny cart. I swiped Elle's message away. With a few clicks, I found the fitting German word: "Wägelchen". A very tiny cart. I saw many beds arranged along the wall: freshly made, empty and white. All this could have been in any hospital in the world. Then I turned to my right and suddenly I could not hear anything besides an odd, zooming sound. My head drifted about freely in the room, like an untied balloon. With my free hand I grasped for the arm of the chair and concentrated on my breathing. I should have eaten more today. I was either about to vomit, or I had fallen asleep where I sat, or Cash was really walking down the gleaming hallway towards me.

He grinned as though it were obvious that I would just grin at him in return. Which I did. I'm such a jackass. I had rehearsed this moment in my mind a million times. And now he was here, and I was acting as though nothing had happened. What might have happened had I *not* looked to my right?

He tugged at his jacket. It was buttoned, but beneath it I could see the blue-green hem of the pullover I had knitted

him. Something was vibrating. Incessantly. It was probably my phone.

"I was looking for you," he said.

Had his voice changed? Or had I just forgotten the sound? I looked away. So Elle had called him. After she had promised . . . Only call him in a real emergency, I'd said. She had promised me. And there was nothing wrong with me! Cash had probably just heard something about "hospital" and "A & E" and rushed over immediately. I imagined how often he had planned to call me – and then discarded the idea. And now, there he was before me. I hated the way I felt when he looked at me.

"What happened?" he asked.

I didn't offer him the seat beside me, but he sat down anyway. At least his annoying grin was gone. What had I ever seen in him? He was not my type at all. Papa would have liked him because he did something with automotive engineering. And my mothers would have liked him simply because he had a car. Which was why I never told any of them about Cash. If he had been a Christian, Auntie Henry would have sealed the deal for our marriage right then and there. Her standards were pretty low. I yawned.

"An elderly man . . ."

Come on, Ada. More words. Put them together in context. In full sentences if you can. If you're going to do something, then do it.

"I was looking at an apartment. The owner took a fall."

Cash nodded, his head tilted to one side, his eyes on the floor. He had folded his beautiful hands together on his knees.

"And you're here with him because . . . ?"

"I was the only other person there."

"I see."

He nodded again. I watched the supple curve of his neck out of the corner of my eye. A hundred years ago, I kissed him there.

"It was his apartment," I continued. "He hurt his head, and now he's only talking nonsense."

"Nonsense?"

"He told me about some banquets and drowned babies and . . . I don't even know. I got scared."

I yawned again. Slowly, the little bumps tumbled across my belly, then they relaxed and diffused. At least Socks was having a good time, I thought. I concentrated on breathing through my "o".

"Is everything okay?"

I nodded without looking in Cash's direction.

"Really?"

I bit my lip. All I wanted was to be back on my sofa. On Elle's sofa. To wrap my arms around a hot-water bottle. The day had been too long.

"Can you please just go and sign me out? They already know everything I know."

But Cash remained seated. When I finally looked at him, he was staring at his feet. I would rather not have spoken with him at all.

"What is it?" I asked.

He rubbed his face with both hands.

"I'm sorry," he said.

I made a dismissive gesture. I did not know what he wanted to apologise for. And I did not really want to find out.

"I . . . uh . . . I didn't know that you weren't ready."

It was quiet for a long time. It felt like a small eternity. The plastic cup crackled beneath the iron grip of my fingers. I blinked. Several times. I was not about to cry in front of him. I had already shed more than enough tears on his behalf.

"Yes," I whispered finally. "You did. You knew. I told you. I told you I was scared."

"Yeah, I guess I didn't hear . . ."

"You heard me."

"I mean I didn't *listen*."

I wanted to be gone. I stood up and my phone fell from my lap. The sound of its falling echoed down the hall. Cash leaped to his feet. I should have thrown the empty plastic cup. I should have kicked or squashed it. I wanted to do so many things. Wanted to? Needed to! Instead, I dropped it into a bin and it vanished beside the other rubbish. Socks was awake, and now I was too.

Away! It didn't matter where . . . so long as I was gone. I just wanted to disappear. Like he had. But there he was, standing in front of me, my phone in his hand. Its broken screen mocked me, as if my day had not been bad enough already.

"Why didn't you just . . . ?"

"Just what? Punch you?

"Yeah. Or maybe . . . I don't know . . ."

I gave a laugh.

"Are you trying to put the blame on me now?"

I pressed my fingers against my eyes. The pressure and the warmth and the play of colours behind my eyelids helped calm my voice. I hated that I had no better answer

to his question. Why hadn't I hit or kicked him? I would have liked to know myself. Why hadn't I even screamed at him? Why hadn't I broken up with him on the spot?

A vein in his temple bulged and throbbed.

"Ada," he said. "I think we already resolved the question of blame, didn't we?"

Resolved? He still didn't understand at all. Did he think he could fix everything with an empty phrase? And besides. Why was I still wasting so many of my fucking thoughts on him?

"What can I say?" he whispered.

The people around us tried their best not to make it obvious that they were listening to our argument.

"How would it be if you just didn't say anything for a while?" I hissed.

Cash nodded. His hair had grown longer. His curls hung down over his face.

"I shouldn't have come at all . . ."

I stared up at the ceiling and bit my lip again. He was lucky that we were in public.

"How can I make it right, Ada?"

I had just said he shouldn't speak at all.

"You can't make it right."

"Yeah, I know. But I mean, what can I do so that . . ."

He leaned forward, but I took a step back. Touching me? Seeking comfort in me? Was he for real? Cash looked down at his feet again.

"There's not going to be a happy ending," I said at last. "You hurt me. And I'm still dealing with it. You being nice to me now isn't going to change that."

I exhaled slowly while he kept nodding. Maybe, just

286

maybe, he would finally understand. I couldn't see his eyes. But it didn't look like he was trying to get away.

"So, if you do plan on sticking around," I added after a moment, "you better be prepared!"

A young nurse was approaching us. She had luminous-pink hair shaved short around her temples. I thought she just wanted to get past us and I moved to one side to give her room, but she turned and spoke to me.

"Excuse me. Are you the relative of Herr Wilhelm?"

The timbre of her voice surprised me. Perhaps they were not a she at all. And who was this Herr Wilhelm? The name sounded oddly familiar . . .

An announcement over the loudspeaker startled me back into the present moment: there, on that Friday evening in the corridor of the hospital. Cash was still here, but there had been a different dramatic situation before his reappearance. Several, even.

"Oh, right, Herr Wilhelm," I answered. "No, I only accompanied him in the ambulance. I don't know him otherwise; the police are looking for his next of kin. As far as I know."

"Well, he's asking for his daughter . . ."

I shrugged.

"I didn't even know he had one."

Cash took a seat then looked up at me, patting the space beside him. I shook my head.

"He said," the nurse . . . but perhaps people still make too many gendered associations with that word – the care-giver – began again: "He said that she was waiting in the corridor."

"Oh?" The corners of my mouth began to frown, and

I raised my eyebrows. "I haven't seen anyone else here for him."

"He said her name was Ada."

. . . . .

I didn't even want to be there. I'd had enough. It didn't matter to me whether the wrinkly grandpa lying in the bed was now ignoring me or whether he really hadn't noticed I was there. It's the same difference, as the Germans would say. I didn't even want to be there, o!

I didn't need to look behind me. Cash had followed me to the room and was seated just outside, waiting for some kind of pronouncement. Before me lay Herr Wilhelm – I hadn't the foggiest idea what he wanted from me. Somehow, again, I'd landed smack between the desires of two men. I found myself wondering: How do they always manage it? Although I knew the better question was: How do *I* always manage it? My eyes were rolling so hard they were giving me a pain in the back of my head. I cleared my throat and said, "Herr Wilhelm," hoping to flavour my words with the message "I don't want to be here."

There wasn't enough light to see his eyes. Perhaps he was already asleep? Or maybe he was deep in thought, observing the sparkle of each individual raindrop on the windowpane? Slowly, he turned his bald head in my direction. With the bandage on his head he looked vulnerable, almost like a lost child. Part of me would have liked to comfort him. Another, far stronger part of me pressed my lips together firmly. He smiled, and I nodded. He kept smiling, but the joy did not extend into his eyes.

"It's nice outside," he said.

Nice in what sense of the word? The rain fell harder; I could barely hear him. And besides the distant, fuzzy lights of the office buildings across the way, there was nothing more to see outside the window. I squinted, but his pause did not last longer than my intake of breath. He was speaking, but not necessarily as though he expected an answer from me.

"Concrete desert far and wide. And yet respectable all the same, I'd say . . ."

His smile faded, as if he were unsure of his next word.

"Urban . . . ?"

He lay sunken in his bed, colourless, without warmth. I concentrated on the view from the window, for the storm was raging and roaring, throwing everything else into chaos. At times I could still hear the revulsion in Elle's words when she had said: "Popping out babies." Popping out, she had said! As if I were some kind of beast! As if she'd punched me in the gut, o! And then Papa snarled in my ear, as cold and direct as if he were standing right beside me: "I sacrificed so much for you, and in return? You spit in my face. Your mother would be ashamed." Ashamed, he had said! I hadn't even hung up the phone. I'd clung to it instead, praying that I had understood him wrong – even after he had long hung up himself. My flooded eyes were threatening to spill over. They burned and quivered. I was clenching and unclenching my fist, nearly ready to punch a hole in the wall. Because Cash was now trying to sob his way out of his guilt.

"Herr Wilhelm," I said.

My voice betrayed nothing. Herr Wilhelm glanced back at me, two tiny question marks dancing in his pupils.

"Herr Wilhelm, what do you want from me?"

A clap of thunder burst above the hospital building and startled him. Or so at least I interpreted the wordless seconds which followed. And so I waited. For a man, again. As if I had nothing better to do. My mouth formed an "o".

The last time I had experienced a rainstorm like this one had been on the day that I had left my mothers. It had been so powerful that the street dogs had all howled. When he finally began to speak again, I had to strain to understand his words. Herr Wilhelm's voice was hardly more than a murmur.

"Actually, I'd like to go outside . . . just by the entrance . . ." He made a walking motion with his index and middle fingers. "Go for a walk. There's something in the air tonight. Isn't there?"

He reached out his right hand to me.

"Would you like to come along?"

His eyelids sagged at the outer corners, and his head bobbed lightly up and down. Where was his toupee? He looked naked without it. I stared at his hand, instead, as I answered.

"No."

"No?"

"No."

"But why not?"

His lower lip began to protrude.

"Herr Wilhelm," I repeated. It sounded more forceful than I had intended. But that wasn't a bad thing. "You told

the nurse . . . the caregiver . . . that I was your daughter. You do know that I am not your child."

His hand was still extended.

"It has thirty-three gold beads," he continued. "Thirty-three! To forty-five!"

My stomach muscles contracted while his eyebrows continued to dance with excitement.

"I'll give it to you!"

"No."

"No?"

"No."

"But why not?"

I finally stepped fully into the room and let the door close behind me. I should have told him that I needed to go and fetch my jacket. He probably would not even have noticed if I had not come back. But his lower lip was quivering and his cheeks were glowing. I took a deep breath while I shuffled through my words, trying to bring them into the proper order. My back was starting to hurt, my pelvis was aching and my feet were starting to grumble. But I was still a great deal better off than he, I thought. I looked down at him. How his still-outstretched hand was trembling, how his eyes were rimmed with red, and his voice broke as he asked me again.

"Herr Wilhelm," I answered. My voice was soft again, thank God. "How are you going to give me something that doesn't belong to you at all?"

I had never seen a face blush so crimson, and the transformation from chalky white to fiery red happened so quickly that I glanced involuntarily at the emergency buzzer on the wall.

"Without me you won't get the bracelet!"

The lost child had vanished entirely, and in his place lay a monster – gnashing its teeth, extending its claws to pounce. His roaring awakened Socks. I rubbed my dancing belly and whispered just loud enough for him to hear me, too: "We'll find a way . . ."

He opened and closed his mouth again and again. He looked like a fish out of water. I tried my best to arrange a neutral expression upon my face, and yet despite his own confusion he still took note of something in the corners of my mouth. I had never been good at disguising my feelings. In the end he shook his head and stared out of the window. He remained quiet as a flash of lightning rent the sky. For a wondrous moment it illuminated the entire room.

"I was told –" he sighed a few seconds later – "to put on . . . when we go out . . . our jackets."

"Who said that?" I asked.

Herr Wilhelm closed his eyes.

"Ada," he breathed at last. But he pronounced it like the English name: "Ay-da." And then he smiled again. This time his eyes, too, were smiling: "She said it would rain soon."

The raindrops were still pounding against the window-pane. Quicker. Harder. I remained standing for a while by the door. Until his right hand – which now lay upon the bed – no longer trembled. Until the lights in the buildings across the way went out. Until I noticed the warm water running down my leg.

EPILOGUE

# Me. We.

During the longest night of the year, blood clung to my forehead and my baby breathed. At last. My tiny princess, my future! She squinted and blinked. The figures and contours before her eyes took shape incrementally. The colours shifted through many darker and lighter shadows, from a uniform grey to a kaleidoscope of tiny, iridescent stars. The rushing in her ears sounded like an eternal Shhh . . . Had it been years or only a matter of seconds? I didn't ask. For soon enough, the realisation would dawn insidiously upon her that she was no longer drifting through the realm of everlasting time. At least that is how it had been for me each time around.

A child!

The sign that I could bring another life into the world had reappeared and was now slumbering beside me. As though it had never been away. Or as though my uterus had been playing a trick on me all along: "That's fairly knocked the wind out of yer sails!"

I laughed myself awake. Pain blossomed across my

body: between, inside, around, even *on top of* my muscles – and not only in those places where I had expected it. A rending, bursting throbbing coursed throughout my lower body, and a seeping bruise began to spread out from my lower back. My throat was raw, the joints of my fingers creaked and I was even sore in the skin behind my ears. But none of that mattered.

She lay on her back, her tiny hands above her head. Her perfect fingernails were soft and delicate. And she snuffled. I was relieved and disappointed at the same time that she did not awaken when I grasped one of her fists. She had my nose. And very clearly Cash's chin. But her curved eyelashes, the peaceful brow, the heart-shaped lips: these things she had brought with her on her own. She curled two of her tiny fingers around my index finger. I had no idea how long I had been lying beside her. After a while, I realised that I had forgotten to breathe. My lungs were already screaming. Sorry, I thought to myself, I was trying not to wake my daughter!

I filled my lungs with stale air, enriched by a waft of disinfectant, gladiolas and rice pudding. Some downright earthy aromas, I thought, considering that a being had just transcended the wall between Asamando and Wiase. Asamando? I scratched my head. Why could I suddenly think only of the Twi words? Eh, eh! The word for Wiase was completely gone. It had been so long since I had spoken Ga. My language was offended. Se wo were fi na wosan kofa a yennkyi!

A constant, quiet beeping persisted behind the snores of two (or maybe three?) other people. I recognised the form of my neighbour in the shared ward by her silhouette

before the window. She was sleeping with her back to me. I turned my head a little at a time, moving through the pain in my neck to see what was to the left of me. The beeping was coming from an old monitor. Green and blue lines were moving calmly across its screen. And then a bit further.

Elle! Seated in a chair by the door, her head on her chest, the exhibition catalogue on her lap. Cash's knitted pullover was spread over her like a blanket.

"Elle!" I called.

I noticed too late that she had headphones on. My neighbour murmured in her sleep and shifted in the bed. I froze – but everything grew quiet again. Elle was hardly moving. Her chest rose and fell in a gentle, peaceful rhythm. The blues and greens of the pullover undulated with her breaths like waves. So, she had found me. And she had stayed with me. Despite it all.

"Thank you," I whispered.

For I finally understood who I was. And while quiet snores entered the silent, shadowy corners which had not yet been filled with our dreams, I turned my head and focused my eyes on our treasure. And then I closed my eyes. And drifted away again.

The quote on the opening page is adapted from:

Kwami, M. et al (1993): *Adinkra. Symbolsprache der Ashanti / Symbolic language of the Ashanti* (Berlin: Haus der Kulturen der Welt).

# Acknowledgments

I begin with a huge "thank you" to the unknown person who, back in the winter of 2020, when I was compiling a list of people who might possibly be interested in translating my German language novel into English, first suggested that I contact Jon Cho-Polizzi. I don't know who this wonderful individual was, but they mentioned Jon's name to Peter Blackstock. Peter dutifully passed Jon's name on to me and the rest, as they say, is history. An equally huge "thank you" to Peter also, of course!

But the biggest thanks of all are reserved for Jon Cho-Polizzi. You are a blessing.

Thank you, dear Jon, for fiercely defending *Adas Raum* at every turn, thank you for your phenomenal tenacity, for your meticulous choices, for your enduring patience and ultimately for this beautiful piece of work. I hope you know I am completely serious when I say that I would never have been able to achieve what you have achieved here. Working with you has been an amazing honour and an absolute joy. I am incredibly proud of this version of my first novel.

Thank you also to everyone who has supported Jon on his quest. Áine McMurtry's rendering of the Berlin dialect into a Northern Irish one is simply fantastic. Thank you, dear Áine, for your generosity and creativity! David Gramling must be the best cheerleader for translators ever. I have never met anyone quite like you, dear David, thank you so much for all your support! Sarah Colvin's promotion of both my literary and essayistic writing is unparalleled. This has included creating supportive environments, online and off, for academic researchers like Jon. I will forever be in your debt, dear Sarah, thank you so much. I am also mentioning Jon's wonderful partner, Viola Tietje, here as, word has it, she probably knows the translation better than any of us. Thank you, dear Viola, for your countless hours on this book. You are seen!

I am also deeply grateful to every single person, including Laura Perciasepe, Markus Hoffmann, Katharina Bielenberg, Myriam Alfano, Stefan Lingg and Karin Graf, who has worked so hard behind the scenes to make this stunning publication possible. Thank you all.

In the original German-language publication, I listed many, many people who somehow inspired or supported me on the journey from the first tentative ideas to the finished product. It is an honour to be able to list their names here again:

Aischa Ahmed, Wazi Apoh, Hans Jürgen Balmes, Manuela Bauche, Barbara Benbenek, Ewelina Benbenek, Willi Bischof, John Boachie Bonnah, Olenka Bordo Benavides, Carina Büker, Clementine Ewokolo Burnley, Ricky Charway, Jamile da Silva e Silva, Dietmar Dath, Tahir Della, Elisa Diallo, Julia Eichhorn, Elena Ficara, Yosime

Flood, Karin Graf, Svenja Gräfen, David J. Gramling, Petra Gropp, Viktorie Hanišová, Tania Hensen, Marcel Inhoff, Catherine Johnson, Sandra Kegel, Hans Koch, Grace Chioma Kupka, Mahret Ifeoma Kupka, Svealena Kutschke, Daniel Lankai Lawson, Stephen Hugh Lawson, Stephen Nii Lankwei Lawson, Victoria Naa Lamiokor Lawson, Svenja Leiber, Dirk Ludwig, Leon Ludwig, Wamilika Mawakha, Jeannine Mayani, Marcin Michalski, Charlotte Milsch, Andrés Nader, Bona Ngoumou, Gonza Ngoumou, Sita Ngoumou, Nana Nketsia V, Valentine Chike Nnamani, Mirjam Nuenning, Dion Otoo, Elijah Otoo, Lewis Otoo, Tyrell Otoo, Anthony Owosekun, Mary Owusu, Nele Pollatschek, Hanno Rinke, Jayrôme C. Robinet, Pasquale Virginie Rotter, Charlott Schönwetter, Joachim Schulz, Asad Schwarz-Msesilamba, Ulla Schweitzer, Irène Servant, Ralf Steinberger, Paul Teschner, Raphael Urweider, Silke van der Velden, Leoní Weber Bordo, Melissa Wessel and Adjo Zorn.

My deepest thanks to all of you. You have all left unmistakable marks in and upon this novel. With all my heart:

Asante ~ Daalu ~ Danke ~ Děkuju ~ Dziękuję ~
Gracias ~ Grazie ~ Medaase ~ Merci ~ Obrigado ~
Oyiwala doŋ ~ Shukran ~ Thank you!

Sharon Dodua Otoo,
November 2022

Born in London in 1972 to Ghanaian parents, SHARON DODUA OTOO is a political activist and novelist living in Berlin. After having published several newspaper articles and two novellas in English, she wrote a short story in German which was later awarded the Ingeborg Bachmann Prize (2016), one of Germany's most renowned literary awards. She is politically active with several civil rights organisations, including the Initiative Black People in Germany (ISD), a Black queer feminist organisation called ADEFRA, and Phoenix. *Ada's Realm* is her first novel.

JON CHO-POLIZZI is a freelance literary translator and Assistant Professor of German at the University of Michigan. He received a PhD in German and Medieval Studies from the University of California, Berkeley, where he was managing editor for the online academic journal *TRANSIT*. His translations have appeared in the Jewish Museum Berlin, the Maxim Gorki Theater, *taz*, *Jewish Currents*, *renk Magazin*, Versopolis Poetry and *Der Spiegel*, as well as in numerous anthologies. He lives and works between Ann Arbor, Northern California and Berlin.